"You know, for a guy who has Emerson Roth exactly where he wants, you're in a rotten mood."

Merriman narrowed his eyes as he continued. "You know what I think? I think you're attracted to her. And you blew your chance with her—big time. Smooth, Garner."

Merriman's words annoyed Eli because they were true. Emerson was a beautiful woman. But more than that, she had spirit, she was smart—and loyal to a fault. He didn't want her to be guilty, but he feared she was.

He wanted her to have a reasonable, moral excuse for the games her family played. He didn't want her to hate him. But it was too late for that. The damage was done.

Eli was relentless; it went with his job. He could go beyond relentless to ruthless when he had to, and he had been ruthless with Emerson.

She would talk to him again tomorrow, because she had no choice.

And he would show her no mercy, because he couldn't.

Dear Reader,

People often ask if my characters are based on real people. In *One True Secret*, the answer is yes and no.

Most of the characters are composites of the real and the imaginary. The heroine, Emerson, owes her beauty and boldness to one of my friends who has the good fortune to have both. But Emerson's other qualities are drawn from a number of different people, some of them members of my family. And part of her is pure imagination.

Still, I confess that one character *is* drawn completely from reality. The only thing that is made up about him is his name.

This character is Bunbury, the overweight gray cat who chirps rather than meows. Bunbury is nearly identical to my overweight gray cat, Hodge, who chirps instead of meows. Hodge could sue me for invasion of privacy and libel, but he couldn't care less about being in a book. Outrage, even mild irritation, would be a waste of his preciously hoarded calories.

His passions are (a) eating (b) coveting the food of others and (c) being petted. He hates the vacuum cleaner, all doors that shut him in or out and, most of all, travel.

As this is being written, Hodge is lying on the dog's cushion, hogging it as he manages to look both sleepy and superior. He will not answer to the name Bunbury, but he won't answer to the name Hodge, either. He's a real cat, but he's also, in every sense of the word, a real character.

Best wishes,

Bethany Campbell and *Hodge*, a Very Fine Cat Indeed.

Bethany would love you to visit her at her Web site, www.bethanycampbell.com.

One True Secret
Bethany Campbell

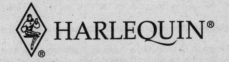

HARLEQUIN®

TORONTO • NEW YORK • LONDON
AMSTERDAM • PARIS • SYDNEY • HAMBURG
STOCKHOLM • ATHENS • TOKYO • MILAN • MADRID
PRAGUE • WARSAW • BUDAPEST • AUCKLAND

ISBN 0-373-71207-3

ONE TRUE SECRET

Copyright © 2004 by Bethany Campbell.

This edition published by arrangement with Harlequin Books S.A.

® and TM are trademarks of the publisher. Trademarks indicated with
® are registered in the United States Patent and Trademark Office, the
Canadian Trade Marks Office and in other countries.

www.eHarlequin.com

Printed in U.S.A.

To Wheels and Mrs. Wheels with affection and gratitude.

Books by Bethany Campbell

HARLEQUIN SUPERROMANCE

*Crystal Creek

CRYSTAL CREEK

I'LL TAKE TEXAS (a novella in the anthology RETURN TO CRYSTAL CREEK)

Don't miss any of our special offers. Write to us at the
following address for information on our newest releases.

Harlequin Reader Service
U.S.: 3010 Walden Ave., P.O. Box 1325, Buffalo, NY 14269
Canadian: P.O. Box 609, Fort Erie, Ont. L2A 5X3

CHAPTER ONE

"I DON'T WANT to talk to those men," Claire said. She sat under the buttercup tree, glumly feeding almonds to the parrot.

"Then don't." Emerson lay stretched on the chaise longue beside the pool. She wore a purple bikini and a green baseball cap. "I'll do the talking."

"For them to come barging in this way? I think it's just—rude."

"Arrak!" said the parrot. "Rude! Rude!"

"They're journalists. It's their job to be rude. Pass me some almonds, will you? I've got the munchies."

Claire rose and handed Emerson the bowl. Then she paused, furrowing her smooth brow. "What'll you do if they get—you know—too pushy?"

Emerson shrugged disdainfully. "Cut 'em into little pieces and feed 'em to Gollum."

Gollum was the alligator who lived in the pond on the back of the property, the acres their grandfather kept untouched and wild. Gollum was six feet long and had only one eye. It was yellow and gleamed with malevolence.

"That's a thought," Claire said, all seriousness. She moved back to the low stone wall under the yellow blossoms of the tree and sat beside the parrot again, crossing her legs. She put her chin on her fist and stared pensively at her sister. "Aren't you afraid you'll say the wrong thing?"

"Nope." Emerson popped an almond into her mouth. "Not at all."

"I'd be," Claire murmured. "I know I'd say too much. Strangers make me nervous. This whole situation makes me nervous."

"Yarrk," croaked the green parrot. "Nervous." He climbed to a lower branch of the tree and hung upside down, cocking his head from side to side.

Emerson peered over her funky sunglasses to scrutinize Claire. Her younger sister was a pretty girl with a sweet face and a gentle air. The Florida sun had streaked her light-brown hair with gold, and her hazel eyes had a faraway look in them.

Emerson loved her sister, but she worried about her. Claire had always been shy, but lately, Emerson thought, her shyness was overpowering her. Claire went outside the estate as little as possible these days and then only to certain places on the Lower Keys.

She stayed home and saw to the needs of their grand-parents, Nana and the Captain. She worked in the garden and walked on the beach and played with her pets.

Claire seemed content with her lot, almost serene. But Emerson didn't want her to hide away from the world, like the Captain. One recluse in the family was more than enough, thank you very much.

After Emerson had fended off the damn journalists, she needed to get to work on Claire's social life. That would take some first-class scheming and wheedling. Well, Emerson was up for it.

A fat blue-gray cat with a white belly and paws waddled out of the coleus and began to rub against Claire's ankles. "Ah," Claire said with real delight, "it's Mr. Bunbury. Hello, Bunbury."

Bunbury flopped onto his back, offering up the consid-erable expanse of his stomach for petting. Claire rubbed him, ruffled and smoothed him, then lifted him onto her lap and scratched his jowls. The parrot, wary, righted himself and climbed several branches higher in the tree.

Claire looked at Emerson over Bunbury's ears. "When do you go to New York again?"

Emerson sat up and began to coat herself with a fresh layer of sunscreen. "In ten days."

"How many paintings will you take?"

"Only the two small ones. I'll take slides of the rest. See what Krystol thinks."

"Krystol's a very good dealer," Claire said. "But Nana's worried about him."

"Why? Because he's asking questions?" Emerson kept stroking the lotion on her thighs. "It's all right. I can handle Krystol. I've been doing it for years, haven't I?"

"Yes, but so many people are asking questions," Claire said, hugging the purring Bunbury. "And now these men—"

Emerson sighed, put the sunscreen aside, and took off her cap. She pulled the pins from her hair, shaking it loose. Unlike Claire, Emerson had dark hair, nearly black, and it was so long it tumbled halfway down her back.

She took off the sunglasses, revealing eyes as dark as her hair. She narrowed these striking eyes at her sister.

"Look, I promised Daddy on his death bed that I'd take care of this family and the business. And I've done it."

"Done it," echoed the parrot, "Family. Done it." He shot Bunbury a suspicious glance and edged still higher.

Emerson leaned forward. "And I'll keep doing it. I know what's at stake here. These paintings aren't *just* paintings. What we have are works of genius. We have a legacy to protect. And I *will* protect it. So, relax."

Claire bit her lip, her expression almost rebellious. "But why'd you have to say they could come to Mandevilla? It's the first time anybody's been allowed here in years."

Emerson stood and made a sweeping gesture. She was

tall and dramatic-looking, as their grandfather had been, and she could get away with such gestures, just as he had.

Her motion was meant to take in all of Mandevilla, the private beach, the pool and garden, the house itself, and the seven acres of tropical wilderness behind it.

"Mandevilla's part of the legend," Emerson said. "The greatest paintings were done here. Famous people came here to visit. Good Lord, Princess Diana came here."

"That was then, this is now," Claire said. "Nobody's come for years."

Emerson put her hands on her hips. "That's why it's important we let somebody see it. To see the place and the new paintings. To stop the damn rumors."

Bunbury spied a lizard and slipped from Claire's lap to stalk it in his ponderous way. Claire didn't try to stop him. Bunbury was too fat and slow to catch anything.

She sighed and picked one of the golden blossoms from the buttercup tree. She twirled its stem between her fingers and stared at it moodily.

"I don't know. An ordinary magazine would be bad enough. But *Mondragon? Mondragon*'s very, very classy—"

"That's why I'm letting them come." Emerson strolled to the diving board, her hands still poised on her hips. *Mondragon, A Magazine of the Arts* was sleek, costly and sophisticated. It didn't shy from controversy or the dark side of the business.

Its managing editor hadn't made a polite request of Emerson. He'd practically demanded that she allow a writer and photographer to visit Mandevilla.

Agreeing was a gamble, a great one, but Emerson took it because she intended to win. The people from *Mondragon* would not use her. She would use them.

"They're classy," Claire admitted. "But they can be ruthless. And this writer, Eli Garner. They couldn't send anybody worse. *You* know what his specialty is."

Emerson walked to the end of the diving board. She knew, all right. His specialty was investigation—and exposé. He had ruined reputations, lives and fortunes. And a few, a very few times, he had saved them.

"I'm not afraid of him," she said.

The parrot worked his way down the tree and climbed onto Claire's shoulder. He rubbed his forehead against her ear. He wanted a kiss.

But for once, Claire ignored him. She stared at Emerson with doubt in her golden-brown eyes. "Maybe you should be afraid, Em. I mean, we do have secrets."

"I'm not afraid," Emerson repeated.

"Awrk!" said the parrot. "Secrets!"

But Emerson paid no attention. She made a perfect jackknife dive that plunged her deep into the blue, blue water.

KEY WEST WAS NOT a quiet town. It was charming, it was artsy and hustling at the same time it was eccentric. But it was not quiet. The least quiet part was Duval Street, which was both famous and infamous.

Shops, restaurants, galleries, ice cream stands and antique stores squeezed together on both sides of the street, punctuated occasionally by a porn emporium or a church. Tourists swarmed, mingling with the tanned and laid-back natives.

Street performers performed, beggars begged and occasionally a chicken with gorgeous plumage strolled regally down the sidewalk. Wild chickens were protected in Key West. After dark, the rock and roll blasting out of nightclubs kept them awake, and the roosters crowed all night long.

So Eli Garner considered himself lucky. He'd found that rarest of things on Duval Street, a quiet bar. It was a big, dim, cavernous place, strangely uncrowded, and the only music came from a bearded man on a tiny stage in the corner. He sang mournful folk songs in a mournful voice, and he sang quietly, which was good, because Eli and Merriman could talk.

Eli and Merriman had never before worked together, but Eli had seen the photographer's work and respected it. The two men had met for the first time a week ago in New York at the offices of *Mondragon.*

Today they'd joined up at the Miami airport and taken the bumpy and jammed commuter flight into Key West. Eli had come from New York, Merriman from Toronto. As soon as they landed, they'd checked into their hotel on the Atlantic end of Duval and dropped off their luggage. Now, sitting in this dimly lit bar, they had their first chance for a real conversation.

Merriman was a muscular, genial man with deep-set blue eyes and straight blond hair that looked perpetually rumpled. He went only by his last name because, he said, his first and middle names were too horrible to mention. He had the odd habit of wrinkling his forehead when he smiled, which was often.

Eli thought he would like Merriman. His only worry was that maybe the guy was *too* genial. This gig would be damn tricky. Was Merriman too easygoing to make the best of it?

Eli took a sip of beer and made his voice casual. "So what do you know about Nathan Roth?"

Merriman gave a good-natured shrug. "Just the basics. Giant of the art world. A golden boy in his heyday. Moved here twenty years ago. Lately, he's gotten reclusive. Hasn't granted an interview in six years. Or been photographed."

Eli nodded. A lean, dark man, his face could seem handsome or dangerous, or both at the same time. He could have credibly passed himself off as an aristocrat or as a high-priced hit man.

He tried to pinpoint how much Merriman knew. "For a painter, Roth's a rich man."

Merriman licked the foam from his upper lip. "So much for starving artists."

"Right." Eli knew Roth's canvases weren't selling at the prices they'd once commanded, but they still sold. But for the past six years, speculation and gossip had circulated about both the work and the man.

Eli raised a dark eyebrow. "You know his son was his manager."

"Till he died. Uh—five years ago." Then Merriman flashed him an abashed grin. "But look. All I know is what I read last week. Modern art isn't my thing. I'm an old-fashioned guy. I like pictures of naked ladies."

Eli's mouth crooked at one corner. Merriman had photographed a series of paintings celebrating women's bodies. He'd done a hell of a job, and he obviously loved the subject. The book was called, simply, *The Female Nude*, and it was equally admired by esteemed scholars and horny teenage boys.

"Roth was an outgoing guy once," Eli said. "But something happened. We don't know what."

"I knew a guy like that once." Merriman lifted his beer mug, signaling for a refill. "News photographer. Real hell-raiser. One day he ups and goes into a monastery in Tibet. Go figure."

Eli wouldn't let the conversation stray. "Roth had a lot of acquaintances. Only one good friend. William Marcuse, another painter. But after Marcuse died, Roth closed himself off to everybody except his family. And they're loyal to him. Absolutely. They don't talk, and they don't want to."

"A wife and two granddaughters, right?" Merriman accepted a frosted mug of beer and nodded his thanks to the barman.

Eli's expression grew more intense. "Roth's son, Damon, handled his father's business. All of it. And protected

his privacy. He was good at it. Since he died, it's the granddaughters' job. They're just as good. Maybe better.''

Merriman cocked his head. "What you're saying is you
want me to be aggressive. But *discreetly* aggressive."

"Right. Take all the pictures you can. Don't be intimi-
dated. Don't offend them if you can help it, but don't let
them push you around."

"I take it nobody has to tell *you* to be aggressive."

Eli let the remark pass. Anybody who thought the art
world was stodgy, highfalutin and boring didn't know it.
He'd uncovered smugglers, forgers, black marketeers,
thieves and killers. In his business, he'd dealt with everything from tomb robbers in Yucatán to looters in Baghdad.

He stuck to the subject of the Roths. "I hear the younger
granddaughter's the more pliable. Less worldly. You may
be able to work her better than the older one."

Merriman looked dubious. "Are you saying come on to
her? Flirt with her? *Me?*"

"Whatever." Eli kept his face and voice impassive.
"These women will pretend to cooperate. We've got to get
past that."

"So what's she like? The younger, pliable, unworldly
one? What's she do?"

"The domestic stuff. She's the stay-at-home one. The
older one handles the business end."

Merriman smiled, and the lines appeared across his forehead, under a lock of sun-gilded hair. "Oh, yeah. She
comes to New York. I hear she's a looker. What's her
name? Emilene or something?"

Eli's face grew more guarded than usual. "Emerson.
Yeah. She's a looker."

He'd seen her once, last year at a gallery opening in
Soho. He'd caught only the briefest glimpse. But in that
glimpse, Eli had seen she was a true beauty: flowing dark
hair, the eyes of a gazelle and the long legs to match. But
though she had a gazelle's grace, the word was that she

also had the protective instincts of a lioness when it came to her family.

Almost as soon as he'd spied her that afternoon, she'd left, simply vanished. Later he heard she'd left because of him.

Like her, he had a reputation. When he went after the truth, nothing stopped him, and he had the scars to prove it. If she thought she could keep things hidden from him, she was dead wrong.

"These people don't live in this town, right?" Merriman asked. "They live on the next key or island or whatever you call these things."

"Three islands up. Mimosa Key. About fifteen miles away."

"Pretty isolated?"

"Fairly isolated. Mimosa's been built up in recent years. But not much. The estate's on a finger of land that juts away from the main body. No close neighbors. People who've seen it say it's a little bit of paradise."

Merriman grinned. "If they're going to team us, this is the right assignment. A little bit of paradise? Couple of women with a rich granddaddy? Beats chasing after criminals and con men. Me, I'm allergic to danger."

"The only danger is that these women hold us off." Eli was concerned about this, but not worried. Not deeply.

"The older one? Emerson?" Merriman said.

"What about her?"

Merriman shrugged. "I heard she's smart, that's all. And she can be tough."

"She's not as smart as she thinks." Eli finished the last of his beer and he wiped the back of his hand across his mouth. "And she may be tough. But she's not tough enough."

THE NEXT MORNING, Emerson sat in the library, curled up in the ancient velvet armchair, her legs dangling over its arm.

The library was on the second floor of the house, and its large glass doors opened to a balcony that looked out on the ocean. The ocean tossed more than usual today because the wind was high, with long, gray clouds streaking the sky.

Books crammed the teakwood shelves, books of every sort, and they were piled on the desk and floor and on the antique sofa where no one ever sat.

A teak counter ran along the east wall, and the wall above it was covered with framed paintings, wild with color and boldly signed Roth. Beneath the counter were cabinets designed to hold magazines, some decades old.

Magazines were what interested Emerson this morning. A fallen stack of them spilled across the wine-colored ottoman, and others littered the carpet.

The library was Emerson's favorite part of the house. It had its own fireplace for the rare spell of winter cold, and an old-fashioned ceiling fan to dispel heat. She loved the feel of being surrounded by books yet being only steps away from the sense of space and freedom offered by the balcony.

This room was Claire's bane, for Claire was neat, and the room defied all her efforts to make it tidy. But Emerson did not mind that the place was a hodgepodge. She found its disorder as comfortable as a pair of old jeans.

A knock sounded at the library door. Emerson looked up from her magazine, her face brightening. She recognized that delicate knock; it was Nana's.

"Come in," she called. The door opened, and her grandmother entered.

Lela Roth was a tiny woman, seventy-three years old. Her hair, once ink-black, was now dark gray, and she wore it in one long braid down her back. Her black eyes, large and thickly lashed, were her most striking feature, and Emerson had inherited them.

Lela's back was still straight, her movements slow but

sure. She spoke with an accent, for she had been raised in Paris. Nathan had always teased that he'd kidnapped her from her strict father and made her his child bride. She was ten years younger than her husband.

"I thought I would find you here." Nana moved to Emerson's side and kissed her on the cheek. "What are you doing?"

Emerson kissed her back, then waggled her magazine. "My homework."

"Phaa!" said Nana. "You're reading things by that man, that Garner person."

"It's important to know your enemy." Emerson rose, gesturing for Nana to take the armchair.

"You do not have much time to learn about him," Nana said, sitting. "He and the *photographe* arrive in an hour. Your sister is going crazy."

Emerson cleared the ottoman and sat by Nana's feet. "My sister's an alarmist."

"I'm a bit alarmed myself." Nana shook her head. "You're sure it's wise to do this?"

"I'm sure." Emerson took the toe of her grandmother's embroidered slipper and squeezed it playfully. "How's the Captain?"

"As usual," Nana said with an expressive shrug. "I've been sitting with him."

"How's the painting going?"

"It goes well, I think." Nana frowned slightly. She had been a great beauty in her day, and now she was an elderly beauty. Even her frown was becoming. It had style.

She tilted her head and gave Emerson a stern look. "But you're changing the subject on me. This man, Garner. This is how you get ready for him? Only looking at magazines? Again?"

"By their works ye shall know them."

Nana tapped her foot scornfully on a copy of *Mondragon*.

"He is like *le requin.* The shark. From a distance I admire his strength. But close I do not want to see him. I do not want his sharp teeth going snap-snap at me and my family."

Emerson took her grandmother's gnarled hand gently between her own. Age had been kind to the older woman except for her hands. Arthritis had swollen and bent her fingers. "Nana, *Mondragon* gave us a choice. They'll do the story with our cooperation. Or without it. We have far more control if we cooperate. Or seem to."

Nana tapped a forefinger to her temple. "This Garner man, he is smart. I have read him. And he is hard. He has moved among criminals, masters of deception. You truly think you are his equal?"

Emerson smiled. "Why shouldn't I be? I have the Captain's blood in my veins. And yours, too."

Slowly, the older woman smiled back. She reached out and smoothed Emerson's long hair. "Ahh. Yes. But be careful. I have seen his picture. He is handsome. That is another weapon. He will not be above using it. *Apel du sex.*"

"Sex appeal?" Emerson's eyes lit with mischief. "Two can play that game."

Nana threw her head back and laughed. Then she grew serious. She gave Emerson a critical look. "You're not wearing *that,* are you?"

Emerson wore very short red shorts and a white T-shirt without a bra beneath. "No. I thought the little white sun dress. With the low neck."

Nana's scowl was elegant in its disdain. She waved her hand in admonition. "*Non, non, non.* So obvious! Be subtle. The blue caftan. With the sleeves that flow. Cover yourself. It is much more provocative. Shouldn't I know?"

With that, she got up and walked toward the door.

Emerson frowned. "I can't. The caftan has a spot on it." It did, a small but dark stain on the bosom.

"All the better," Nana said loftily. "It will look less studied."

With that, she was out the door and was gone.

Emerson rolled her eyes, thinking, *I will not wear something with a spot on it. Why it'd look as if I didn't care a bit what impression I made—*

But then she grinned. "Damn," she said softly. "She's right. Exactly."

WHEN IN THE TROPICS, rent a convertible and don Ray•Bans; this was Eli's philosophy. Except, of course, in certain parts of the tropics, where it was more prudent to rent a Humvee and wear Kevlar.

He drove north, up Highway 1, while Merriman stared at a map of the Keys in perplexity.

"How many of these islands are there?"

"Around eight hundred or so."

Merriman shot him a disbelieving look. "Get real. There aren't eight hundred on this map. No way."

"A lot are too small to chart. Only about thirty are inhabited."

Merriman looked at the map again, frowning. The Keys stretched 120 miles from Key Largo, the northernmost, to Key West, the farthest south. "There's only this one highway connecting them? That's it?"

"That's it," Eli said. "One highway in and out."

The convertible, a red Chrysler, was crossing a long bridge. Merriman grimaced uneasily. "These damn bridges go over the *ocean*, man."

"Right." Eli nodded calmly. "The Overseas Highway. Forty-two bridges. Great feat of engineering."

Merriman was unimpressed by the great feat. "What if there's a wreck or a traffic jam or something?"

"You're stuck."

"What if a bridge collapses? Or washes out?"

Eli shrugged. "Same thing. You're stuck."

Merriman's expression became a bit queasy. "At breakfast I heard people talking about a hurricane warning."

"Tropical storm. It was downgraded."

"Technicalities," Merriman grumbled. "I heard the word *evacuation*. That this thing might hit the Lower Keys."

"And it might not. It's been diddling around out there for a week. People are tired of worrying about it." Eli gave him a measuring glance. "I didn't take you for a worrier."

"I'm from Toronto," Merriman protested. "We don't have hurricanes. Well, there was one, but it was before I was born. Look, if we have to evacuate, and planes are grounded, *this* is the only way out? One dinky road?"

"Relax. It's hurricane season. There are always watches and warnings."

Eli had played waiting games with hurricanes before. They could change course swiftly, and the storm Merriman was fretting about might never touch Florida.

But right now, the photographer was eyeing the sky with suspicion. It was blue, but gray clouds were sweeping in from the south. The wind made the palm trees bend northward, fronds streaming.

"Don't worry about the damn weather," Eli said out of the side of his mouth. "We're nearly there. Another five minutes, we'll be at Mandevilla."

"Maybe they have a storm cellar there. Maybe they'll share it."

"Most people don't have cellars on the Keys."

Eli turned down a graveled road. Scrub pines and lingam vitae trees grew in a wild tangle on both sides of the road, blocking any view beyond them.

They came to a high iron gate. On either side of it stretched a wall of limestone, six feet tall. Its top was jagged with gray coral that had been cemented into place. Eli stopped beside a limestone kiosk with a speaker. Next to it was a mailbox with no name on it.

They were close enough to the ocean to smell the salt, and under the rush of the wind, Eli heard the murmur of the waves, low and even. Merriman looked about warily. "All of a sudden we're in the middle of nowhere."

"Yeah." Eli recognized the trees growing along the wall. They were poisonwoods, the Keys' equivalent of poison ivy. Along with the sharp coral, they were there to discourage outsiders from climbing the wall.

Merriman said, "I get the feeling that they really *don't* want visitors."

"There's a couple of million bucks worth of art behind those walls," Eli murmured, gazing at them. "You can bet this place has some high security."

He pushed the button beside the speaker, which crackled into life. "Yes?" A woman's voice, low and rich, came through the static. "Who is it?"

"Eli Garner and Merriman from *Mondragon Magazine.* We have a ten o'clock appointment to speak with Miss Roth. Miss Emerson Roth."

More static. Again the woman's voice. "All right. Come to the front entrance." The speaker went dead.

Half a minute passed, then the gate creaked open. The road grew narrower and bumpier, and then, as they rounded a curve, they clattered over a rickety metal bridge that crossed a gully. It was shaded by a grove of tall trees that stood like sentries.

At last they saw the house, almost completely screened by a row of royal poincianas and oleanders. The lawn had a scruffy look. It needed mowing, and its green came as much from weeds as grass.

Eli drove past the trees with their red and white flowers, and for the first time, saw the house clearly. He'd seen it dozens of times in photos, of course, but the photos were old.

The place, no mansion, was smaller than he'd imagined. Although not decaying, it had an air of having seen better days. Still, it was made of blocks of granite, and looked as solid as a vault.

It was the setting, not the dwelling that drew the eye and held it. The house stood on a slight rise, facing a magnificent view of the Gulf. For two hundred yards, the lawn extended, ragged and dappled with wildflowers. Then the lawn gave way to a stretch of clean, dun-colored sand.

The waves pounding the beach were more gray than blue today, but in the distance was a scattering of small islands so green that they seemed jewellike. Out in the cove, Eli saw a dolphin jump and smiled in spite of himself.

Merriman whistled. "What's that they always say about real estate? Location, location, location."

Eli didn't answer. He stared out over ragged grass and flowers, past the beach to where the sea met the sky in a hazy blue-gray line.

"If you're going to be a hermit, this is a great place to do it," Merriman said. "A little piece of paradise is right."

But paradise is showing signs of wear, Eli thought, his gaze drifting back to the house.

The paint on its wooden trim was peeling from the salt air, and a large crack zigzagged up the cement walk that led to the front stairs. The roof of the porch sagged slightly. The flame-of-the-woods shrubs flanking the porch on both sides sprawled untrimmed, an uncontrolled mass of fiery blossoms.

"Scenery's one of the hardest things in the world to shoot," Merriman grumbled almost to himself, his eyes still on the waves. He looked as if he was already calculating how he'd have to do it.

Eli put his sunglasses back on. "Come on. You can figure it out later. Let's get the introductions over with."

He got out of the convertible, and so did Merriman, who followed him up the walk with obvious reluctance. He wanted to play with his viewfinder so much that his face was pained as he stared at the vista.

Eli noticed hairline cracks in the floor of the porch and that the old-fashioned doorbell seemed tarnished by years of sea salt. The white paint of the front door was peeling, like the trim.

He pressed the bell. He heard it chime, echoing within the house. He glanced about the house and saw no sign of anyone. Surely there had to be a groundskeeper or yardman, with this much land.

No one answered. *She knows we're here,* Eli thought with cold irritation. *All right, baby, play your games.* He rang again, leaning on the bell a little harder, just to annoy her.

They waited a full minute, Merriman still gazing at the sea and lost in silent concentration. Eli was about to hit the bell a third time, giving it all he had, when the door swung open.

There she stood. Emerson Roth.

Eli went blind to everything else. His ears buzzed, his forehead turned numb and a rush of excitement surged through his veins.

She was tall and— Great God, he was a writer, and he couldn't think of a word for her. Yes, he could. Ravishing. She ravished him. She overwhelmed and bewitched him— for an eon that lasted fully a second. He yanked himself back to sanity.

Everything about her face was good, the rounded cheekbones, the straight nose and the intriguing mouth with its hint of a smile. Her hair fell in a dark, lush cascade. But it was her eyes that struck him. Depthless, exotic, they reminded him that her grandmother, too, was an exotic woman.

Emerson wore a long plain gown of something crinkly and silky. It was a vivid turquoise blue with full sleeves that came almost to her fingertips. The garment covered her from collarbone to ankle. It only hinted at the curve of her breasts, but the hint was excellent.

"Hello," she said in a voice that was surprisingly human. "You must be the people from *Mondragon*."

She thrust out her hand with an air of stoic resignation. "I'm Emerson Roth."

He took her hand and was relieved that it didn't shoot sparks and lightning bolts through his system. It was a medium-size hand, firm and strong.

"Eli Garner," he said gruffly. "And this is the photographer, Merriman."

He actually had to elbow Merriman, who'd kept staring at the ocean. "Oh," Merriman said. "Pleased to meet you." He shook her hand and went back to taking imaginary pictures of the sea.

"I won't ask you to come in," she said. "Not today. We'll sit by the pool. Follow me."

She passed him and descended the stairs. He smelled the fleeting scent of sandalwood. The wind lifted and tumbled her long mane of hair, fluttered her sleeves.

As she'd passed, he'd noticed a small dark spot on her gown, over the left breast. It was hard to pull his gaze away. Didn't she know the spot was there? Or did she think so little of her visitors that she didn't care?

CHAPTER TWO

HEAD HIGH, Emerson led the way to the patio's gate and unlocked it. She did not so much as glance at the two men behind her, but her heart beat a herky-jerky rhythm.

Merriman, the photographer, didn't alarm her. He seemed to have surrendered completely to the visual charms of Mandevilla.

But she sensed a menacing edge in Eli Garner. He had what she thought of as gunfighter's eyes, keen and permanently narrowed in watchfulness.

Yet he was handsome, as well. Nana was right; this was a man with sex appeal, possibly more than should be legal. She must be on guard against it.

She let the men enter the patio, then followed, closing the gate behind her. She turned to face them. They both stood by the pool, whose water glittered and quivered like a live blue gem.

She walked to the white wrought-iron table and stood behind the master chair, setting her hands on its back to claim it for her own. It was the largest of the four chairs, thronelike. It would give her the air of command.

"Sit," she said in a no-nonsense tone. "Please."

Merriman, busy gawking at the foliage and flowers, mechanically sat in one of the smaller chairs. Giving her a calculating glance, Eli Garner took another.

He was lean with strongly carved features. His high cheekbones seemed sharp enough to cut diamonds. His dark hair waved nearly to his collar, and he was so tanned that he looked more like an outdoorsman than a writer.

She gave each man a cool smile. Merriman, gazing entranced at the hibiscus tree, didn't notice. Eli returned the smile but made it several degrees cooler than hers.

Before they'd arrived, she'd placed a silver tray on the table. On it were a carafe of turquoise crystal and three matching goblets.

"Lemonade?" she asked. She meant to be hospitable, but only minimally.

"No, thanks," murmured Merriman. He was absorbed by the garden's flowers.

"Please," said Eli, not taking his eyes from her.

She filled two of the goblets and handed him one. A gold pocket watch lay on the tray beside the remaining glass. She opened it and set it on the table so both he and she could see its face.

"I said I'd talk to you for an hour today. I'll begin by stating the ground rules." She turned to Merriman. "You can take all the exterior shots of the house and grounds you want. On your other visits, you may take pictures of the paintings, the studio and some of the more interesting family pieces. No pictures of the family itself."

Merriman seemed to jerk back into reality. He blinked his cobalt blue eyes. "Not even you?"

"No pictures of the family," she repeated.

He shrugged amiably and went back to contemplating the flora.

She faced Eli Garner, whose gaze stayed fastened on her with unnerving steadiness. "I'll be the main person you'll talk to. Day after tomorrow, my grandmother will speak with you for half an hour. No more."

One of Eli's brows lifted, just a trace. "I hope she's not unwell."

"No. Her health is fine."

"Will I talk with your sister?"

"No. She doesn't choose to speak with you."

He sat back in his chair and sipped from the goblet. She noticed that he had a tattoo on one sinewy forearm. It was a picture of a dancing Hindu god with four arms and an elephant's head.

Emerson recognized it—Ganesh. The sight unsettled her, for she had an expensive figurine of Ganesh in her bedroom. He was the deity invoked to help overcome obstacles. She'd bought the figurine when she'd made her first solo trip to New York to take over her father's job.

It agitated her to see a symbol she'd chosen for herself etched on the arm of a man she thought of as an opponent. She pulled her gaze away. *Don't think about it.*

He ran a knuckle over his chin thoughtfully. "Your sister is shy, perhaps. Maybe she's picked up a reclusive gene from your grandfather."

This was close enough to what Emerson feared about Claire that she blinked in irritation. "No. She doesn't choose to speak to you. That's all."

His mouth crooked in a mocking smile. "This isn't going to be much of an interview if you just keep repeating yourself."

Don't let him control this conversation, she told herself sternly. She tilted her head, gave him a flirtatious glance. "Why don't you ask me questions that don't force me to repeat myself?"

He nodded as if he were humoring a troublesome child. "All right. Your father was your grandfather's agent. He knew he was a very sick man. He trained you to take his place. Did *you* know how sick he was?"

"Yes," she lied. She hadn't known. He'd always had a weak heart, but his decline had come swiftly and inexorably. Learning he was doomed had made her feel as if she were dying, too. But she would not tell that to this stranger, this intruder.

She was saved from elaborating on the lie by Merriman.

"There're some interesting cloud formations blowing in. If you don't mind, I'd like to start those exterior shots. Go down and take a few from the beach. You'll excuse me?"

"Of course," she said and gave him her most dazzling smile. He didn't seem to notice. He stood and pulled his camera from its case as he went out the gate.

She turned her attention back to Eli, who was still watching her as a cat watches a particularly tricky mouse. She smiled at him, hoping coquettishness might make him forget that she was journalistic prey.

"We were talking about my father. We were a close family. And private. That's why I'm not very good at being questioned. I'm afraid I give a bad interview."

For all the effect it had on him, she might as well have smiled at a boulder. "Your father died of cardiovascular disease. Is this something that runs in the family?"

She sidestepped the question. "My father was born with a heart defect—congenital, not hereditary. He looked very healthy. Strapping, even. But he always knew he might not live to old age."

She and Claire had known that, too, from the time they were little girls. But they hadn't *realized* it. People would say, "Damon has a heart problem." To Emerson and Claire, the words generated a vague fear about something that seemed far away and was not truly possible.

Eli frowned. "Your mother died when you and your sister were quite young. Would you tell me about it?"

Oh, hell, she thought, *how can I try to flirt when he keeps asking questions about everybody I love dying?*

She decided to use tears. She could cry at will if she thought of sad things. Her father had always said she could have been an actress. So she thought of her father's funeral and her mother's, and the tears welled up.

She tossed her hair as if exasperated at her own weakness. "I really don't like to talk about those things."

To prove it, she let a tear spill over and slide down her cheek.

He stared at the tear with the air of a scientist examining an interesting bug. He pulled a clean handkerchief from his back pocket and held it out to her. "Could you try? To say just a little?"

She let two more tears fall then, her voice breaking, said, "No." Stalling for time, she added, "I'll be all right in a few minutes." She dabbed the tears away but kept clutching his handkerchief as if one more such question would reduce her to a sobbing heap.

The dark eyes studied her, but she thought she saw unexpected sympathy in them. He reached out and put his hand over one of hers. "Sorry," he said gruffly. His touch sent unexpected tingles through her.

She looked down, astonished that he'd do such a thing. She found herself gazing at the Ganesh on his arm, dancing on one foot, his four arms waving merrily. Eli's hand felt good wrapped around hers—it actually felt comforting—but she drew back as if unready for such intimacy.

"Excuse me," he said frowning again. "I didn't mean to be forward."

"It's all right. It's just that remembering makes me emotional."

His expression was slightly dubious, but he said, "Let me see if I have it straight. After your mother passed away, your family came here. You lived with your grandparents. Your grandfather's agent retired that same year, and your father took over his job."

Emerson nodded her head yes. She sniffled and squeezed the handkerchief. Her fingers still prickled from his touch. "Yes. Felix Mettler was the agent. We called him Uncle Felix. He died, too. Of pneumonia. Fourteen years ago."

That, she thought, was information Eli probably had anyway, and it wasted his time. She stole a glance at the watch.

He'd been here a full ten minutes, and he hadn't pried anything out of her yet.

She was doing well, she told herself. She was doing just fine.

This man wasn't so formidable, after all.

FOR TEN MINUTES Eli had let her fend him off. If he gave her five more minutes, she'd get cocky. And when she got cocky, she'd get careless. And then he'd spring his trap.

She was an amateur, but he had to admit she was good. For a few disturbing seconds, he'd believed her tears were real. Well, they *were* real, but his gut instinct was that she'd summoned them by willpower.

So she'd played the tears card, which was dirty fighting, and he'd played the sympathy card, which was just as dirty, but it gave him an excuse to touch her. Because from the moment she'd opened the door, he'd *wanted* to touch her. He wanted it so much his blood pounded with it.

Good Lord, but she was something. When she pulled her flirtatious act, he had to control his expression until his face ached from it.

Now he toyed with the blue goblet as it sat on the table, turning it first one way, then the other. For a moment he didn't allow himself to look at her. Why hadn't Merriman fallen down at her feet and begged to take her photo? Was he gay? Crazy? Was it possible he was the world's only blind photographer?

"So," he said, his voice neutral. "Your grandparents had a big part in raising you."

"Mmm. Yes. They were wonderful. In every way. He was such fun, and she was so sweet—"

He cut her off as he kept playing with his glass. "Did you know, when you moved here, that your grandfather was a famous artist?"

"My sister and I knew he was an artist. I don't think we

understood he was famous. To me, *famous* meant being on television. Or in movies. Mickey Mouse was famous. Mel Gibson was famous. We knew the Captain was kind of important, but we didn't know why.''

He let her babble in that vein a bit, knowing she thought she was running down the clock. He would treat her gently for a while, asking simple questions. He stared at the light dancing on the blue goblet and tried his best to look harmless.

"And his nickname was the Captain because he grew up around boats? In Maine, yes?"

"Yes. His father had a fishing boat. When he went off to college in New York somebody nicknamed him the Captain. It stuck.''

"But he didn't finish college. A bit of a rebel, wasn't he?''

"Yes. Most good artists have a rebellious streak. He took off to see the world. He wanted to study non-Western art. And to go to Paris. Don't all painters want to go to Paris?'' She sounded relieved, as if these questions weren't as bad as she'd feared.

Eli stole a look at her, and the sight of her slammed him like a blow. She sat in that ornate white chair, wearing that simple, perfect turquoise gown and holding a goblet the same color. Something really was wrong with Merriman. Very wrong.

His breath stuck in his chest, but he got his question out with no change in tone. "He went to north Africa first?"

She nodded, and he watched her lips as she answered. "Morocco. Egypt. Tunisia. Algeria. Oh, yes. He spent time in all of them.''

"And then he went to Paris and met your grandmother…"

"Yes.'' She didn't elaborate, and Eli knew better than to push much further. Nathan Roth had always been vague about how he had met and married his wife. She had avoided the spotlight, even in the days her husband had gloried in it.

Still, Eli had to seem to *try*. "I've heard conflicting stories. That she wasn't actually born in France. That her family came from Egypt? Algeria? Morocco?"

Emerson smiled vaguely. "That's something you should ask her."

He allowed himself to smile back. "Will she tell me?"

She raised the goblet to her mouth. "Perhaps."

"Tell me," he said, "when you were a child, what did you think of the paintings? Or is that too personal for you to say?"

The will-o'-the-wisp smile touched her lips again. "I thought they were squiggles. Pretty, but just squiggles. I didn't know why people bought them."

He nodded to encourage her. "Now you do. Because you sell them."

"No. The dealer sells them. Gerald Krystol. He and I talk over the prices and so on. I'm only the agent."

"What do you think of the paintings now?"

She sat a bit taller in the chair. A look of pride crossed her face. But there was something more, as well. He realized it might be love. "They're great. They're a national treasure."

Suddenly, she rose. "Would you like to walk on the beach? It's one of the Captain's favorite places. This may be your only chance. The weather's supposed to get worse the next few days."

He gazed up at her, her gown rippling in the wind. His throat tightened. "Yes. I would."

"Then come with me," she said, moving toward the gate. She turned and glanced over her shoulder, then made a beckoning motion.

Suddenly he wondered if he really *was* the one in charge here. He followed her as if powerless to do otherwise.

COMING BACK from the beach, Merriman met Eli and the
Roth woman on the path. He grinned, feeling uneasy. She
was pretty, but in too flamboyant a way. He liked faces that
were subtler; they were more interesting to him.

Besides, Emerson Roth struck him as too edgy. She and
Eli had been engaged in a complex fencing match from the
get-go. Eli might relish such games, but Merriman did not.

He said to Emerson, "I'd like to do some more exterior
shots, but closer up. That okay with you?"

Her eyes went wary, but only for a split second. She gave
him a nod of permission. "As long as there are no people.
Not even the groundsman. And he's been told not to talk
to either of you."

"I understand," said Merriman, mentally adding *Your
Highness*. He saw Eli looking her over, as if trying to figure
out exactly who lived behind that glamorous face. Merriman shrugged a goodbye to them both, then trudged back
up the path. The wind was rising, and the clouds rolling in
thicker and darker.

The pool area had a garden next to it, and the garden
lured him. He liked the lushness of its tropical flowers, their
startling spectrum of colors.

But he stopped before reaching the house and glanced
again at Eli and Emerson Roth. Their backs were to him.
Beyond them, the sea stretched, colored like steel, and the
sky had turned dark gray. Even the sand looked grayish.

Eli wore wheat-colored jeans and a red shirt. The woman
was a splash of turquoise beside him. Except for the muted
greens of a few plants, he and she offered the only bright
colors; they caught the eye and held it.

To hell with it, he thought. Permission or no permission,
he'd take a few shots. She couldn't object to having her
back photographed could she? He raised the camera and
snapped them, one, two, three times.

Then he turned toward the house and let himself in
through the iron gate. He sniffed the air and could scent the

smell of oncoming rain mingling with the heavy fragrance of the flowers. He walked slowly through the garden until an unbelievable tree caught his interest.

The tree was huge, but looked as if dozens of smaller trees had grown together, fusing into one. From above it dropped dozens of new roots to the ground, so that it seemed like a one-tree jungle. It was surrounded by a colorful stand of other plants.

He tried to make his way around this bizarre tree, to see it more closely. But then a flower caught his eye, a peculiar flower of gold and purple and scarlet.

Momentarily distracted, he dropped to his knee and began to take shots of this odd blossom. Suddenly he heard a rustling in the foliage. It sounded like the rustling of something *large.*

Merriman went still as a stone, wondering if the Keys were so tropical that they harbored things like anacondas or man-eating pythons. He knew there were alligators or crocodiles, but would they come this near to a house?

The rustling came closer, and Merriman held his breath. Of course, alligators crept around buildings—weren't there always horror stories in the paper about them eating pet poodles and the occasional hapless tourist?

He vaguely remembered, from watching *Peter Pan,* that alligators had yellow eyes and could move with lethal speed. Something made a scuttling sound, almost next to him now, and Merriman whirled and stared down—into a pair of glinting yellow eyes.

After a split second of horror, he was relieved to see that the eyes belonged to the fattest cat he'd ever seen. Blue-gray, with a white nose, breast and paws, it stared at him with a disdain as massive as its body.

Well, thought Merriman, if he couldn't snap the family, he could snap the family cat. This rotund beast had a fancy collar, and a tag shaped like a mouse. *Say cheese,* thought Merriman, looking through the lens.

Then, from behind his tree, Merriman heard light footsteps. The cat heard them, too, and cocked its head in that direction. It hunkered lower to the ground, as if trying to hide.

"Bunbury! It's no good. I see you."

The voice was feminine and breathless—and nearby. More rustling, and the animal cringed lower, its ears flattening. A pair of slender hands struggled to grab the cat by its fat middle.

Merriman found himself looking into a young woman's face. Her eyes widened, and her mouth formed a small, perfect O of shock.

"Oh, goodness," she breathed, and she looked paralyzed, crouched there, her hands motionless on the cat's gray fur.

Merriman lowered his camera. The sight of her was like a kick in his chest. She was lovely. Her hair was the dark golden brown of honey, and so were her eyes. Her skin was a paler shade of honey, and she wore a T-shirt that matched her hair.

A woman made out of honey, Merriman thought illogically, but his system, ignoring logic, said *Yum.*

She seemed in dismay, almost terror. "You can't take my picture."

"I—I wasn't," he stammered. "Just the cat's."

"You can't take the cat's picture." Her voice was panicky.

"I'm sorry," Merriman said with all the sincerity he could muster. He meant it. She was such an appealing creature, the last thing he wanted was to upset her. "I didn't know the cat was here. When I saw him, it was an automatic reflex. I didn't mean—"

She snatched the cat up and clutched it protectively against her breast. She seemed too upset to gather her thoughts. "He's not supposed to be out here. I was supposed to get everything inside."

He couldn't stop looking at her. "Everything?" he echoed.

"All the animals. I couldn't find him. You know—cats."

"I know cats. Yes. Independent. I used to be one. I mean, I used to have one. Do you want me to help you? He looks heavy."

"No. No." She struggled to rise, but she was trying not to crush the foliage and still balance the cat. She had her arms wrapped round him under his forelegs, so he was staring at Merriman over the great mound of his belly. He looked like King Henry VIII.

The woman almost lost her balance, so Merriman sprang to his feet, putting out a hand to steady her. She went stock-still. "I didn't *know* you were out here," she said. "I looked out and saw Bunbury—"

He kept his hand on her upper arm, just to make sure she was all right and to convey his concern. "Bunbury is?"

"The cat." She swallowed. "I didn't see any people. Why were you behind that tree?"

"I never saw a tree like that. I just wanted to look closer."

"You were squatting down behind it, hiding," she accused. Her cheeks had flushed an enticing pink.

"There was a flower. A strange flower. That one." He pointed an accusing finger at it. "I was kneeling to take a picture, that's all."

She hugged the cat more tightly to her. It screwed up its face in protest and emitted a sound that was more like a hoarse chirp than a meow. Merriman realized the woman was staring just as intently at him as he was at her. He still had his hand on her arm, but she made no protest, so he was happy to keep touching her.

Her face was gentle, not flamboyantly pretty like her sister's, but pretty with a natural sweetness that almost hypnotized him. Her hair was brushed in a soft wave away from her face and hung nearly to her shoulders.

"I'm Merriman, the photographer," he said, extending his free hand. "Please shake hands so I know you forgive me for startling you. I apologize. From the heart."

From a heart that ached oddly and pleasantly, he realized. She looked doubtful, but then tried to reach for his hand. But that entailed juggling the cat, who protested with another of his weird, grating chirps.

"Let me take him for you," Merriman said, scrambling to get one arm around the cat. He managed, and Bunbury dangled like a sulky sack of grain in his hold.

Almost shyly, Merriman offered his hand again. She studied it, then, far more shyly, took it. He stared down at her, tongue-tied. Her grasp was light and cool, yet firm.

"I'm Claire Roth," she said. "I—I saw you walking down on the beach. I didn't know you'd come back here."

Merriman reluctantly let her draw her hand away. She was edging back from him, clearly about to make a quick escape. He didn't want her to go. Desperately, he said, "The flowers—the trees. I'm taking pictures, but I don't know what I'm taking pictures *of*. This tree—what is it?"

"A banyan," she almost whispered.

"It looks like sixteen trees grown together. Those things dropping down, are they roots, or just vines? How big will the thing get?"

"It's all one tree. Yes, they're roots. It could grow a hundred feet tall. But it probably won't."

Her eyes rose to the sky. "Storms." She looked worried.

"Hurricanes?" He should have glanced at the sky, too, but he didn't have to. He could sense the morning darkening and the wind rising. And he couldn't stop taking in her face.

A gust of wind lifted her hair, revealing a delicate ear that had never been pierced. She nodded. "Hurricanes. Tropical storms. We lose branches."

Something about her made him feel giddy as a schoolboy. "There's a watch or a warning. Does it scare you?"

She nodded. "A little. I—I need to go in now."

"I'll carry the cat," he offered.

Her expression went uncomfortable, and hastily he added, "Only to the door. That's all. Do you have to go in? I'd sure like somebody to tell me the names of all these plants."

He was pleased to see her hesitate. She shook her head. "I didn't mean to talk to anybody."

"I wouldn't ask you anything personal," he vowed, forgetting that he owed any loyalty to Eli. "If you could just tell me the names, and I could write them down. Like that thing— I don't know what it is."

Still clutching Bunbury in a one-armed hold, he pointed at the peculiar flower of purple and gold. "I'll get back, develop all this stuff and not know how to look it up."

She still acted as if she had reservations. But she said, "It's a bird-of-paradise." She paused, then said, "Some people say it looks like a bird in flight. It's unusual, because it's actually pollinated by birds, not bees."

"*Really,*" Merriman said, as if this was the most fascinating fact he'd ever heard. Perhaps it was, coming from her lips, those words about birds and bees.

He rubbed the cat's stomach so it would stay peaceful. Merriman tilted his head toward a climbing vine with ornate lavender flowers. "And those? Orchids?"

She pushed a wayward lock of hair from her cheek. "No. They're passionflowers."

He rubbed the cat harder. "Passionflowers. Why are they called that?"

"Well…" She still seemed torn about lingering, but clearly she loved the plants and wanted him to appreciate them. "It's kind of a complicated legend…"

"I'd love to hear it," Merriman told her with so much sincerity that it made him dizzy. He rubbed the cat until it had no choice but to purr in sensual pleasure.

EMERSON KICKED OFF her sandals so she could walk in the damp sand and dodge the surf when it came foaming onto the beach. It was a game she'd played since childhood, and she loved it.

This, she calculated, would force Eli Garner to keep his distance and try to question her against the wind and over the roar of the waves. That, or he'd have to shed his own shoes and a considerable amount of dignity to stay at her side.

She was surprised when he undid his sandals and set them next to hers. He rolled his jeans up to his shins, stuck his hands in his pockets and strolled to the sea's edge beside her as if it were the most natural thing in the world.

But today the sea was not playful. The waves that came rolling in were rough, and they did not so much collapse in a froth on the sand as throw themselves on it in assault.

The wind was cool and whipped Emerson's long skirt around her. She had to gather it up and clench its hem in her fist. This left her legs bare to the knee, and Eli gave them a glance that seemed coolly interested. She wished she'd worn capri pants.

The wind blew her hair about, and his, too. He had thick hair, longish and wavy. He reached into his pocket and put on his sunglasses. They gave him a masked look.

She sidestepped a wave more aggressive than the rest and accidentally bumped into him. The water surged around her calves, and she nearly lost her balance when the spent wave pulled seaward again.

His arm shot out to steady her, settling on her waist, bracing her so she didn't stumble. It seemed a perfunctory gesture, brief and businesslike. His hand fell away almost immediately. She was glad. His touch implied an intimacy she found dangerously intriguing.

"Careful," he warned.

"I didn't realize you were that close," she grumbled.

"I have to stay close to hear you. Looks like we've got some weather coming."

She glanced at the far horizon. There, the clouds were almost black, and a gray veil seemed to spill from them: rain.

She said, "They've upgraded the storm back to a hurricane. It's in the Caribbean and moving fast."

He studied her from behind the mask of his sunglasses. "Hurricane? When did they upgrade it? It was still a tropical storm when we left Key West."

"I heard it on the radio right before you came." She tried to smooth her streaming hair. "It's growing. And picking up speed."

"Does that scare you?" he asked.

Few things frightened Emerson, and she hated to admit that anything *could* frighten her. But hurricanes did. She tried to sound philosophic. "Hurricanes are the price you pay for living here."

"That didn't answer the question."

Damn, he must sense her uneasiness. "Only a fool wouldn't respect a hurricane. But it doesn't scare me until I know it's close. I've seen what they can do."

"So have I. So what do you do when one's coming at you?"

"The usual. We have emergency supplies. A propane stove, lanterns, the whole disaster kit. Even a special room. We hope for the best and close the hurricane shutters."

He looked at the dark horizon, then back at the house. "Maybe you should shut them soon."

She tossed her head. "Frenchy will. As soon as you leave."

"I see. And Frenchy would be…"

"The groundskeeper and maintenance man."

"Frenchy, I take it, is French?"

"No. Frenchy is Norwegian."

"Then why's he called Frenchy?"

"I don't know. Things like that happen in the Keys."

He seemed to reflect on this. She added, "He won't talk to you under any circumstances. He's signed a confidentiality agreement. An ironclad one."

Take that, she thought. But at that moment, she had to dodge another wave and once again nearly collided with him. Why did he have to stay so close?

But he didn't seem to notice, and he changed the subject. "So this is the beach your grandfather loved so much."

She caught his careful wording. "He still loves it," she said. "There's no need to use the past tense."

"He still comes here?" Eli asked, just casually enough.

"Of course." She pushed her hair out of her eyes. "It's the main reason he bought this place. Maybe we should turn back. This isn't a nice day to be here."

"I don't mind." His gaze swept up and down the beach. "It's private here. Very private."

"Yes. It is."

"No immediate neighbors. I looked at it on a detailed map. To the south, a mangrove swamp. To the north, a mangrove swamp. To the east, a long tract of wild country that your family owns. And to the west, the Gulf."

She shrugged. He walked so close now that strands of her hair flicked and danced against the shoulder of his shirt. Her gauzy sleeve, damp with spray, blew against his tattooed arm.

She stopped. "The wind's getting higher. I feel it. We'll turn back now."

She walked to his other side, no longer wanting to play tag with the water. She moved out of its reach, letting her skirt fall to her ankles again.

He kept even with her, and he tilted his head toward the cove. "You'd have a tough time getting here by boat, if I read the charts right. It's shallow with a rough bottom. Almost impossible to land here."

"That's right," she said, quickening her stride toward home. "So if a sightseer should come—"

Or a snoop— she added mentally.

"—he could only see this spot from a distance. That wall of trees hides the house. All he could see is the top of the house rising over the branches. Or somebody on this beach."

"Not many people come sight-seeing," she returned defensively. "People come to the Keys to fish and boat and party. Not to see an aging painter."

"I don't know about that. I did."

He smiled at her. He had an interesting mouth, a full lower lip for so lean a face. The smile was knowing, and there was a dare in it.

She ignored the dare. "My grandfather's famous in the art world. But to the general public? He's not a celebrity."

His maddening smile stayed in place, bracketed by wry lines. "He used to be. People would see his pictures in the glossy magazines, *Vanity Fair, Vogue.*"

A prickle of apprehension rippled up her spine. "It got old for him. Stale. He found that sort of thing less and less attractive."

He stopped, and she started to walk on without him. "Wait," he said.

She stopped, but turned to stare at him in challenge. "What?"

The wind ruffled his hair, the clouded sky reflected in the lenses of his sunglasses. He held up his hand, as if signaling her to stay. "Hold on a minute. Seven years ago, your grandfather threw himself a birthday party. He'd done the same thing for years. The guest list was twenty-one people. If I remember correctly."

He remembered correctly, all right, curse him. But Emerson gave him a smile of false sweetness. "Yes?"

"But six years ago, no party. None. And none since. He basically withdrew from the world."

She'd known it was coming and was only surprised he hadn't zeroed in sooner. She raised her chin. "He decided to focus more on his family and his work. His dearest friend, William Marcuse, died of a heart attack that year. It affected him deeply, especially since my father had a heart condition, too. So the Captain decided to devote himself to what mattered most. Besides that, my grandmother is a retiring woman. The social life was always a strain on her."

It was a speech she'd rehearsed carefully and delivered just as carefully. She had said exactly the same thing before, and she never changed it. Still, she found her hands clenched into nervous fists and realized she held her back uncomfortably straight.

His gaze seemed amused. "It was very considerate of Marcuse to die when he did. He provided an excuse. It's very convenient that your grandmother was always reserved. She also provides an excuse. But, Miss Roth, it's time to stop the lies."

"What lies?" she asked, feigning indignation.

He took off the sunglasses. His eyes, hard as obsidian, met hers. "No one outside your immediate family admits to talking to your grandfather for six years or seeing him closely. Something's happened to him. Something bad. Everyone suspects it. It showed in his art then, and it's showing more now. Much more."

She clenched her fists harder. She felt her face turn stiff. The salt spray stung her eyes and pricked like tears.

He smiled at her like a man who holds all the winning cards and knows it. "What happened to your grandfather? What have you worked so hard to hide? Everyone knows there's a secret, Miss Roth. Everyone. What is it?"

CHAPTER THREE

FOR A MOMENT, Eli thought his bluntness had caught her unprepared. He was wrong. She turned from him, laughing, and began to walk again.

"You're trying to be dramatic, Mr. Garner. You talk as if we're running some terrible conspiracy. You're in the wrong field. You should write fiction."

He caught up with her, but she wouldn't look at him. She faced into the wind, chin high. She had a nice profile, with a nose that came close to being pert, especially when she stuck it up in the air, like now.

He bent close to speak in her ear. "Nobody's talked to your grandfather for years. Not even by phone."

She smiled as if to herself. "He never liked the phone much. Ask people who knew him."

"I have," Eli said. A strand of her hair blew across his cheekbone, tickling him. "That's true. He wasn't crazy about the phone. But he'd use it. Until six years ago, this coming fall. Sometime around September. What happened?"

She turned and looked him straight in the eyes. "Do you really want to know what happened? Time happened. My grandfather went deaf. It came on suddenly. It was irreversible. Hearing aids can't help him. Deaf men, Mr. Garner, don't use phones."

"You've dropped hints in New York about that," he accused. "It's a nice excuse, but a little too pat. A man doesn't withdraw from society because he's deaf."

She showed him her profile again, as if she found him tiresome to look at. "Deafness can be isolating. My grandfather was a wit. He enjoyed conversation, making jokes. Now he's uncomfortable in social situations. He loses patience. He feels left out. He doesn't like people seeing him that way."

She said it with such passion and conviction that he almost believed her. "Did he consult specialists? If so, whom? Can they confirm your story?"

Her tone became one of weary impatience, as if she were talking to an imbecile. "Of course he did. In Palm Beach. Dr. Joseph Z. Feldman. One of the best. But Feldman died four years ago. Had a brain aneurism playing golf. On the eighth hole. You can check it out."

Oh, Eli liked that, the little detail about dying on the eighth hole. He imagined it would check out. But he didn't believe her. He brought his mouth close to her ear again, and again her hair tickled his face like silky feathers.

He said, "Four years is a long time. Doctors make breakthroughs all the time. Hasn't your grandfather been to a specialist since?"

"No. He refuses. He's resigned himself to his condition. He's a stubborn man."

And you're a stubborn woman. Damn stubborn.

"He must see some doctor, a man his age. Does he have a personal physician?"

She shot him a disapproving glance. "Yes. But his name is none of your business. He wouldn't talk to you anyway. There's a little thing called the Oath of Hippocrates. His dealings with his patients are confidential."

He wanted to stop, seize her by the shoulders and shake the truth out of her. He also wanted to stop, seize her by the shoulders and kiss her until…until he didn't know what. He jammed his hands deeply into his pockets.

"I've been doing background checks for a month," he

said. "And I can't find anybody in Key West who's seen him up close for five years. Not even at a doctor's office."

She gave a small, derisive laugh. "There are doctors up and down the Keys. Not just Key West."

He cocked his head in the direction of the ocean. "People boating used to see him from out there. Walking on this beach. Not anymore. Sometimes they see him riding in some sort of all terrain vehicle. There's speculation that he *can't* walk."

"I told you, Mr. Garner—time. He's eighty-three. He wears out more easily than he used to."

Eli decided it was time to get tough. "When you or your sister or your grandmother needs a prescription, you get it filled at Killian's Pharmacy in Key West. But you never get anything for your grandfather there. A man his age never needs a prescription?"

She stopped, wheeling to face him. "Excuse me—how in hell do you know about our prescriptions?"

Her eyes flashed dangerously, and the color in her cheeks rose even higher. He smiled, because he knew it would make her angrier still. "I told you. I've been checking."

"How do you know we go to Killian's?" she demanded. "How?"

He shrugged. "Claire's picked up prescriptions there. And other stuff. Makeup. Perfume. Laundry soap. Even kitty litter. She must like one-stop shopping. And sometimes she pays by credit card."

Her lips parted in disbelief. "My God, you've had a detective on us, haven't you? Snooping in our credit cards. And you got somebody at Killian's to talk about us. You bastard."

"Six years ago your grandfather had sinus problems. He needed a prescription nasal spray. He also had a recurrent rash. He used a prescription salve. He was prone to backaches. He had a prescription painkiller for when it got bad. Has he been miraculously cured of all that?"

She made no answer. She glared at him so contemptuously that he was impressed.

He raised an eyebrow. "Or do you just make sure that you buy his prescriptions someplace else? And pay cash, so that you don't leave a paper trail, the way Claire did?"

Her lip curled in disdain, and she made a sound deep in her throat like a small, warning growl. Turning from him, she stalked toward the path that led back to the house. He stayed by her side, and he didn't let up. "You drive to Marathon at least once a month. You go grocery shopping there. Why? Why drive forty miles to Marathon instead of fifteen to Key West? Because the Winn-Dixie store there has a pharmacy? I think so. But the pharmacists there are a tight-lipped bunch. Not like a certain person at Killian's. It's amazing the information you can buy for a hundred bucks."

She stopped in her tracks again, and this time he thought she was going to take a swing at him. "You're a disgusting excuse for a human being. Low, rancid and disgusting."

"And you're beautiful when you're angry." He smirked. "A cliché. Sorry, but it's true."

"You had somebody follow me to Marathon?"

"No. The detective had somebody follow you."

"Don't play word games with me, you odious toad."

"Then don't lie. Why go to so much trouble to cover up what drugs your grandfather takes?"

"Go to hell," she said. "This interview's over. And don't come back tomorrow. I'm not talking to a low-down sneak."

"Ah," he said with satisfaction. "But we have an agreement. You signed it with *Mondragon*."

"Take your agreement," she snapped at him, "fold it five ways and shove it where the sun won't shine."

She stamped toward her sandals, snatched them up and jammed them onto her feet. And she was off, walking up the path so fast she almost loped.

He didn't have time to put on his own sandals; he went right after her. This was a mistake. The path was rough, and littered with burrs that cut his feet.

But he kept up with her anyway. "You have a contract, and you have to honor it," he said, all teasing gone from his voice. "Besides that, you *need* to talk to me."

"When we get to the house, you get in your car and get off our property. Or I'll throw rocks at you. I swear it."

He had no doubt she meant it. "You need to talk to me, because you need to know what else I know. If I can find these things out, so can other people. And I know some interesting things. You can discuss them frankly. Or I can publish them and say you refuse to explain. That would be damaging to you. And to your grandfather. To your whole family."

She speared him with another of her killer glares. "I said don't come back. I meant it."

She lifted her skirt to avoid a short, burr-laden bush. He couldn't stop himself. He grasped her by one forearm and forced her to halt.

She jerked as if he'd seared her with live wires. This time she was going to hit him. In a flash, she raised her open hand and drew it back to slap his face.

He caught her wrist. "Stop," he warned, getting angry himself. "And listen. I'll be back, and you'll talk to me, and you'll talk straight."

She narrowed her eyes in pure malevolence. "And if I won't talk?"

He brought his face close to hers. "In that case, I'm going to have to implicate you and your family in a million-dollar scam. So you need to talk to me if you want to prove that you aren't in the middle of the biggest fraud in the art world."

MERRIMAN FASCINATED Claire. He'd put Bunbury down so he could take notes on the flowers and shoot more pictures, but he'd patted and rubbed and caressed the cat so thoroughly that Bunbury was clearly in love.

He stayed next to Merriman, rubbing against the man's leg and purring. Claire hadn't thought the cat would take to strangers, for he hardly ever saw any.

But she saw few herself, and she, too, took to Merriman. He seemed shy and friendly at once, a mysterious combination. And he acted so *interested* in everything she said that she found it easy, even pleasant, to answer his questions.

"It's a coral vine," she told him as he knelt to shoot a vine covered with dark-pink blossoms. "The flowers look like a string of hearts. Some people call it the Chain of Love."

He snapped three shots, then wrote the name in his notebook. He looked up and gave her a bashful smile. "Chain of Love. That's a pretty name."

His smile was intriguing. It was straight, not curved like the grin of the Cheshire cat. And when he smiled, for some reason, his forehead wrinkled, so that his smile looked... thoughtful.

He had thick dark-blond hair that wouldn't stay put; it stirred constantly in the breeze. He was handsome in a way that was both boyish and rugged.

He pointed at a white-flowered vine, strung with similarly shaped blooms. "Is this another kind of Chain of Love?"

He looked so earnest that she almost smiled herself. "That's a bleeding heart. In some places they use the flower to cast spells."

The wind rippled his hair so it fell over his forehead. "What kind of spells?"

Maybe she shouldn't have brought that up; a blush heated her face. "Spells to...attract something...that you, uh, desire."

"Could I take a sprig?"

She tilted her head in puzzlement. "What for?"

"A souvenir. Something real. Not just pictures."

She licked her lips nervously. He watched the movement as if it hypnotized him. "I guess," she breathed.

"I'll take the pictures first." He moved nearer the vine, Bunbury pressing against his knee. He clicked the shutter three times and jotted a note in his tablet. Carefully, he picked a section of vine hung with delicate flowers. He tucked it in the buttonhole of his blue shirt.

Then he gave her such a long look that she felt more embarrassed than before. He said, "I don't suppose you'd let me take your photo."

"Oh, no," she said, alarmed. "I couldn't do that. We don't want our pictures in any magazine."

"Not for the magazine. For me. To remember you. Nobody else would see it. I promise."

She shook her head. "No. I couldn't do that."

"I'd really like to," he said. "On my word of honor, it wouldn't be for publication."

"No," she repeated. "I can't. I don't even know why you're taking pictures of the flowers. They could be anybody's flowers."

"They're your flowers," he said.

"Not really. I just help take care of them. They belong to my grandparents."

"Maybe they inspire your grandfather's paintings. His paintings are colorful. Strong colors."

She turned and stared at the banyan tree. "I can't talk about him. Or the paintings."

"You don't have to," he said. He put his tablet aside and rubbed Bunbury's back. His expression went solemn, as if he was thinking hard. "Will I see you tomorrow?"

Confusion filled her. "No. Probably not." But she had wanted to say yes. She had wanted to say it very much.

"The next day?" he persisted.

"No. I shouldn't be here now. I should go back inside."

She got to her feet and went to pick up Bunbury, but the

cat was pressed so affectionately against Merriman's thigh that her hand brushed the man's leg.

She'd knelt so that her eyes were now on the same level as Merriman's. "Would you go out with me?" he asked.

She froze, her hands on the cat's bulging middle. The question was extraordinary. "What?"

"Would you go out with me?" he repeated. "I wouldn't pry into your family's business, I swear. I'd just like to be with you. I know it—"

The gate clanged as Emerson burst through it. She stopped and stared in anger at Claire and Merriman kneeling so closely together. Beyond her, standing outside the gate, Claire could see Eli Garner, his expression fierce.

"What's this?" Emerson demanded. "Claire, you were supposed to stay inside."

Claire, usually mild-mannered, was offended by her sister's tone. "I came out to get Bunbury."

"Have you been talking to this person?" Emerson glared at Merriman.

"I told him the names of some plants," Claire said.

"You—" Emerson pointed at Merriman. "Your hour here's up. Leave now."

"Emerson," Claire objected, "there's no need to be rude. He hasn't done anything."

Emerson ignored her. She shook her finger at the photographer. "I said time's up. Leave. You and your sleazy friend."

"Emerson!" Claire was shocked. She'd never seen her sister so imperious.

Merriman stood, picking up his tablet. "I'll leave," he said calmly. "And your sister's right. I asked her about the banyan and the flowers. That's all we talked about."

Claire, too, rose, clutching Bunbury. Merriman turned to her. "Goodbye. And thank you. I hope I'll see you again."

"I—I hope so, too," Claire stammered, amazing herself. Then Merriman was leaving, and Claire felt a sense of something almost like bereavement. He nodded to Emerson. "Good day, Miss Roth. I'm sorry to have upset you."

As soon as he was out of the gate, Emerson slammed it behind him.

"Em! Why were you so hateful?" Claire protested. "He's a nice man. He really is."

"Nice?" Emerson fumed. "Those men are treacherous. They want to ruin us."

Claire shook her head stubbornly. "I can't believe that about him. I won't."

"You will when you know the truth. Come inside. Nana's got to hear this. We need to have a council of war."

"War?" Claire echoed, horrified.

"Yes." Emerson said it with ferocious conviction. "War."

"GOOD GOD," Merriman complained, "what did you do to that woman? What did you say to her?"

As the car passed through the gates to the estate, rain began to fall in fat, cold drops. Eli glowered at the sky as if even the heavens had decided to punish him. "I told her the truth."

"What truth?" Merriman asked, pushing his hair out of his eyes. "Hey, put the top up, will you?"

"I told her that *Mondragon* had a detective investigating them. And he found out some strange things."

He punched the button that brought the convertible's top up. He punched it savagely because it suited his mood. The top rose with a smooth whir.

Merriman stared at him with an expression of disgust. "A detective? You never told me that. I'm surprised she didn't knock your block off."

"She tried," Eli said from between his teeth. He still remembered how swiftly she'd drawn her hand back to slap him. And his feet hurt from walking on burrs. He was still barefoot, his feet scratched and bleeding.

"I don't blame her," Merriman said. "Why'd you tell her? It was sure to rile her."

"I had to tell her so she'd stop trying to stonewall me," Eli said. The car clattered over the rusted metal bridge. "She doesn't like it, but I've got her where I want her, and she knows it. That's why she's mad."

"Great. I was just starting to get somewhere with the sister, and you make me seem like a…spy or something." Merriman swore and stared glumly out at the rain.

Eli frowned at him. "Get somewhere with her? You mean you were actually getting information out of her?"

Merriman shot him a dirty look. "I don't want information. I like her. I've never met anybody like her. And now you've queered it. She'll think I'm a weasel."

Eli grimaced in disbelief. "You *like* her? You're supposed to be a professional. We're here on a story. She's part of it. If she talked to you, what in hell did she say?"

"We talked about flowers. I patted her cat. She seemed to trust me, but now—"

"You petted her *cat?* You talked about *flowers?* Does the word *journalism* have no meaning for you?"

"I'm just the guy who takes pictures. You're the investigator."

"Before you saw the broad, you were singing a different song," Eli accused.

"She's not a broad," Merriman retorted. "She's a lady. Now I'll probably never see her again—thanks to you."

"My heart bleeds."

Merriman narrowed his eyes. "You know, for a guy who has Emerson Roth exactly where he wants, you're in a rotten mood. You know what I think? I think you've got the hots for her. And you blew your chance with her—big time. Smooth, Garner."

Merriman's words annoyed Eli because they were true. Emerson Roth was a beautiful woman. But more than that, she had spirit, she was smart…and loyal to a fault. He

didn't want her to be guilty of high crimes and misde-
meanors, but he feared she was.

He wanted her to have a reasonable, moral excuse for
the games her family played. He didn't want her to hate
him. But it was too late for that. The damage was done.

Eli was relentless; it went with his job. He could go beyond relentless to ruthless when he had to, and he had been
ruthless with Emerson.

She would talk to him again tomorrow because she had
no choice.

And he would show her no mercy. Because he couldn't.

THE THREE WOMEN sat in the living room. It was a large,
airy room, and most days light flooded through the big windows.

But the sun was hidden in the gloom of fast-moving
clouds, and rain beat against the glass. Emerson sat alone
on the white couch, and Claire sat in the rattan rocker,
looking atypically rebellious. Nana got up from the armchair and switched on the Tiffany lamp.

She turned to face the two young women. "So, Em, what
did this detective tell the Garner man?"

"I don't know," Emerson admitted unhappily. "That's
why I have to talk to him again. To see how much he
knows."

Nana moved to the Queen Anne chair and sat down,
looking small but regal. She twined her gnarled fingers together. "They looked at our credit card records?"

"Yes," Emerson said bitterly. She'd warned them to be
careful with credit cards. Emerson herself was careful even
with checks. She paid cash whenever possible.

She cast an accusing glance at Claire. "Why did you
charge our prescriptions so often? Why didn't you *think?*"

Claire, clutching the arms of the rocker, kept her air of
defiance. "I thought we only had to be careful about the
Captain."

"I worried for years that we'd slip up," Emerson snapped. "I *told* you we couldn't be too careful."

Claire's defenses wobbled. "Em, I made a mistake. I'm sorry. But my mind doesn't work like yours. For me, it's exhausting, watching every move I make. It's confusing. It's nerve-racking. It's paralyzing."

Nana shook her finger gently at Emerson. "She made an innocent faux pas, Em. Do not scold. It does no good to squabble."

Emerson felt a surge of guilt for rebuking Claire. She knew that the family secrets preyed on Claire, that they gnawed at her nerves and undermined her confidence.

Claire was retiring, like Nana. Emerson took after the Captain. The Captain had been so bold it was breathtaking. But now he could no longer be bold, and his job fell to her. She was daring, she was quick-witted, and, like the Captain, she could play a part and play it well.

Yet Eli Garner was a formidable opponent. It was possible he was too formidable. Had she met her match? The thought terrified her. Not so much for her own sake, but for her family's. Their future and their welfare depended on her. She was their protector, and she loved them passionately.

She let her gaze meander over the room's walls. The paintings hung there, and she loved them, too. They were striking and so full of life they seemed to glow with it. It was her duty to protect them, too, all that vivid, glorious work signed Roth.

She turned to face Claire. "I'm sorry, too. It's just… upsetting. To have people prying. Spying on you."

Claire winced and nodded. Nana said, "Em, someone followed you to Marathon, when you went to get the Captain's medicine. Do you suppose he even followed you to the pharmacy counter?"

"Yes. He must have."

The thought of being stalked and watched gave Emerson

a sick feeling in the pit of her stomach. What else had the informer seen?

Nana squeezed her fingers together more tightly. "They may have watched the beach from out in the cove. They may have seen the Captain from there. They may have even photographed him."

Emerson swallowed. "I know. A good telephoto lens— I wonder how much they could see, what they could tell about him?"

"Let's hope very little," Nana said. "We've always been discreet."

But not discreet enough, Emerson thought bleakly. *What else did Eli Garner know?*

Claire said in a small voice, "What can we do?"

Emerson smoothed her hair, which was still tousled from the wind. At the front of the house, she heard a scraping sound, and then a rattling and banging. Now that the outsiders were gone, Frenchy must be fastening the hurricane shutters in place.

"The first thing," Emerson said, forcing her voice to sound calm, "is to talk to the Captain. I'll go to him."

Nana shook her head firmly. "No. I will. It's best if I do." She started for the door. But she paused for a moment and stared at the paintings on the walls. Emerson thought she saw tears glint in the older woman's eyes, and a knot rose in her own throat.

Slowly, looking tired, Nana left the living room.

When Claire was certain Nana was out of hearing, she looked warily at Emerson. "I suppose you're going to tell me not to talk to the photographer again."

Emerson remembered the sight of the two of them crouched by the cat, staring raptly into each other's eyes. The photographer had initially struck Emerson as harmless. He'd seemed truly smitten by Claire, and she by him.

Merriman might be as bad a scoundrel as Eli. Or he

might not. But it seemed wrong to give Claire orders as if she were a child or an incompetent.

"Suit yourself," she told Claire. "But be careful. Do you want to see him again?"

Claire didn't answer immediately. She sat looking up at the painting over the mantel. Then, softly, she said, "Em, don't you get tired of it? Of living this way? Sometimes don't you think it would be better if we could just...tell the truth?"

Emerson wanted to say yes. It would be much better for Claire, who was not a creature formed for deception. It would be better for her, too, because maintaining the illusion took all her effort and energy. It ruled her life.

But she and Claire were not the only people caught in this complex web. There was Nana, there was the Captain...and there was more, much more at stake.

"We'll tell the truth someday," she said, rising and going to the window. "But not yet."

"But how can you throw this Garner man off the track?" Claire asked.

"I'll find a way." Emerson said it with a confidence that seemed perfect. But it was false. Secretly she was more frightened by Eli Garner than by anyone or anything she had ever encountered.

CHAPTER FOUR

ELI DROPPED Merriman off at the hotel, grabbed his swim gear, then drove back north. He spent the afternoon at the best stretch of public beach in the Keys, Bahia Hondo.

The wind was high, the rain intermittent. The beach was deserted, which suited him fine.

His scratched feet hurt. The sand irritated them, and the salt water stung them. He didn't care. The pain distracted him. He didn't want to think about Emerson Roth, or her sweet-faced sister. He thought of them anyway.

Neither did he want to think about his own life, but he couldn't stop himself. For years he'd gone from place to place, trying to solve puzzles. Some of the puzzles were unsolvable. Others were foolish, mere hoaxes or pranks to be exposed.

On occasion Eli's work was dangerous. He had a scar on his chest from a bullet and one on his back from a machete. He'd been shadowed in Kuwait, beaten in New Delhi and drugged in Paris. He was still recovering from the caper in Yucatán, and he was not recovering swiftly. The machete wound still ached, and sometimes his fever came back.

The life of an investigative reporter was much like that of a soldier. It could be ninety-eight percent boredom and two percent terror. Sometimes he was tired of both.

His work could be disturbing as well as dangerous. If he had been hurt from time to time, he'd hurt others in return. He'd stripped them of their honor and watched the law strip them of their wealth, and sometimes their very freedom.

Some of the people involved were criminals, and he didn't mind what happened to them. But others were misled or deluded or desperate, and some were simply innocent bystanders.

There was a puzzle about the Roths, and it was a troubling one. But what was its nature and how culpable was Emerson Roth?

Sick of brooding, he waded into the churning waves. The sea was too rough to swim in comfort. He did anyway, the salt stinging the soles of his feet. Then he sat alone on the beach, throwing pebbles at the choppy waves and letting the rain pelt him.

When the rain began to pour down in earnest, he put on his street clothes in the little changing room, then limped back to his car. He hadn't eaten, so he stopped at a rustic restaurant on Cudjo Key.

Few customers were inside, and none out at the garden tables, where the tropical trees waved their branches in the wind and flowers were beaten down by the assault of the rain.

Outside, workers fastened hurricane shutters, cutting off the view of the garden. The waitress was blond, busty, middle-aged, tanned to a crisp and friendly. She called him "hon" and said her name was Brenda.

"You here on vacation?" she asked, setting a plate of red snapper before him.

"No. I deal in art," he said. It wasn't exactly a lie. He switched the topic to her. "You lived here long?"

"All my life," she laughed. "Born and bred here. Where're you from?"

"I'm based in New York, but I travel a lot," Eli said.

She raised a heavily penciled eyebrow. "Art dealer, huh? Lotta galleries in Key West."

"Yup." That was no lie, either.

Brenda looked philosophical. "Well, hope you got your

work done and are headin' home. We're gonna have a big blow, I'm afraid.''

"It feels worse," he said. He hadn't bothered to turn on the car radio.

"Looks like its headin' for Cuba. Folks'll be evacuatin'.'' Brenda nodded in the direction of the highway. "That road out there's gonna be mighty crowded. Ugh. Head north now, and you can get a head start.''

He shook his head. "Can't. I got an appointment tomorrow I can't cancel. Took too much work to get it. Local artist.''

She looked curious, so he thought he'd push further. "Nathan Roth.''

Her expression went dubious. So did her tone. "You're talking to Nathan Roth?''

"His family, not him.'' Eli did a good imitation of looking sincere and troubled. "Something may be up with him. Nobody's seen him around for a long time.''

"You're tellin' me," Brenda said. "He used to be in here every weekend. This was one of his favorite places. Liked the live music. Good-natured guy. Come here with that little wife of his. She hung back, but he'd get a few beers in him, be life of the party. Then…poof.''

"Poof?''

"He stopped coming. Just like that. Poof. Like he'd vanished.''

"Why?''

She gave an elaborate shrug. "I don't know. There are rumors.''

He frowned and made his expression more concerned. "Can you say what? The outfit I represent is worried. They've heard rumors, too.''

Conflict played across her face. "I don't know," she said at last. "People think maybe it's his health.''

"His hearing? One thing we've heard is that he lost his hearing.''

"No," she said immediately. "More serious than that."

He looked at her as if he'd just discovered his guardian angel. He'd given this look to women many time before, and it usually worked.

He said, "That's what we're afraid of. You're the first person I've met here who's actually known him. What do *you* think happened to him?"

She tapped her forehead. "His mind going? Something like that, maybe? He was kind of forgetful the last few times I saw him. And...sometimes he was different. Once he argued that I didn't add up his check right. But I had. He got it all wrong."

Eli felt his chest contract, and a chill played under his skin. The woman hadn't said it outright, but she'd hinted clearly. This was the gossip growing and spreading through the art world about Nathan Roth: something had happened to his lively and creative mind.

And his family was hiding it.

Eli stared deeply into Brenda's mascaraed eyes. "That's what we've been wondering, too."

She shook her head sadly. "He's getting on in years. These things happen. What is he, eighty-something?"

"Eighty-three. Tell me, what do you think of his work?"

She made a gesture of exasperation. "Look, I liked him as a guy. But his pictures were just a bunch a wiggly lines. They didn't look like anything to me. I'm sorry, but that's the truth."

"It's okay," Eli said. "Lots of people don't care for modern art. It's no crime."

She shook her head. "I just don't understand it, is all. Nathan's, his was kinda pretty—the colors, the shading I guess you'd call it. But some of the stuff out there, it looks like a little kid did it. Or even a chimpanzee, for God's sake."

He gave her a half smile to show he understood. "You're not the first person to think so."

She pointed to a brightly colored ceramic fish on the wall. "That, to me, is artistic. You look at it, you know it's a fish, right?"

"Right." He paused. "Nathan's granddaughter's still putting his work on the market, you know. She says he's still painting."

Brenda's face hardened. "Oh. *Her.*"

Her reaction pricked Eli's interest. "Emerson Roth? You don't like her?"

"She comes in here once or twice a month. To buy takeout for Nathan. He still likes our shrimp and scallops. I always ask her how he is, why he doesn't come around. She just says he's fine, then gives me the brush-off. Sometimes men try to get friendly with her. No dice. Guess she thinks she's too high and mighty for the likes of us."

Eli wondered. Emerson could give a fine impression of an ice princess. But was it snobbery that kept her from getting close to the locals? Or fear?

He stroked his chin thoughtfully. "If Nathan's…not himself, could he really still be painting? Do you think so?"

The woman rolled her eyes. "Hey, I said he painted wiggles. How hard is that? He could probably do it with his eyes closed. Oop. 'Scuze me. Those folks want to check out."

She bustled to the cash register. He gazed after her, a sturdy, kindly woman full of common sense. Perhaps she had hit the nail on the head. Were Roth's new works only parodies of what he'd once done, but nobody had caught the sad joke of it?

Were they the scribbles of a mind in dementia? But the dementia was a secret, and the paintings kept selling because once the man had been a genius?

Stranger things had happened in the art world. But if it was true, did it mean the paintings were worthless? And did that make Emerson Roth a first-class con artist?

He pushed his dinner away only half-eaten. He paid his

bill and left Brenda a ten-dollar tip. Then he drove south toward Key West, into the darkness of the gathering storm.

MERRIMAN WANDERED alone around Duval Street. He'd bought himself a light raincoat, but hadn't bothered with a hat.

The rain flattened his unruly hair, ran down his face. Plenty of people were in bars, forgetting their troubles or the weather reports or both. They forgot loudly. He could hear the blare of their conversation and music when he passed the open doors.

He wasn't tempted to join them. His mind was on Claire Roth. He had a mind made for images, and hers had him enthralled and kept him haunted. Hers was more than pretty face. It was an innocent's face.

Eli Garner couldn't suspect *her* of anything...could he? Maybe the rest of the family was involved in something shady. Not Claire.

Merriman believed that he could read faces. In hers he saw something so unspoiled and guileless it almost gave him a religious experience, except she also set off the most primitive of his desires.

Had she been going to agree to see him again? Or refuse? He wanted to believe she felt what he did. Did he dare phone her? He walked faster to try to burn off his indecision.

The streets were not nearly as bustling today. They weren't empty, but the human traffic was nothing like the throngs of yesterday.

Merriman made his way to Mallory Square, where crowds usually gathered every afternoon. They came to celebrate the sun going down and cheer when it sank beneath the rim of the ocean. Merriman had heard it was a carnivallike atmosphere, with street performers, vendors of crafts and souvenirs, popcorn stands, drinks and hundreds of tourists.

But this sunset celebration was clearly going to be a dud. The sun, hidden behind streaming clouds, was a no-show. So were many of the street performers. The flames of the fire-eater would be whipped too much by the wind. The man who suspended himself in the air from chains would have lashed back and forth like a pendulum. Dominique the Cat Man wouldn't chance his beloved trained cats jumping through a fiery hoop—too dangerous.

The popcorn stands were battened down. The crafts tables had been folded up and carted away. Only a few acts played to small knots of people hunched against the rain. No drunken college boys would be leaping off the pier in an excess of celebration.

Then the rain began to pour more wildly. The man with the trained dogs packed up to leave; the bagpiper moaned and screeched his last and the spectators darted for the nearest shelter.

The weather was getting wild, all right, Merriman thought, and it made him nervous. He turned to slosh back down Duval to his hotel room. Now stores were shutting early, windows were being boarded up and the streets were nearly deserted.

The wind had torn loose palm branches and they swept along the street, like brooms being wielded by ghosts. Petals were flying off the flowers Claire had told him were bougainvillea. They reminded of him damp butterflies fluttering to escape.

What was this storm doing to Claire at Mandevilla? She'd said it frightened her a little. It was worse now. Would she and her family try to ride it out in the old house, or would they evacuate the way some people were talking about doing?

He had to phone her, to find out how she was. And to ask if she would see him again. He didn't want to call from any of the bars or restaurants—they were too noisy. He made it back to the hotel and up to his room.

He was cold from the rain, so he took a hot shower, then wrapped a towel around his middle and padded to the bed. He sat down and dialed the number of Nathan Roth's house. Eli had given it to him. He held his breath, hoping against hope that it would be Claire who answered.

CLAIRE COULD TELL that this storm had Emerson worried.

She knew because Emerson had been in the library, pulling together important paperwork and documents. She would not have done that unless she thought they might have to leave.

Now Emerson was in the kitchen, checking batteries in half a dozen different appliances and muttering to herself. When the phone rang in the living room, she called to Claire, "Get that, will you? Maybe it's Frenchy."

Frenchy was not a native of Key West, but his wife, LouAnn was. LouAnn had an eerie instinct about hurricanes, Frenchy claimed. He had promised to keep them informed if her hunches and vibes told her danger was coming.

Claire swallowed and picked up the phone. She'd brought the two guard dogs, Doberman pinschers, inside again. Emerson hadn't wanted them running loose when Eli and Merriman were there. Fang, who hated storms, pressed against her knee, not wanting to leave her. Bruiser slept on the hearth rug, oblivious to the weather.

"Hello?" Claire said, expecting to hear Frenchy.

But the voice was not Frenchy's. It was one she'd never heard on the telephone before, yet she recognized it immediately.

"Claire? Is that you, Claire?"

It was the photographer. Her heart bounded like a frightened hare. "Yes," she breathed, her heart still trying to run away.

"This is Merriman. Are you all right out there? I was worried about you."

She took a deep breath, eased to the living room door and shut it, so that Emerson wouldn't overhear. "We're fine. I—I've been worried about you."

He laughed. "Me? Why?"

"We're used to this. You're not."

"They say it could be headed right for us," Merriman said.

Claire was touched. He sounded truly concerned. "They've said that before. And this one keeps stalling."

"Has one ever hit? Head-on, I mean?"

"Not badly for many, many years," she answered, echoing what Nana used to tell her. "Long before we were born."

"I thought I heard that recently..." His voice trailed off, uncertain.

"Georges in '98," she admitted. "It wrecked some boats on Houseboat Row in Key West and that was sad. It did more damage to the neighboring Keys, but no fatalities, thank heaven. We're not really all that hurricane prone. Honestly."

She took a deep breath. She didn't usually make speeches that long.

He didn't sound convinced. "That's not what I'm hearing people say."

"People like to exaggerate," she said. She smiled, realizing that *she* was reassuring *him*. It was a nice feeling.

"Then you're staying put?"

Claire stole a look at the closed door and thought of Emerson's gathering of papers and documents. But nothing had really been said yet about going.

"Probably." Claire hesitated. "But if it bothers you, you should evacuate."

"We're supposed to be at your place tomorrow," Merriman said, determination in his voice. "If you're there, we'll be there. *I'll* be there. Will I see you?"

She felt her face burn, her stomach flutter. "I don't know."

His tone grew pleading. "Did your sister tell you not to? Look, I'm not the investigator on this story. I just take pictures. Would it help if I talked to her?"

Claire swallowed. "She said it was my choice. But...I don't know if I should."

"Yes," he said with feeling. "You should. I know you should. I think you know it, too."

Claire thought of him kneeling in the garden by Bunbury. She thought of the man's tousled hair, his serious blue eyes, his forehead that furrowed so thoughtfully when he smiled. She remembered his kindness to Bunbury and his deference to her.

Claire had been pursued before, and she hadn't liked it. The men had been arrogant or leering. Merriman was different. When he looked at her it was with a sense of wonder, as if he respected and admired her.

"I—I don't even know your first name," she said.

"I haven't got one."

"You don't?" This revelation shook her slightly. What sort of person had only one name? She could think of only rock stars and cartoon characters.

"My first and middle names were horrible," he admitted. "I went to court and had them dropped. I don't know what my parents were thinking. So I'm just plain Merriman."

"Well..." She pondered it.

"Do I need to have a first name to see you?" He had a strange, endearing desperation in his voice. "I'll get one."

She smiled. "No. Merriman is fine. Don't you even have a nickname?"

"No. But you can make up one if you'll let me see you. Will you?"

"You'll be too busy taking pictures. Emerson said you can look at the inside of the house tomorrow. At least, the first story."

"Could you be the one to show it to me? Explain what I'm seeing? You were helpful with the flowers. You could do it again, inside."

She paused. "Emerson will do it."

Merriman persisted, but his persistence was gentle. "She'll have her hands full with Garner. She'll have no time for me. Would you?"

Do you want to see him again? Emerson had challenged. *Suit yourself.*

She did want to see him again. So much that she didn't feel like her usual self at all. In two days he would be leaving, maybe forever. She couldn't bear not to see him at least one more time.

"I—I'll try," she stammered, dazed by her own daring. "But you can't ask me about my family. You *can't.* You have to promise."

"I promise." She heard a harsh rattling noise in the background. "Drat," Merriman said. "Somebody at the door. Garner, probably. He's been out wandering. I have to go. Claire, thank you. I'll see you tomorrow. Good night."

"Tomorrow," she said, still feeling dazed. "Good night."

She listened to the click as he hung up. Her chest felt as if it were full of winged things, struggling to be free. As she hung up the phone, she thought, *What have I done?*

"YOU'VE done *what?*" Emerson demanded when Claire told her.

"I'm going to help show Merriman around tomorrow. He phoned and asked. He was very nice about it."

Emerson stood in the doorway to the living room, her hand on her hip. She wanted to snap that of course he acted nice; he was trying to dig up all the dirt he could.

But something in Claire's face stopped her. A kind of radiance shone from it, and Emerson had never seen

Claire's cheeks so pink. So she didn't zing out a sarcastic answer.

"Be careful what you say," she muttered.

"I will, I promise. But he's not like the other one. He's not like Eli Garner at all. He's…different."

With mixed feelings, Emerson realized that Claire was actually taken by this man. Up to now Claire had never had a real boyfriend…and she was twenty-five years old!

The men who had chased Claire had frightened or repelled her. The ones she admired, she admired from afar and in silence. Over the years, the few male friends she'd had were gay. Not flamboyant sorts, but boys as sensitive and almost as shy as she was.

Yes, it was high time Claire got interested in a man. But, Emerson fumed inwardly, why this one? He might be "nice" and "polite" as Claire hoped, but his alliance with Eli Garner made him suspect.

She trained a gaze on Claire she hoped didn't show her very real reservations about the man. "They're only going to be here an hour, you know."

A sly man can do a lot of damage in an hour, Emerson thought. *Especially to someone like Claire.*

"I know," Claire said, with a hint of defiance. "And so does he."

"Shall I tell Nana about this decision? Or do you want to do it yourself?."

"I'll do it myself," Claire said in the same tone. "Is she upstairs?"

"Yes." Emerson didn't have to tell Claire not to discuss the matter in front of the Captain. Extreme weather excited him. When the wind was high, so were his emotions.

Claire started upstairs. Fang stayed pressed close to her, as if only she could protect him from the storm. Emerson sighed, shook her long hair and ran her fingers through it.

Nana's reaction, like Emerson's, would be mixed. For a long time Nana had been wanting Claire to mingle more.

But with the enemy? Emerson knew Eli was the enemy. Merriman seemed a gentler, more head-in-the-clouds sort, but was he really trustworthy?

She gritted her teeth. If Merriman used or betrayed Claire, Emerson would kill him, just plain murder him in cold, vengeful blood.

On impulse, she snatched up the phone. She glanced up the stairs, making sure Claire was out of earshot. Then she looked at the number Eli had scribbled on his card and dialed it, stabbing the phone buttons militantly. She wanted him to know she was capable of skinning him alive and nailing his hide to the wall.

He answered on the second ring, his deep voice lazy. "Eli Garner here."

Drat! His voice sent a quiver through her midsection. "This is Emerson Roth. I want to talk to you."

"Ah," he said, "I was just wanting to talk to you."

"Me?" she asked, taken aback.

"You. And your family. I'm watching weather reports. The hurricane."

"Oh, *that*." She spoke as if the storm was trifling, although in truth it had her deeply worried.

"Yeah, *that*." He said the word as snidely as she had. "It's getting worse, veering closer. There's talk of an evacuation order for the Keys. It may come tonight."

"They can't *enforce* it," Emerson said. "They call it an order, but they can't make people with solid homes go. And storms are unpredictable—"

"Like women?"

She squared her jaw. "If the hurricane scares you, Mr. Garner, I suggest you run. Get out while the getting's good."

"Ah, but I have an appointment with you tomorrow. I wouldn't miss it for the world. Providing your house is still standing, of course. And you're still in it."

"We'll be here," she vowed. *But we may not stay.*

"You're determined not to evacuate?"

"I don't plan on it." This was a lie, because she'd spent all evening planning for it. Nana and the Captain wouldn't like it, but she considered herself responsible for them. She would do whatever she had to do to keep them safe.

"On TV," he drawled, "it said that usually twenty-five percent of the population wouldn't leave, no matter how bad things get. You know what that tells me?"

"That we're a hardy breed."

"No. It tells me that at least twenty-five percent of you people down here are certifiably crazy."

"Probably a conservative estimate," she shot back. "But I didn't call you about the weather. I want to talk about your photographer."

"Oh. Merriman."

"Yes. Merriman. He phoned my sister tonight."

"Isn't she allowed to take calls? Or is there a new law— Merriman can't make them?"

Damn you, Emerson thought, wishing she could twist the phone cord around his neck. "They're both adults. They can talk to whom they please."

"That's very generous of you. This afternoon you acted more like you were her keeper than her sister. And poor Merriman. You kicked him out. But now you've relented? How magnanimous."

"I kicked him out because he was with you," she retorted. "*You* were anything but a gentleman."

"True. While you were every inch a lady. In spite of your threat to throw rocks at me."

He's impossible, Emerson thought. "My sister is a sweet and naive girl. If your photographer is cozying up to her to get information from her, I'll make him rue the day he was born."

"You're a very protective woman. And a passionate one. Fascinating."

She took a deep breath to calm herself. "Did you put him up to it? Is this part of your 'detective work'?"

"You called your sister a girl. She's not a girl. She's a woman, and a lovely one. Merriman is honestly smitten with her. He apparently likes the quiet, innocent type. Me, I prefer a woman with some fire."

"I mean it, Garner. If Merriman is trying to use Claire, if he hurts her in any way, he's going to be dealing with *me*."

"Um. And you have fire. Lots of it."

"And if he hurts her, I'm holding *you* responsible."

"Punishment? You're talking punishment? You'd strip me down, tie me up? Put me in handcuffs? Do something with a whip? What would you wear? Spiked heels and a garter belt?"

Emerson fought against grinding her teeth. "Don't be a smart-ass. You heard what I said. And if you keep being suggestive, I'll report you to your editor. For sexually harassing me."

That shut him up. For fully two seconds. "Touché," he said. "I'll take your advice, but I'd like to give you some in return."

"What?"

"If that hurricane stays on course, it could hit soon, and it could hit fast. I suggest we don't drag these interviews out for two more days. That I talk to you and your grandmother tomorrow. Then Merriman and I will be out of your beautiful hair—excuse me—your hair. And you should think about getting your family someplace safer."

"I know what I'm doing," Emerson said.

"I was in Hurricane Iniki in Hawaii," Eli said. "It turned from an ordinary storm into a killer in a flash. Nobody expected it to hit, but it did—with less than twenty-four hours' notice. It left one in three families homeless. I was in Honduras when Hurricane Mitch hit. It killed thirty-two people."

He paused, as if letting his words sink in. "I was reading the stats in the Miami paper tonight. The Keys aren't just due for a bad hit. They're long overdue."

She bit the inside of her cheek, knowing what he said was true.

He went on, his tone dead serious. "I'd like to come early tomorrow. Is nine too early? Then Merriman and I can hit the road. It's going to be a tough drive getting out of here."

Emerson knew he was right. The highway was only two lanes in most places. If an evacuation order came on too short notice and matters got out of hand, it could create a gigantic and desperate traffic jam.

"Nine will be fine," she said, trying to show no emotion. "And you'd better book a hotel inland. Rooms are going to be hard to get."

"I know," he said. "And I'd suggest you do the same. Just to be on the safe side. And I say that out of true concern."

"This isn't the first time I've been through this, you know."

"I don't want it to be the last, either. I've got flaws. But being an alarmist isn't one of them. See you in the morning."

He hung up, leaving her in a solemn, worrisome mood. Her anger at Merriman had mostly evaporated. He would be gone before noon tomorrow. And so, thank God, would Eli.

She listened to the wind lashing the house. Its shrill whine had risen to a wail now, and the wail, she knew, could turn into a roar, and if that happened…

The phone rang, startling her. She picked up the receiver, hoping it wasn't Eli calling back. It was not. It was Frenchy.

"Miss Roth," he said, "I'm not gonna be there tomorrow. LouAnn's gettin' nervous. We're headin' north. She's seein' signs that it's gonna get bad, sure thing."

"What signs?" Emerson asked. She knew the real natives read things in nature she could not.

"The way the birds are actin'. The land crabs are movin' to higher ground. Then she saw a line of ants walkin' straight up the wall. She said, 'That's it. We're gettin' out of here.' She's usually right, Miss Roth. You might not want to ride this one out."

An atypical anxiety skittered through her nerves. "But there's no real evacuation warning yet."

"Not yet," Frenchy said. "The missus says there will be. Did you notice the poincianas today? Losin' leaves. Yep. The signs are all there."

"Thanks, Frenchy. I appreciate your concern. Let's hope it's a false alarm."

"I'm hopin'. But it's better to be safe than sorry. Night, Miss Roth. You take care."

"You, too, Frenchy. Take very good care."

She hung up. She thought. She listened to the wind. She heard a branch crack outside, a large one.

She picked up the receiver again and started dialing hotels in Fort Myers. Fort Myers would be less crowded than Orlando. The family could leave tomorrow, as soon as Garner and Merriman were gone. She would need to find a hotel that allowed pets.

Claire would never go without the animals...never.

And she must register under her or Claire's name, with no mention of her grandfather. Nobody must recognize the Captain. Or see what had happened to him.

CHAPTER FIVE

ELI AWOKE AT DAWN.

The room felt strange. The very air felt strange. *He* felt strange, full of minute prickles.

He rose, wearing only his briefs, and went to the window. He pulled aside the heavy drapes and squinted outside. The sky was fiery red, clouds glowing like flames as far as he could see.

Red sky at morning, sailor take warning.

Out in the harbor a tanker swung back and forth, even though it was anchored. It was like some ponderous beast straining to break its leash. *My God, what force of wind could move a ship that big?*

Closer to shore, waves were breaking, high and rough, although the rain had lessened. Smaller boats bobbed insanely, and two looked in danger of swamping. Eli saw palm trees, their supple trunks bending, their fronds flying like streamers.

The hotel was well built, but he could hear the wind thumping at the thick outer walls, as if warning it wanted in. Instinctively, he stepped back from the plate glass. He switched on the television.

A news anchor with tired, basset-hound eyes said the hurricane was still stalling west of Cuba's coast. It could weaken as it crossed Cuba and be downgraded to a tropical storm, then dissipate somewhere at sea. Or it could strengthen and suddenly bear down on the Keys.

Or it might veer, merely skirting the Lower Keys and

whirl over the Gulf toward Mississippi or Louisiana. It might do any of these things. In Cuba there were already mass evacuations—hundreds of thousands of people.

The order to evacuate the Lower Keys might come at any time. Stay tuned, the announcer said.

Eli swore under his breath. He snatched up the phone and dialed Merriman's number. When Merriman answered, he sounded out of breath. "Wow. Have you seen the sky? I was out on the balcony taking shots of it."

"On the balcony, you idiot? I thought this storm scared you."

"It does, but man, those colors—the reds, the oranges. Did you see that weird yellow streak snaking along?"

"Did you see the weather report?" Eli asked from between his teeth.

"Yeah, they've got a radar shot on right now. Cool. It looks like a big parrot head, red and yellow and blue. It's even got an eye like a parrot."

That's the eye of the storm, Eli wanted to snarl. He needed to shake Merriman out of his happy trance of seeing pretty pictures. "Get dressed. It's seven-fifteen. I'm phoning Emerson Roth to tell her we're coming early. Then we split. I got a feeling the evacuation order's coming."

"I've got to shower and shave—"

"Do it fast."

He hung up, then he dialed the Roths' number. Emerson answered immediately. He thought he heard tension in her voice.

"Look," he said, "Merriman and I are going to leave for your place as soon as possible if that's okay with you."

"Fine," she said. "You need to be getting out of here."

He ran his hand over his bare chest. "What about you? Are you going? Or staying?"

She hesitated, but only for an instant. "I can't say yet." Then she added, "My grandmother's nervous. She may not be able to say much to you. She may not want to speak to you at all.''

Inwardly, he cursed. ''Nervous about the storm?''

''Yes. So respect her wishes,'' Emerson said curtly. ''Whatever they are.''

She hung up on him before he could protest. Talking to Lela Roth was part of the agreement. What in hell was Emerson trying to pull now?

In disgust, he turned to head for the shower. But the voice of the basset-eyed announcer stopped him. ''The Monroe County Director of Evacuation has declared a state of emergency. Residents of the Lower Keys have been issued an evacuation order, effective immediately. I repeat, the Lower Keys are to be evacuated immediately....''

EMERSON SWUNG open the back door. Eli stood there, looking grim, and he had the sort of dark, angular face that could look grim indeed. His eyes were so intense that they seemed to blaze through her.

Behind him, Merriman hunched, eyeing the sky, the collar of his red windbreaker turned up against the rain. It was coursing down steadily again.

''Come in,'' she said. ''How was the trip? Is the highway crowded?''

Eli wiped his feet and tried to shake the drops from his hair. ''Not bumper to bumper, but the traffic's heavy.''

Both men entered and she gestured for them to sit at the kitchen table. She'd taken pity on them and brewed a fresh pot of coffee. ''Have you had breakfast?''

''We didn't take the time,'' Eli said, pulling out a chair and sitting.

''I've got coffee cake and fresh sliced pineapple. It's not much, but we're not big on breakfast around here.''

''That would be wonderful.'' Merriman sounded truly grateful. Then his face went both serious and hopeful at once. ''Is Claire around? Will she be here?''

"In a little while." Emerson poured the coffee. "She has a few things to do first."

She did not say that she and Claire had been up since four in the morning, taking down the paintings, covering them and loading them in the panel truck. Right now, Claire was frantically boxing up sketches.

She could feel Eli's eyes on her. This morning she had been too busy to bother to dress for anything but work. She wore a pair of cutoff jeans and a stretchy T-shirt of hot pink. She felt half-naked compared to yesterday.

Eli said, "There's a car parked out there. It's got a caduceus sticker on the back window. There's a doctor here?"

"Our neighbor. He dropped in to check on Nana as a courtesy. He knows she doesn't like storms. And besides that she's had some bad news. A personal matter. It doesn't concern you."

She set coffee mugs down before the two men. Eli said, "You know about the evacuation order."

She turned to the refrigerator and opened the door. "I know."

She tossed her head as if the order didn't matter. Early this morning she'd used a gold barrette to pin back her hair, but it was coming loose, hanging about her face in strands. She hoped she didn't look as harried as she felt.

"No decision yet?" Eli asked.

She spooned the pineapple chunks into dishes. "Actually, I think we may," she admitted. "So the sooner we finish our business, the better. You've got questions? Start asking."

She sliced two pieces of coffee cake and thrust them into the microwave. She realized that her back was rigid, her shoulders tense.

Eli said, "First, what's this about your grandmother not talking to me? She agreed to it."

"My grandmother's elderly. I told you, she's upset."

"I'd be gentle with her," Eli said.

Unlike the way you are you with me, she thought, her shoulders knotting more tightly. She picked up the two dishes of fruit and set them down sharply on a silver tray.

She strode to a set of drawers and pulled out silverware. "Besides," she said, slapping forks down beside the pineapple, "when my grandmother's upset she reverts to French."

"I speak French." For the first time something like a smile played on Eli's lips.

"Or sometimes even Arabic," Emerson said, trying to fend him off. "If she's *very* upset. And she is."

"I speak Arabic. Enough to get by."

Damn! Emerson thought, and gave a slight jump when the microwave buzzed.

"So *might* she talk to me?" he asked as she put the coffee cake and plates on the tray.

"I'll ask her after you've eaten. Come into the sitting room. Follow me. Bring your coffee."

She picked up the tray and carried it through the living room and into the cozy little sitting room. The windows were shuttered, but two sconces with shades of amber glass cast a golden glow.

Emerson set the small bridge table with breakfast and gestured for the men to sit. She sat herself, crossing her arms. She shot Eli a challenging look.

He said, "Where'd we leave off? Oh, yes. There are rumors about your grandfather."

She shrugged one shoulder. "There are rumors about Elvis. That he's alive and living in Michigan."

Merriman ate hungrily, not seeming to listen. He kept his eyes on the door to the living room, watching, also hungrily, for Claire.

"How long have you been up?" Eli asked.

She blinked in surprise at the question. "What?"

He looked her in the eye with unnerving steadiness. "I

asked how long you've been up this morning. And what have you been doing?''

"Since just before you called," she fibbed. "I was making a list of what we'd need to do if we do evacuate. I was just putting some important papers together when you got here.''

He shook his head and sighed. "You're a good liar, Emerson. But not good enough. Have you looked at your watch lately?''

She jerked her chin down and was jarred to see that her watch's face was cracked. It had stopped at 4:35. She must have struck it on something while she was packing the van and not even noticed. For once, she could think of nothing to say.

He nodded knowingly. "I'd say you've been up for a long time. Doing something physical, doing it strenuously. Moving things. Loading paintings is my guess.''

He'd caught her. She tried to escape. "I wanted to be prepared if we decided to go.''

"You'd decided when I called this morning. You'd already been hard at work. You've got two bruises on your hands that weren't there yesterday. You've chipped a nail. You've got a fresh scrape right under your knee. And a couple of smudges here and there. Why did you tell me you hadn't made up your mind?''

"Because it's none of your business," she retorted. But she was rattled that he could deduce like Sherlock Holmes.

"It's my business to find out if you lie," he contradicted. "And you do. You weren't going to hustle your family into that panel truck of yours and head north with no preparation. Not you.''

"How do you know about my truck?" she demanded, then wanted to bite her tongue.

"The detectives told me. It's big enough to hold quite a few paintings. And you're not about to leave those paintings behind. They're too valuable.''

"They're my grandparents' income. And more than that, they're works of art."

He tilted his head slightly. "Whose works of art, Emerson? Certain experts have noticed...differences."

"I don't know what you're talking about." But she knew; she was only playing for time. Her heart rapped in anxiety.

He leaned closer. "The works are smaller. For a while the details got less bold, almost shaky. Uninspired, is what one critic said. Derivative. Almost as if someone was imitating him. Imitating him very well. But not brilliantly."

Emerson fought against trembling. She told herself she was prepared for this man, these questions. But looking into those keen eyes, she wasn't so sure.

She drew a deep breath. "When the Captain lost his hearing," she said, "he went through a period of depression. It showed in his work. Depression's bad for inspiration, Mr. Garner. The work *was* derivative in a way. He's been imitating his old self."

"Has he? Or is somebody being paid to do it? And to keep quiet about it? You've made some big withdrawals of cash in the past five years. Is that why?"

This question angered her, and she felt the blood rise hotly to her face. "That's an insult. A double insult. You've been snooping in our banking, too. That's unconscionable."

"So's fraud."

The word *fraud* struck her like a blow, stunning her. But suddenly she realized that Merriman had begun to pay attention to the conversation, and he didn't like it.

"Hey," Merriman said, putting his hand on Eli's arm, "take it easy, will you? I mean, this isn't a courtroom. We're guests in this house."

Eli glared at him. "You're here to take the pictures, that's all. *I* ask the questions."

"I can quit right now and leave you without any pictures," Merriman warned.

Eli shook off his hand. "You've got a contract."

Merriman's brow furrowed. "Contracts can be broken."

The door to the sitting room opened, and Claire came in, with Fang cowering against her knee. She looked at Merriman, and Merriman looked at her. The atmosphere in the room changed.

The tension didn't dissolve, but it was nearly crowded out, forced into the corners. Emerson was grateful to Merriman for defending her, and relieved that Claire had interrupted the conflict, but she realized that one kind of voltage had replaced another.

Claire and Merriman could barely take their eyes off each other. They both seemed to glow from within. They smiled shyly. Claire managed to give Emerson the briefest of glances. "I just came from Nana. She wants to see you."

"Yes. Well, excuse me." Emerson leaped to her feet and made her escape.

Behind her, she heard Merriman say to Claire, "You were going to show me the house?"

"Yes." Claire's voice was happy and breathless. "Oh, *yes*. We can start with the living room. I can show you the studio, too, since you have to leave today."

EMERSON RAN UP the stairs two at a time. The library door was open, and she saw her grandmother sitting in the worn velvet armchair, weariness in every line of her body.

Dr. Willard Kim sat on the ottoman by her feet. He rose and patted Emerson's shoulder. "It's very unfortunate about your grandmother's mother."

Emerson nodded. The timing could not be worse.

"She has some sedatives left from her last prescription," he said. "Claire found them. I've had Lela take one for traveling. The Captain may need one, too. I've told Claire the dosages and written another prescription to be filled in Fort Myers, if necessary."

"Thank you, Doctor."

He drew his cell phone from his pocket. "I need to make some calls. I want to phone my wife and tell her I'll be home soon. I also need to check in with the Key West shelter. They don't have a doctor assigned there, and they may need one. Even an old duffer like me."

Emerson smiled. Dr. Kim was a diminutive gray-haired man, married to a nurse. They would not leave the Keys in any emergency. They might be needed.

He bent, putting his face close to Nana's. "Try to relax. I'll be back shortly, my dear."

He left. Emerson sat down on the ottoman and took Nana's gnarled hand. She stared into the older woman's eyes. They were sad, but not reddened. She hadn't wept. "How do you feel, Nana?"

Nana tried to smile but didn't quite succeed. "About my poor mother? I am resigned. It would be less painful if troubles didn't come in packs, like wolves. Ahh, that is life's way."

Nana had learned late last night that her mother had been taken very ill in Algeria. Fatima was an old woman, past ninety. She had married when she was sixteen, had her first son when she was seventeen, then another son, then Nana.

Nana had not seen her mother in over fifty years. The two were estranged, and there was much bitterness on the mother's side. But Nana's brothers kept her informed. Habib had phoned last night from Paris to say the older woman might have three months to live, perhaps three weeks, perhaps even less.

"I'm so sorry about everything happening at once," Emerson said, truly sad for Nana.

Nana squeezed her hand. "My mother has lived a long life and a good one...except for me."

"I'm sure she loves you in her way," Emerson said.

"And I love her in mine. But I also loved the Captain. I defied her and I went with him. I would do it again."

"The house," Emerson said. "Does it bother you, leaving it? We never evacuated before."

"A house is a thing. It's a big box to hold smaller things. The only things I care about are the paintings. Even more than that, I want you girls and the Captain safe. That is what is important." She sighed. "Yes, I'm ready to leave."

Emerson moved closer to her, put her hands on Nana's shoulders. "The men came early, Eli Garner and the photographer."

Nana sank more deeply against the back of the chair. "Yes. You said they would. I'm ready to talk to Mr. Garner."

Emerson clasped the frail shoulders more tightly. "Nana. I don't think you should. He's very suspicious. He accused me of fraud."

Nana waved away the thought. "I will tell him this is not the time to talk to him. He's not a fool, he'll see it's true. His suspicions can wait. The hurricane will not."

"Nana, are you sure? He can be aggressive. He might try to rattle you, to shake you—"

Another dismissive wave. "Dr. Kim has given me a pill for my nerves. I'm calm. Bring Mr. Garner to me. What I have to say won't take long."

"You're certain?" Emerson feared Nana was overestimating her own strength.

"I'm certain."

Emerson kissed her on the cheek and left the room. She saw Dr. Kim in the hallway, frowning as he listened to his cell phone. She smiled weakly at him and descended the stairs.

ELI WATCHED HER as she moved down the steps, her hand trailing on the mahogany banister. She kept her gaze cast downward, as if she knew he was there but refused to acknowledge it.

Eli had followed Claire and Merriman into the living

room, but they took no more notice of him than if he were a shadow. Now Claire stood by the fireplace, softly explaining that the marble mantel had come from a two-hundred-year-old house in Saint Augustine.

The big dog still huddled against her leg, quivering, his stub of a tail between his legs. Another dog, calmer but watchful, lay before the fireplace. A green parrot had flown in from somewhere and landed on Claire's shoulder. It took a strand of her golden-brown hair in its beak and toyed with it.

Merriman was dutifully snapping pictures of an antique sofa, a modernistic tapestry, a sleek chrome statue. But Eli could tell all Merriman really saw was Claire. And although she spoke of this or that curio or architectural detail, the real object of her attention was the photographer.

Eli had listened to her, noted the mixed but striking decor of the room. He would remember it all, for he had an excellent memory. But he recorded the details mechanically, for his true focus was now on Emerson.

She reached the bottom stair and raised her eyes to meet his. Something deep within him staggered, but he forced his face to stay impassive.

"My grandmother will talk to you, after all. I'll take you to her."

"This phone is going weak," Dr. Kim grumbled. "I'll try it from outdoors. Danged contraption." He strode toward the front door, still frowning.

"Use ours," Emerson offered.

"Or mine," said Eli.

"I need to master this thing," he replied in disgust. "Technology. Argh." Still muttering, he stepped outside to the front porch.

Emerson turned and started back upstairs. Eli followed. He said, "You left three of your grandfather's paintings in the living room. You didn't pack them. Why?"

She glanced coolly over her shoulder. "So you could have pictures of them. I left a few in the studio, too."

"You'd have taken them down as soon as we left?"

"Exactly."

"They're older pieces. From before he changed."

She didn't respond to his statement. Instead she said, "That was Dr. Kim who went outside. You won't get any information out of him, so don't try."

"I didn't intend to try."

He didn't have to ask about Kim. He already knew about the man from the detective. Retired, Kim had moved to the Mimosa Key from New York five years ago. A retired neurologist, he was also an art lover and an old friend of Nathan Roth.

Now Kim lived just three miles from the Roths and was their only frequent visitor. Eli was certain that he served the Captain as a private physician.

Emerson opened one of the closed doors. Eli followed her into a room that was obviously a library, crowded with books and smelling faintly musty.

An elderly woman sat in a wine-colored chair. Her hands were knotted by arthritis, and her face was lined, but he could see she had once been a great beauty.

Her eyes were like Emerson's, large, dark, thickly fringed with lashes. And they must still be sharp eyes. She did not wear glasses, and when she looked him over, she seemed to do it minutely.

"Nana, this is Eli Garner, the reporter. Mr. Garner, my grandmother, Lela Roth."

Lela Roth's expression was both weary and solemn. "I would shake hands, Mr. Garner, but it is painful to me. So I will simply say hello."

Eli found himself making a small, informal bow. It was the sort of thing he never did, but somehow this woman seemed to deserve it. "I'm honored, Mrs. Roth."

"You've made a long trip," Lela Roth said. She had an

exotic accent, partly Parisian, partly Middle Eastern. Her voice was neither cracked nor quavering, but almost melodic.

She gestured toward the sofa, which was covered with stacks of books. "I would tell Emerson to clear a place for you to sit. But unfortunately, we must postpone your interview. I have had bad news about my mother. And—" she indicated the shuttered windows "—this terrible storm is upon us. I haven't the spirit in me to talk at this time. Nor the strength. I hope you have it in your heart to let me break my promise for now. We will speak another time, if you would be so good."

Emerson kept her face blank, but her eyes smouldered her message: *Be a gentleman and go away. Or you're no better than a vulture.*

Eli looked again at Lela Roth, who had an air of dignified resignation. At first it had struck him as odd that a woman this elderly could still have a parent living. But Lela was seventy-three. Her mother could be ninety, or even a hundred.

Lela had spoken with such sincerity that he did not doubt her. He said, "I'm sorry that I came at a bad time. But you'll talk to me later?"

She sighed and nodded. "Yes. Later. You can return when things are…normal. I hope you will return to this house. It has stood through many a storm. I hope it will do so once again."

"I fervently hope so, too, Mrs. Roth," he said. "I'll be in touch." He threw Emerson a pointed glance. "I'll let you get on with preparations to evacuate. I wish you a safe trip."

"And I wish one to you and your companion," she replied.

She gave Emerson a nod. And Eli knew the "interview" was over. He was dismissed.

Emerson walked to the door, watching to make sure he

was following her. Again he found himself making a stiff, impromptu bow. It seemed the right thing to do.

He left the room, and the doctor was coming up the stairs. "I need to give the Captain a wakeup call," he said to Emerson. "He's sleeping late. That's good. He'll need to be rested for the trip."

Emerson murmured her thanks. Eli could see Merriman and Claire in the studio. The nervous dog stayed close to Claire, and the parrot still sat on her shoulder. Merriman was taking pictures of an old poster announcing the opening of an exhibition of paintings by Nathan Roth.

Emerson tensed at the sight of people in the room, obviously displeased. She moved quickly on. Eli heard the sound of the doctor knocking at the Captain's door.

"Are you satisfied?" he asked. "Was I gentleman enough?"

"It will have to do. But you needn't come back. Talk to her on the phone. *She's* not deaf."

"It's not the same as talking face-to-face."

"You've done that. She's kept that part of the agreement. She's met with you. The interview can be done by phone."

They'd reached the first floor. Eli said. "Your grandmother seems a remarkable woman."

"She *is* a remarkable woman."

"You take after her." His gaze traveled up and down her body. "Physically, that is."

He couldn't help himself. He couldn't look enough at her.

She crossed her arms. "I resemble her *physically?* You make that sound like both a compliment and an insult."

"I meant it as a compliment. She's still lovely. How could it be an insult?"

Her expression clouded. "Because she's a great lady. I'm not."

"She seems like a woman of integrity."

Emerson put a fist on her hip. "Right, and I don't. You implied I'm a crook, as I recall."

He frowned. He was a man who saw things clearly. He could read character, and he could smell lies. The scent of lies was all over this house. But he had been thrown off track by Lela Roth. Perhaps he had misread her. But he didn't think so.

As for Emerson, he wasn't sure he could read her at all. He wanted to pull her closer, stare more deeply into her enigmatic eyes. But he tensed and forced himself not to touch her.

He said, "You seem like a woman who—" He shook his head in frustration.

"A woman who *what?*" she demanded.

"A woman who'd do anything for the people she loves."

She tilted her head in sardonic challenge. "Anything...including fraud?"

At that moment, the wind gusted, hitting the house so hard the walls trembled, the lights dimmed and the very air seemed to shake as if a huge, taut string had been plucked.

From upstairs came a bursting thud and the shattering of glass.

Emerson's body jerked in surprise and alarm. Eli took a step toward her, an instinctive urge to protect her. She stared up the steps in horror.

Eli was stunned. Was the hurricane making itself felt this soon? Was it possible? He seized Emerson by the arm and hauled her into the kitchen, where there were fewer windows to break.

"Let go," she protested. "It was only a gust. Frenchy must not've fastened a shutter tight enough."

He didn't let go. He gripped her just above the elbows, and for emphasis, he pulled her nearer. "You need to get your family out of here. But I'm not through with you. Not by a long shot. Something's going on here. And I'll find out what. I guarantee you."

The wind's shriek had died back to a dull, rumbling growl. Emerson glared at him. "You're obsessed. And I *won't* talk to you again. I'm reporting you to your editor. Now, I need to check upstairs. So go away. Just take your friend and—"

Suddenly Claire appeared in the doorway, panic on her face. "Emerson! Oh, Emerson!"

Emerson stiffened in Eli's grasp as if she were a trapped animal, temporarily paralyzed by fear. His first thought was that the shuttered library windows had burst, sending shards of glass through the air like flying knives. Lela Roth could have been cut, badly.

"Emerson," Claire said brokenly. "It's the Captain— he's gone, Em! He's *gone!*"

CHAPTER SIX

EMERSON STARED AT Claire in disbelief, unable to speak.

"Nana's hurt," Claire said in a choked voice. "And the Captain's not in his room. Is he down here?"

Emerson shook her head, dazed. "No. I haven't seen him. Nana's hurt?"

"The glass in one of the French doors. Something hit the shutter, broke through. The panes shattered—"

"And Nana?" A terrible image flashed through Emerson's mind, her grandmother, lying in a pool of blood and glass.

She swayed, barely realized that Eli had moved to her side and put his arm around her—was, in fact, helping support her.

"Her cheek g-got bloodied," Claire stammered. "Some other cuts, but little ones. Dr. Kim's helping her."

"Will she be all right?" Emerson's knees felt insubstantial, as if they were dissolving. Without realizing it she had braced her hands against Eli's chest for support.

"Yes, yes." Tears welled in Claire's eyes. "But, Em, where's the Captain? Dr. Kim knocked on his door. When there was no answer, he went in. And the Captain's not there. I don't know whe-whe-where he *is*." She began to weep.

Claire's tears galvanized Emerson, bringing back her strength. She broke away from Eli and moved to Claire, griping her shoulders. "He *must* be here somewhere."

Claire shook her head. "No. We looked in all the other

rooms. His pajamas were on the floor and the closet door was open. His cane's gone. And if he isn't down here—''

Claire broke down and hid her face in her hands. Emerson shook her to ward off hysteria. "Of course he's down here. Where else could he be?''

"Outside," Claire sobbed. "He might have gone outside. Oh, Em. What if he wandered off in this—this—''

Fear pierced Emerson like a blade. The Captain had always loved storms. He had a romantic nature, and rough weather exhilarated him. He would stride about in the rain and lightning like Lord Byron, driving Nana into anxious fits.

Emerson shook Claire again. "We'll look downstairs. Maybe he's in the sitting room. Or out in the sunroom. We'll look. Come on.''

She seized Claire by the hand and started to pull her toward the sitting room. At that instant, she became aware of Eli. All too aware.

If they found the Captain, Eli would see. And their secret would be out.

But they found no sign of the Captain in the house.

He had vanished.

ELI HELPED THE SISTERS search for Nathan Roth. Merriman came downstairs and joined them. Eli had plenty of questions, but he didn't ask them.

He figured they were about to be answered, whether the women liked it or not. If they hadn't seemed so frantic and tense, the search might have amused him. He helped them peer behind sofas, search the depths of closets, even look in a large brass-bound sea chest.

They might have been hunting a perverse and disobedient child. Or, thought Eli, a man in his second childhood.

When they'd searched the kitchen, Emerson heaved a sigh ragged with frustration and raked her hand through her hair. It had come undone, and fell in dark waves around her face.

She squared her jaw and said, "We haven't checked the garage."

"Or by the pool," Merriman said. "I'll go look there."

Eli didn't like the idea of searching among the Banyan roots and foliage and vines in the driving rain. Even less he liked the thought of finding Nathan Roth floating facedown in the swimming pool.

Still, he was about to volunteer to go with Merriman, but Claire took the photographer by the arm. "I'll help."

Merriman's brow furrowed, and he put his hand over hers. "He might be hurt."

"Then he'll need me," she answered, raising her chin.

For the first time Eli realized that Claire might have unsuspected steel in her. It was Emerson who now looked the more frightened.

Merriman tilted his head in Eli's direction. "You stay with her. We'll look in teams."

Eli nodded. Merriman put his arm around Claire, and the two of them left through the back door. Emerson bit her lip and tried to look as if she needed nobody, as if she was in perfect control of herself. But Eli could see she wasn't.

Back straight, Emerson marched to the door that led to the garage and flung it open. Then she stopped abruptly, as if frozen into place, staring. Eli, right behind her, stared over her shoulder.

The garage was a triple one, cavernous and gloomy. The customized panel truck was parked farthest away, and next to it was a dark-green Volkswagen van. But the space next to the Volkswagen was empty.

The garage doors gaped, completely open. They let in the howl of wind, the whipping of the rain. Broken palm fronds scuttled along the cement floor.

"Oh, no. No." The words came from deep inside Emerson, a primal moan. She put the heel of her hand to her forehead and closed her eyes as if she felt dizzy. She seemed about to sink to her knees.

Eli stepped to face her and took her by the upper arms. "What's wrong?"

Emerson tried to square her jaw, but couldn't. It trembled. She opened her eyes, and they swam with unshed tears. "He's taken his little ATV. He's out there... somewhere."

She stared bleakly out the yawning doors. The rain was like an endless curtain billowing crazily in the wind. Through the gray rush of it, Eli saw the palm trees bending, their fronds flying like flags that fought against being torn away.

Two of the smaller poinciana trees were broken, their trunks snapped nearly in two. Large branches littered the sodden lawn, small ones tumbled over it and leaves blew through the air in flurries.

"He's out there. He could get killed out there." She'd started to tremble, but it wasn't from the chill of the wind.

He wanted to draw her to him, wrap his arms around her, hold her close. But she was already pulling back from him, angry at herself. She scrubbed the back of her hand across her eyes and stood as straight as she could.

"I've got to find him."

Eli wouldn't release her. "No. I can't let you go out there. Merriman and I will go."

She pushed against his chest. "No. You wouldn't know where to look. He doesn't know you. He might—"

She stopped, as if she'd said too much. "You wouldn't know where to look," she repeated stubbornly.

He held her fast. "He might be frightened of us? Emerson, for God's sake, tell me the truth. Has he lost his mind? Does he have some degenerative disease? Is he out there, wandering around not knowing what he's doing?"

"No! That's not it, at all." She shook her head, glaring at him fiercely.

Dr. Kim came into the kitchen, his wrinkled face grim. "Emerson, you haven't found your grandfather?"

Her mask dropped, her expression showed pure desperation. She forgot even to fight Eli's grasp.

"He's gone. He took the ATV. I don't know where he could be. I have to find him."

Dr. Kim shook his head. "My dear, you must get your sister and grandmother out of here. This storm is the worst I've seen since Georges. It's not safe for them to stay here…or you."

"I won't leave my grandfather! I *won't!*"

Merriman and Claire came into the kitchen, the wind and rain gusting behind them. Both were drenched, and Claire shivered in the crook of Merriman's arm.

"No sign of him," Merriman said. "Some big branches are breaking off your banyan. One's already knocked down part of the fence—"

He stopped, looking at Emerson's stricken face. "What's wrong?"

She explained in a halting voice. Claire's knees buckled, but Merriman held her, both arms around her now.

Emerson broke away from Eli, and he watched as she went to Claire, taking her sister's pale face between her hands. "He'll be all right. I'll find him. You stay with Nana."

Dr. Kim was a small man, but he suddenly became formidably stern. "Claire, I've told your sister that you and she and your grandmother need to leave. This is a dangerous storm, and I fear it's going to get worse. I'll call 911 to alert them about your grandfather."

"Call," Emerson retorted. "I'm staying. And Nana won't go if she knows the Captain's lost."

"She doesn't know, and I don't want her to," Dr. Kim snapped back. "She's close to collapse now. I gave her another half a tranquilizer. I want you to get her to a safer place, and she won't go if she knows the Captain's missing.

I can't stay here with her. I've already been called for an emergency at the shelter. I'm going to meet my wife there. They need us. I'm sorry.''

Eli saw a small, fierce war ripping Emerson apart. But she kept her spine straight, and this time she didn't let her chin quiver.

She brought her face close to Claire's. ''Claire, you'll have to take her. Get her and the paintings to Fort Myers. I have rooms reserved under your name. Tell Nana I'm following in the Volkswagen with the Captain as soon as I've shut the house up.''

''I—I—'' Claire stammered. ''Yes. Okay. Yes. I—I—''

Eli saw her reluctance, her fear, her uncertainty. The detectives had told him that Claire did not go out a great deal, and she seldom drove over twenty miles from the house. The thought of getting her grandmother safely through one hundred and twenty miles of jammed highway must be her worst nightmare.

''Merriman,'' he said. ''Take her. You do the driving.''

''Absolutely,'' Merriman said. He turned to Claire. ''I won't let you go alone.''

She gazed up at him as if he were a knight on a white horse. ''I—I have to take the animals,'' she breathed. ''I can't leave them.''

''Then we take them,'' Merriman said. That made Claire stare at him as if he were Sir Galahad himself. Even Emerson seemed impressed. She put her hand on Merriman's rain-damp arm and said, ''Thank you, so much.''

Eli was disgusted to feel a small stab of jealousy.

But Merriman the Valiant was all business. ''What about Mrs. Roth?'' he asked Kim. ''Can she make it downstairs, or should I carry her?''

''It would be safer for you to carry her,'' said Dr. Kim. ''She's conscious, but woozy. She may drift in and out of sleep. I'll walk down with you, explain to her what's happening.''

"I'll gather the animals," Claire said. "W-we have tranquilizers for them, don't we?" she asked Emerson. "In case we ever had to do this?"

"Upstairs. In our bathroom," Emerson said. Claire dashed off.

"And change your clothes," Emerson cried after her.

Eli was alone with her again. He eyed her dubiously. "You really mean it? You're going out looking for him?"

She tossed her head as if the decision was simple. "I know this place. I know how he thinks. I'll find him."

"I'll help you," he said. He *had* to say it. He couldn't leave her alone to do this. It was too dangerous.

She didn't look at him as if he were a knight. She looked at him as if he were crazy. "I don't need your help."

He stepped closer. "You don't know that. What if he's fallen? Or something's fallen on him? Or he's badly hurt? You may need all the help you can get."

Sparks danced in her eyes. He knew what she was thinking. That he wanted only to learn Nathan Roth's secret. That his motive was anything but noble.

He moved closer still and took her right hand in his. "All right. From this moment, until your grandfather's safe, whatever happens, whatever I see, whatever I hear is off the record. Unless it becomes a matter of *public* record."

She looked at him suspiciously. "I don't know what you mean."

"Look, I don't know the story on your grandfather. Maybe he thinks he's Woody Woodpecker. Or Napoleon. Fine. We get him back, nobody finds out about the truth about this little episode, I never tell. I promise you that. I'll shake on it." He clasped her hand more firmly to prove he meant what he said.

"But what do you mean by that other thing—public record?" she demanded.

"Public record. Some weather channel's down here taping the hurricane. Your grandfather appears in front of them, waving his hands and yelling, 'I'm Woody Wood-pecker.' Or Napoleon. And people recognize him. Then the world knows. There's no more secret.''

"Let go of me," she said from between her teeth. "I've got to get my rain gear."

"Is there some that'll fit me?" he challenged. "Because I'm going with you."

"Oh, God," she cried in exasperation. "Is your damn story that important to you?"

"No," he said. "But I think you are."

Her eyes widened. He looked at her lips. Irrational as it was, he wanted to kiss her. He wanted it so much he ached.

But Merriman came into the kitchen, carrying Lela Roth. The woman looked frail and dazed. Her head wobbled sleepily. She looked small as a child in the big man's arms.

"Em," she said in a slurred voice. "This is all so—"

Eli released Emerson so she could go to her grandmother. "Confusing?" Emerson suggested, stroking Lela's fore-head. "Yes. But it'll be all right soon. You go with Claire and the animals and the paintings. This man will take care of you. I'll close up the house and bring the Captain. We'll just be a few miles behind you."

She lied so beautifully, Eli thought. She did it so well, and for a good purpose. He fervently wished all her lies were for a good cause, but he feared they couldn't be.

"What about you?" Merriman asked Eli.

"I'm staying with her." He nodded at Emerson. "And the Captain," he added. "We'll join you as soon as we can."

"Good," said Merriman.

"Good," said Dr. Kim. He blew a kiss to Emerson and started toward his car.

Emerson kissed Lela. "Get in the panel truck, Nana. I'll say goodbye again before you leave."

Her eyes met Eli's. "I'll help reload the truck," she told him.

His heart did something strange and unexpected in his chest. He would stay with her. He wondered just how many kinds of fool he was.

CLAIRE AND EMERSON had done a hell of a job packing the panel truck, Merriman thought. The paintings were neatly stacked upright, supported on both sides, and protected by shields of corrugated cardboard and blankets.

A cache of emergency supplies was loaded, along with a suitcase for each woman and for Nathan Roth. Wordlessly Emerson pulled out hers to make room for Merriman's. She moved the truck's back seat, made sure her grandmother's seat belt was fastened and kissed her on both cheeks, then the mouth.

"I have to start shutting up the house, then get the Captain ready," she said. "I love you, Nana. We'll see you soon."

Lela Roth nodded uncomprehendingly. "It's all so…" she said, but her voice trailed away to nothingness. Emerson kissed her again, then came and embraced her sister.

"We have to start looking. We'll leave by another door so that Nana won't see. Good luck, Claire. Have a safe trip."

The two women held each other tightly. "Good luck," Claire tried to say. It barely came out. "Try to find him."

Emerson stood taller. "I *will* find him."

To Merriman's surprise, she came to him and set a light kiss on his cheek. She took him by the hand and looked into his eyes. "Thank you. Thank you so much. Take good care of them."

"I will," he promised her. He didn't tell her he had no experience with hurricanes or evacuations and had no idea what might lie ahead. He only knew he would protect Claire—and those Claire loved—with the last drop of his heart's blood.

"Good luck." He shook her hand. "I hope to see you soon."

She nodded curtly. "You will. We have to go now. We have to hurry."

Then she disappeared inside, Eli following her. Merriman stuffed his luggage and photo equipment into the space Emerson had just unloaded.

But getting people and inanimate things into place, Merriman realized, was the easy part. The hard part was adding two Dobermans, an overweight cat and a parrot to the cargo. The parrot's cage had a cloth over it, but the bird squawked anyway.

"Good morning," he kept screaming surreally. "Good morning!"

Merriman helped stuff Bunbury the cat, drowsy and looking pie-eyed from his tranquilizer, into his cat carrier. The two dogs were more problematic. Claire had only six tranquilizers to get them all the way to Fort Myers.

She said she had to dole them out carefully. Bruiser, who was calm and ate anything, gulped his down as if it were a treat. Merriman had to help Claire with Fang, who was nervous and suspicious.

Merriman held the dog and pried his jaws open. Claire petted Fang and popped the pill into his mouth, then Merriman clamped the jaws shut until the dog swallowed.

"Mission accomplished," Merriman said. Claire, still trying not to cry over leaving Emerson and her grandfather, gave him a shaky smile.

"Let's get them in their carriers and get on the road," Merriman said. He released Fang and pulled the first dog crate nearer.

Fang inched away from them and spit out the pill. Merriman had never known dogs could spit. He was ready to force-feed the pill to Fang a second time, but Bruiser stepped forward and gobbled up that pill, too.

"Oh, no," Claire said, horrified. "The longer Fang's in

the car, the worse he gets. I'd better save the others for when he really gets upset.''

''Whatever you say,'' Merriman replied and began wrestling the reluctant Fang into his crate. It was a struggle, and once the door was shut, the dog began to whimper and scratch the bars to get out.

Bruiser, in the meantime, had already plunked to the ground, looking dazed. Somehow, at last, Merriman got all the animals into the truck.

They set out into the blinding rain, the rumbling wind.

Merriman, a few days ago careless and unattached, had come to Florida to take some interesting pictures and catch a few rays of sun.

Now he found himself in the confines of a panel truck that held several million dollars worth of paintings, an ailing elderly woman, a dog that was passed out, a dog that was having a nervous breakdown, a cat that looked drunk, a screaming parrot...and a woman he supposed he must love, or he wouldn't be doing this.

A huge gust of wind shook the whole truck, and Merriman could barely see, though the windshield wipers whipped back and forth.

''Good morning!'' shrieked the parrot. ''Good morning!''

Fang moaned and scratched his cage.

Merriman stole a glance at Claire. She was sitting rigidly, not allowing herself to look back.

He said, ''Everything's going to be all right.''

He prayed he wasn't lying.

EMERSON WAS GLAD she didn't have to see the truck leave. She feared watching it go would have undone her. Her throat locked with suppressed emotion.

She had practically tossed an old sou'wester at Eli. It had once belonged to the Captain, but she couldn't find the hat that went with it, nor the overshoes.

Her good raincoat was a tan, silky thing more suitable for Fifth Avenue than the battering storm outside. She slipped into an ancient set of faded brown waterproofs that she'd had since high school.

She zipped the jacket, pulled up the hood and tied it securely. She supposed she looked like a beige ninja, but she didn't give a damn.

Once, like the Captain, she had liked to prowl through storms, glorying in the power of nature. Sometimes they had slipped off together to do it, much to Nana's consternation. She remembered where he and she had hiked then. She hoped that he had headed the same way today.

"You need a hat," she told Eli.

"No. I'll turn up my collar. A hat'd just blow off."

She was in no mood to argue. She snatched a fanny pack from the top shelf of the clothes closet and strapped it on. "Come on."

"What's that?" he asked, squinting at the fanny pack.

"A first-aid kit. Nana used to make me carry it when I'd take a real hike."

Emerson strode to the sunroom and ground her teeth when she saw it already had four broken windows. The tile floor was slick with rain and littered with glass. She should have cracked open all the windows to ease the air pressure. Now it would have to wait.

She struggled to get the slider door open, and Eli had to throw his strength against it, his shoulder grazing hers. It opened a few inches and the wet wind rushed in, but it hardly mattered. Rainy gusts were already pouring through the shattered windows.

Emerson pushed with all her muscle to force the door completely open, but Eli took a step back. He stopped helping.

"Come on," she cried, half-frantic. "You can't see this side of the house from the drive. We can be out looking before Claire even gets started."

He set his hand firmly on the door's metal frame, showing he didn't intend to cooperate. "Some questions first." He had to raise his voice over the rolling grumble of the gale.

"I don't have time for questions," she snapped. "Oh, go away. Who needs you?"

"Questions," he said with finality. "And you need me. You can't even get this door open alone."

She glared at him. His thick hair was already damp and dancing with the wind. The angles of his face had hardened into implacability. "First, where are we going?"

Emerson didn't have time to waste arguing. "There's sort of a gazebo, back at the edge of the mangrove swamp. We used to go there and watch the rain."

He didn't move, his arm still barred her way. "Your grandfather—what kind of shape is he in? What are we dealing with? If he sees us, will he resist coming with us? Would he hide? Is he in his right mind?"

Inwardly, she swore. She had to stop lying. If they were lucky and found him, Eli would see. There would be no more hiding.

"There was a car accident. In Tahiti. Six years ago. He's partially paralyzed. His mind's good—very good for his age. But he has moods. He can only walk with a cane. And then not far."

"What do you mean for his age?" he demanded. "And his moods? What are his moods like?"

She hung her head. "Sometimes—especially lately—he gets a bit confused. Sometimes…a bit…depressed. Or annoyed."

"Okay." Eli gave a nod of resignation. "It helps to know. And if he's not at the gazebo?"

"I—I know some other places."

"All on this property?"

"Yes."

"He wouldn't head for the highway?"

"No." She was certain of that.

"Then let's go," he said. He heaved the door open and took her by the hand. She almost resisted, but his hand was warm, strong and reassuring. She decided to hang on to it.

They made their way down the concrete steps and into the maelstrom.

THIS IS INSANE, Eli thought. When the wind gusted, it had to be sixty miles an hour. At its slowest, it must be close to forty.

He had the sickening feeling that it was going to get worse. He held one arm up to shield his eyes, and the other he wrapped around Emerson.

She was a strong woman, sure of foot, but twice she'd staggered. So he held her tightly, trying to keep his body between hers and the brunt of the gale. The path, rough already, was littered with broken limbs and wet, swirling leaves. She staggered for a third time and threw her arm around his waist.

Under calmer circumstances, he'd have liked that. He'd have liked it a lot. But now he just kept thinking they were both crazy, and she was crazier than he was. She seemed all defiant willpower, with no fear except that of not finding Nathan.

Eli wanted to find Nathan, too—for her sake. She refused to entertain any thought of her own safety. If he hadn't been there, and the gusts knocked her down, he had the feeling she'd keep on, crawling on her hands and knees if she had to. She was a woman possessed.

Eli, not possessed, could see plenty of danger. The path led into scrubland. On both sides he could hear trees being torn apart by the charge of the wind, their limbs cracking like gunshots.

Sticks, chips of wood, strange pieces of unidentifiable trash flew through the air like missiles. Something struck him on the cheek. He thought he was bleeding, but he couldn't tell.

Something, a fragment of branch, struck both his hand and her shoulder. She flinched, but didn't cry out. He should have insisted she stay back at the house, but she never would have agreed.

And he couldn't have found his way without her. Twice the path forked. And, while he could see but dimly and only a few feet ahead of him, she knew exactly where to go.

As for finding her grandfather, her instincts might indeed be strong enough to lead her to him. But was she allowing herself to think of what dangers the old man might have met?

An ATV was light. The wind, especially that great gust that had hit, could have ripped it out of Nathan's control, sent him tumbling into some thicket or ditch. He might have collided with something, a fallen branch or trunk. He might have become stuck and tried to walk.

She'd said sometimes he was confused. He could wander deeper and deeper into the mangrove swamps. A weak and disoriented man could drown there.

She'd said Nathan was sometimes depressed. Was that why he had gone out into the storm? Because he was tired of what his life had become?

The wind surged, the worst so far. A palm frond struck them both and flapped against them, like a bizarre sash binding them together.

Emerson gasped, seizing Eli with both arms around his middle, and burying her face against his chest. He stripped the frond so the wind dashed it away. He'd stopped, holding Emerson tightly.

He winced as something small, dark and boxy went tumbling through the air, just missing his head. What? A birdhouse perhaps? Of all the ways to die, he'd rather not go like that.

Hear what happened to Garner? Killed by a birdhouse, poor chap. Knocked his brains completely out.

He clung to Emerson, realizing how vulnerable they were. And so, somewhere, was Nathan—if he was still alive.

Emerson shuddered against him. Perhaps the same dark thought haunted her. Or perhaps the wind and wet and chill and danger were starting to take their toll on her.

Around them, branches popped like a fresh flurry of gunfire. It was like being in a damn war, he thought. He pressed his mouth against Emerson's hooded ear. "Are you all right?" He yelled to be heard.

And then, the gust passed, and the wind, though fierce, roared less hungrily. She raised her wet face to him. "Yes. Let's go. It's not much farther."

She pulled away awkwardly, as if in fatigue, but kept one arm around his waist. Together they wove down the path snarled and jumbled with debris.

At one point, a stream of water had formed, shallow and narrow, but swift, blocking their way. Emerson was long-legged, but not *that* long-legged. Besides, she was already unsteady. Such a fast flow of water could knock her off her feet.

He swept her up into his arms, and she didn't protest. He crossed the stream in one determined stride, then carried her a few more paces before she shouted in his ear for him to put her down.

Reluctantly, he did. She steadied herself and didn't protest when he kept one arm round her. Again she slipped her arm round his waist. "It's just around that curve," she said, out of breath.

She forged on somehow, frequently wiping the rain from her eyes. He kept tight hold of her and marveled again that she would have gone out into this watery hell alone.

She might be duplicitous, but she was the bravest woman

he'd ever known. And how strong must be the love that drove her? He marveled, too, at that.

Then she stopped. He stopped, too. There, in at the edge of the mangroves, was a clearing. The sparse grass was flattened and strewn with wreckage.

In the middle stood a peculiar structure. It was built much like a gazebo, but of solid concrete. A gazebo was usually a light and delicate-looking structure. This one, anything but delicate, was still handsome, a beautifully designed octagon with eight cement pillars.

In the center was a square table of concrete, flanked by two concrete benches.

But otherwise, it was empty. There was no sign of Nathan Roth.

CHAPTER SEVEN

EMERSON'S HAND flew to Eli's chest, and she sagged against him. Her eyes, dazed and disbelieving, were fixed on the empty gazebo.

"He's not here. I was sure…" Stricken, she could not go on.

"Damn! Damn!" She tried to block sorrow with anger. It didn't work. She choked out one more "damn," then collapsed against his chest, crying.

"Hey," he said, wrapping his arms around her. He laid his face against hers; her skin was startlingly cold. "You said you knew other places. Come in out of the rain. We'll talk."

The gazebo had a low wall around three-quarters of its base. The wall rose only three feet high, but they could huddle against it and find shelter. Though the roof had lost patches of its shingles, it still held. That, too, would help.

He guided her inside, and they sank down, side by side, against the most protective wall. She'd fought back her tears, but her expression was one of devastation. He draped his arm around her shoulders.

"Hey, tough stuff, buck up. You said you know this place, you know him. What's your next guess?"

She took a deep breath and raised her chin. "He wouldn't go to the beach. The sand's blowing too hard. He'd stay on one of the paths. If he took a right instead of a left at the next fork, he might have gone to the blue hole."

"What's the blue hole?"

"It's a little freshwater sink. The water's an extraordinary blue. He—he and I used to like to go there to see the wildlife." She paused, remembering. "And throw rocks at the alligator."

He almost laughed. "Throw rocks? Alligator?"

"Not to hurt him. Just to make him afraid of people. Some people feed 'gators. That's wrong. They get bold. They'll come into your yard. Attack pets. People. The Captain knew better. He didn't want that."

She said this with such longing and fondness, Eli's heart twisted.

"So that's where you learned to throw rocks so well," he said, trying to tease a smile from her.

She gave a solemn nod. Then she tried to wipe the rain from her face. "Oh, when did he slip out? When?" Shaking her head, she said, "It must have been when you and I and Merriman were in the sitting room. Claire and Dr. Kim were upstairs with Nana. He could have got downstairs and slipped into the garage through the kitchen. Oh, God."

She stared at the gazebo's wet and littered floor for a long moment. Then she squared her shoulders. "Let's go. It's less than a mile."

She tried to rise, but he put his hand on her shoulder and held her in place. "Wait," he said as kindly as he could. "You've pushed hard. Rest."

"I don't have time," she objected. "He needs me."

"You won't find him if you exhaust yourself. You were starting to falter toward the end back there."

She stared down again, frowning defensively. "The ground's slippery."

"And getting worse. If we find your grandfather and I have to carry him back to the house, I can. But I can't carry two of you. Get your second wind."

She slid him a disapproving look. "Please. Don't use the word *wind*."

He smiled. "Ah. Your spark's dampened but not quenched. Good."

She wiped back a strand of hair that had escaped from her hood. "I don't quench easily."

"No," he said. "You don't." Her waterproof jacket and pants no longer looked waterproof. The sheer force of the rain looked as if it had penetrated the nylon.

Her face was wet and drawn, but still beautiful. He studied the gleam of her damp cheeks. "So," he said, "tell me about this place. Your grandfather built it?"

She leaned her head back against the wall. "He had it built. He helped design it. He wanted it to stand in a storm like this." She looked up at the beams of the roof.

He followed her gaze. She said, "These places usually have weak roofs. Wind fills them like a sail and takes them."

She nodded. "He had all sorts of things done. It's braced and strapped, and it has guardrails to catch the wind, like the roof on the house. It should hold even in a hundred-mile-an-hour wind."

"Why'd he build it?"

"For picnics. And for a quiet place of his own. He loves the ocean, but he loves the mangroves, too. He grew up where it was always cold. He loves everything down here."

"Even the alligator?" he joked, trying to buoy her up.

Emerson turned her face and looked him in the eyes. It gave him an excited, jittery feeling in his stomach. "Even the alligator. If the 'gator got aggressive, somebody might shoot him. Or call wildlife authorities to relocate him."

"Where do you relocate an aggressive alligator?"

She smiled. "The Captain used to say to the luggage factory."

He smiled, too, even though he was wet and chilled and worried for her. She sighed, then went silent. He drew her closer, wishing he could give her more warmth.

To his surprise, she laid her head on his shoulder. *My God,* he thought.

The wall against which they rested was a poor haven, but he was grateful for it. She must be, too. Perhaps that's why she'd made such a seemingly intimate gesture. She found it comforting to lean against another body—anyone's.

He should not take it personally. But he did. Eli, not a tender man by nature, felt a surge of tenderness for her. It shook him more than the dull rumble of the wind.

She said, "I hope Claire and Nana are all right."

"They will be," he said, though in truth he could promise nothing.

"Merriman's a kind man."

"Yes."

"It can be hell evacuating from down here."

"He'll take care of them." Eli paused. "Your sister? He'd do anything for her. He's pretty taken with her."

She blinked the rain from her eyes. "Yes. She's taken with him, too. It happened fast."

He swallowed. "They say it can."

"Yes. They say…"

I should kiss her, he thought. *Hell, we might die out here. I don't want to die and never have kissed her.*

But suddenly she drew away from him, and he knew the moment had passed.

She looked out toward the path. "The wind's dropped," she said.

She was right. Its roar was dimming, like that of a train growing more distant. The trees lashed less violently. The rain poured, but it no longer gushed.

An approaching hurricane was like a live thing, Eli realized. A shapeshifting monster that charged, then paused, stalking more slowly. The wind was like its breath, heaving in huge cycles.

With luck, the thing would change its course. At least it

might weaken. With no luck, it would gather force and hurl itself straight at them.

Emerson struggled to her feet. "Come on. We've got to try the blue hole."

Eli rose, too. "Right. Let's find him."

He said it with a heartiness he did not feel. But he would stay by her, even if she decided to walk straight through the gates of hell.

IT HAD TAKEN Merriman half an hour to reach the highway. A mammoth branch had fallen across the road. He'd had to shove, tug and drag it out of their path. Claire insisted on helping, though the wind whipped her poncho until it was useless.

"You're scratching your hands all up," Merriman yelled at her.

She ignored him. "This must have fallen after Dr. Kim left. It must have just come down. We're lucky it didn't come down on *us*."

Merriman gritted his teeth and hauled at the thing with all his might. From somewhere came enough adrenaline for him to do it. The damn thing moved a good three feet. He strained again, and the limb lurched another two feet, leaves rattling crazily in the scud of the wind.

He could edge the truck around it now. He grabbed Claire by the elbow, steered her to her door and held it fast against the push of the gale. He got in himself. Fang was whining and scratching. The parrot was screaming, "Good morning! Good morning!"

Lela sat in the back seat, nodding groggily. Merriman put the truck in gear and eased around the flailing leaves of the branch. "Do you have a first-aid kit?" he asked Claire.

She nodded and opened the glove box.

"Take care of your hands," he told her.

"You're bleeding worse," she said, drawing out the kit. "I'm only scraped a little."

Merriman glanced at his hands. He was indeed oozing blood, but not a lot. "Fix yourself up first. I don't want to stop until we have to."

Where he had to stop was the point the side road met the highway. The traffic snailed along through the torrents of rain, an endless parade of it. It was bumper to bumper and creeping only one way, north.

He swore under his breath. It was ten minutes before a kindly motorist let him into the sluggish line. While he waited, Claire tended to his cut and scraped hands.

Her touch was gentle. Her hair hung in wet tendrils around her face. Her expression was of stress mixed with sympathy. She was the sweetest thing he'd ever seen.

He'd walk to Fort Myers if he had to, carrying her and Grandma, too, with the dogs and cat strapped to his back and the parrot cage balanced on his head.

"Does it hurt?" she asked, dabbing antiseptic on a scratch.

"No," he lied.

She kept her head bowed, repacking the first-aid kit. It was at this moment that the charitable driver let him onto the highway. Merriman steered into place and found that the traffic was moving at approximately five miles an hour.

"I know this sounds stupid," Claire said hesitantly. "But...but I think you're a real hero to do this."

He grinned, embarrassed. He shrugged, unable to think of anything to say.

The parrot could. "Sounds stupid!" he squawked.

Merriman's grin died as Fang began to howl.

"Stupid!" cried the parrot.

The dog howled more miserably.

Merriman thought it wasn't easy, this hero business.

EMERSON AND ELI fought their way through the rain, their arms around each other's waists.

Eli might be ruthless, she thought, but he had guts. She hated to admit it, but she might not have made it this far without him. Physically, he was very strong. She was not used to leaning on anyone, but she had leaned on him this morning and done it often.

Was it still morning? Her watch was broken, and she didn't want to spare breath to ask Eli the time. It seemed they had waded through this crazed downpour for eons, perhaps forever.

It didn't matter. She had to find the Captain. She loved him with all her heart, and he was in trouble. He *needed* her.

She put up her free arm to shield her eyes. The wind was rising again, and the scrub on either side of the path swayed as if trying to fly out of the earth. Leaves and twigs spun through the air; once again there was the crack and rip of branches breaking.

She stumbled over a broken limb and would have fallen, but Eli caught her. Both his hands seized her waist, and as she steadied herself, she squinted, panting, up at him.

Drenched, his thick black hair lashed in the wind. Rivulets of water ran down his face. His mouth was set in an impressively stubborn line, his eyebrows drawn together in concern.

"Emerson, how much farther? You're starting to stagger again."

She forced herself to straighten up and throw her shoulders back. "Not much farther. Come on."

She pulled herself half-free of his grasp and lurched onward.

But he stayed next to her, looping his arm around her again. He put his mouth close to her ear. "Is there any shelter at the blue hole? It's getting bad again."

She turned, her cheek grazing his. For a split second, his

lips were barely an inch from hers. Quickly she moved to speak in his ear. "Some stone outcroppings."

That was all she had breath to say. The largest outcropping was an uneven shelf perhaps fifteen feet long. At its highest, it rose only a few feet, but it ran in a direction crosswise to the wind. On the protected side her grandfather would take refuge.

She was certain she would find him there.

He might be hunched over his ATV, or he might be crouched, shivering, on the ground, but he would be there.

He would be cold and soaked and frightened, that part would be terrible, but he would be there. And she and Eli would take him to safety.

But when the path curved to reveal the blue hole and the low wall of rock, Emerson blinked in shock, and her heart withered as if it were dying.

Her grandfather was not there. There was no trace of him or the ATV.

Emerson could not move. His absence was huge, paralyzing. It was as if the storm had eaten him.

NO NATHAN ROTH? Eli thought. No surprise.

He had hoped Emerson was right. But hope was a different thing from belief. Emerson had believed, and now she acted poleaxed.

He took her by the shoulders and shook her to bring her back to life. She looked at him without comprehension.

"Come on," he said urgently. "We'll check the other side."

Trying to understand the geography of the place, he squinted at the blue hole. It was more like a seething gray cauldron, the water whipped to frenzied wavelets and sending sprays of mist into the air.

On the far side of the blue hole, a thicket of young palms bent torturously in the shear of the wind, their fronds tearing. The rain made it impossible to see beyond them.

He said, "What's beyond those palms?"

"Nothing," she said dully. "Scrub."

"Could a man like your grandfather negotiate his way through it?"

"No."

She said it with such utter hopelessness that Eli cursed Nathan Roth. The old fool was probably dead. He was breaking this woman's heart and putting her into peril.

But Nathan would feel no pain, no more anything and was probably lying somewhere in this patch of wilderness, lifeless as a clod.

Perhaps that was what was dawning on Emerson. Eli studied her expression. Her numbness was starting to give way—to what? Despair? Sorrow? Or an even greater determination to keep searching?

"Come on." He put his arm around her again. "Let's look."

He guided her toward the rugged shelf of stone. If Nathan Roth was there, he would not be alive. If he had been lying on the windward side of that wall, he would have been beaten mercilessly by the wind and rain this last hour. He would not have survived.

But the windward side, too, was empty.

Eli steered Emerson back to the leeward, sheltered side and had to force her to sit. Again, she seemed stunned. He sat beside her, not knowing what to say.

He wanted her to go back to the house. He wanted to load both their suitcases in the Volkswagen. He wanted to get the hell out of this place before the wind tore it off the coast and sent it flying out to sink in the ocean. He wanted her safe in Fort Myers and united with her family.

But beside him, Emerson put her face in her hands and began to sob. "Oh, hell," he said with a harsh sigh. He cradled her in his arms and said what he didn't want to say.

"Go ahead. Cry it out. You'll feel better. Then we'll go

find him. You know of other places he might be…don't you?''

"Yes," she choked out. "It's just that—" She couldn't finish the sentence.

"I know, I know," he said. "You were sure he was here. It's all right. We'll keep going."

Gradually, her crying eased. She gasped a few times, her forehead pressed against his chest. The last gusts of wind had finally whipped her hood off, and her wet hair blew in a dark dance. He tried to smooth it.

Emerson took a deep breath and raised her face to his. "I'm sorry."

He shook his head. "Don't be."

Her chin trembled, but he could see her determination coming back.

"You know," she said, her eyes on his, "for a man who's so awful, you're really wonderful."

This is it, he thought with a pleasant ache. *I'm going to kiss her.* He lowered his face to hers. Her lips parted slightly.

But suddenly, barely audible in the grumbling thunder of the wind, a ringing noise sounded. "My phone!" Emerson exclaimed, transformed. She jerked away from him and groped under her rain jacket for her cell phone.

"Maybe it's Claire," she said. "Or maybe— Hello?"

Eli, frowning in frustration, watched her expression change as she listened. It went from cautious to disbelieving surprise, then joy. "Oh!" she kept exclaiming. "Oh!… Yes!… Could you? Can you?… Yes, oh, yes! I *love* you!"

She shut off the phone, and turned back to Eli. "The Captain's alive. Dr. Kim found him on the road, almost to the highway. He's taken him to the shelter. He's suffering from exposure. But he should be fine. Oh, Eli, he's all right!"

She threw her arms around his neck, her hair flying, her face shining.

And Eli finally got to kiss her. He kissed her for all he was worth.

EMERSON HAD KISSED Eli out of sheer exultation. Exultation of one sort turned into another sort. His face felt warm against her cold one, and his mouth, that sinfully good-looking mouth, seemed to fit hers to perfection.

He laced his fingers in her drenched hair, drawing her face closer to his.

His lips moved against hers with growing intensity. She'd kissed him on impulse and in celebration. It hadn't occurred to her that he might kiss back so well, or so thoroughly. Her mind went wavery, her senses became jumbled, her body grew warmer.

But she pulled away. She had promises to keep. "Dr. Kim said he'd keep this quiet. But only on the condition that I left for Fort Myers immediately. Oh, Eli. He's safe. Let's go home. And then let's leave."

Reenergized, she got to her feet, tugging at his hand. He rose with her. "He's all right," she repeated, as if still convincing herself of the truth of it.

"Why didn't Kim call sooner?" Eli asked, staying closed to her.

"He tried. He couldn't get through on his cell phone. He borrowed one at the shelter." She frowned thoughtfully. "Maybe that's why I haven't heard from Claire. I should try to call her."

"Wait till we get back to the house," he said. "It's starting to gust again."

She nodded. Walking with the wind was easier than walking against it, but it still buffeted and shoved them. She heard more trees limbs snapping. For the first time she let herself think about how dangerous it was out here. And how far they were from the house.

"I dragged you out here for nothing," she said. Guilt was not an emotion she often indulged in, but she felt it now. Eli had put his life at risk for Nathan—and for her.

"You didn't drag me," he said, holding her tightly as

they dodged a fallen scrub pine. "I wouldn't let you come out here alone."

She looked up at him gratefully. His shoulders were hunched against the wind, and he frowned in concentration. "You're a better man than you pretend to be."

He cast her a sideways glance that was unreadable. "I don't understand. If your grandfather was on the road, and they left the ATV there, why didn't Merriman see it? Why didn't he get in touch with us? Or the authorities?"

She flinched as the wind thumped her back, knocking her closer to Eli.

"The Captain didn't want to leave it. He was afraid someone would steal it. So Dr. Kim just drove it far enough into the woods so it couldn't be seen."

"Hardly a rational fear, is it? That somebody's going to be out stealing ATVs in a hurricane."

The question forced her to remember what she'd conveniently forgotten too often on this journey. Eli Garner was a reporter, bent on prying out what was best kept hidden.

"I told you," she said. "He gets confused sometimes. I don't want to talk right now. It takes too much effort."

He nodded and said no more. Heads down, they walked as fast as they could toward the house. But now Emerson wondered if she'd been wrong when she'd said, "You're a better man than you pretend to be."

Maybe the opposite was true: he was pretending to be better than he was—far better.

THE SIGHT OF the house heartened Emerson. She could see the broken shutters of the library banging crazily in the wind, see the roof had lost shingles. A gutter had torn loose and swung back and forth like a giant scythe.

The trees and shrubs were battered and broken. The stone birdbath had tipped over; the flowers were torn into ruin.

Half of the boards of the privacy fence around the pool had blown away. Those that remained tilted and sagged drunkenly.

But her home still stood.

Once inside, she felt a tumultuous mixture of emotions. Relief—it was good to be shielded from the tearing wind and not to be chilled to the marrow by the rain. It was such intense relief, she wanted to collapse, just to lie on the familiar rug before the hearth and weep. Weep because she was home again, because the Captain had been found and because the rest of her family was on its way to safety.

But she also felt an almost panicky urgency to escape. The winds beat the house like madmen banging on a drum. The storm could get worse, far worse. Sometimes hurricanes brought storm surges, great walls of water that could wreak more destruction than the strongest gales.

She tried not to let herself think about the surges. But they could be monstrous enough to engulf a whole key and sweep strong buildings out to sea.

So Emerson did not stop to take a warm shower or brew a pot of coffee—though miraculously both electricity and water were still working. She only shed her sodden clothes, dried herself with a towel—it seemed the most wonderful towel in the world to her—and put on dry clothing.

She took time to fill the bathtubs with water, in case they became trapped at Mandevilla and water was cut off. She prayed fervently that this wouldn't happen.

Eli had changed clothes in the garage. He helped open the windows a half inch to equalize the pressure in the house. He took care of the first floor, she the second. He and she packed the last of the paintings in the back of the Volkswagen and loaded it with bottled water and other emergency supplies.

MERRIMAN HAD BEEN on the highway almost an hour and a half. In that time the car had crept perhaps twenty-five miles. The line of traffic would move forward a hundred yards, then stop. Then it would go in a slow roll forward, as in a rush hour traffic jam.

The air in the truck had grown sultry, but Merriman hated to run the air conditioner and chance overheating the motor. They couldn't open the windows because rain would spew in.

At one stop, he stripped off his jacket, and Claire helped him struggle out of the sleeves. His T-shirt was damp with sweat. Modest as she was, she'd undone one button on her blouse. This was the only thing that had cheered Merriman up in two hours. He stole his glances carefully so he wouldn't embarrass her.

During some stops, he tried to get through to Eli on his cell phone, but he couldn't connect. Claire tried hers, hoping to reach Emerson. She had no better luck.

At one stop she loosened her dozing grandmother's blouse, then stayed turned in her seat, to fan the older woman. She kept crooning little songs to calm the nervous Fang. It worked fairly well. She had a lovely voice, low and melodious.

The parrot was another matter. Now he kept quiet for long stretches of time, but then he would squawk angrily and screech strange words and phrases. Claire tried to quiet him, but the parrot wouldn't be soothed. At best, he would fall into another mercifully silent sulk.

The traffic started to move again, and Merriman switched on the air conditioner, hoping a few minutes might cool the interior. Just then his phone rang.

Eagerly, Merriman clapped the phone to his ear. "Hello?"

"It's me…Eli. We're back at the house. Dr. Kim found Nathan Roth trying to get to the highway. He took him with him into Key West to the shelter. He suffered from exposure, but he should be fine."

"Great news. Tell Claire. I'll give her the phone."

Claire's face brightened. "The Captain?" she asked hopefully.

Merriman nodded, and he couldn't help grinning at her happiness.

Eli said, "Listen, Merriman. Emerson doesn't want her grandmother to know we have to leave Roth behind. He's better off with a doctor than on the road with us. You and Claire are going to have to keep the facts from her for a while. Emerson will explain to Claire. We're about to leave. We'll join you in Fort Myers. How's the traffic?"

"God-awful. A snail's pace."

"Maybe it'll speed up. Okay, put Claire on will you?"

Merriman handed her the phone. She listened to her sister and her eyes filled with tears of joy and relief. By the time she finished talking, the traffic had stopped again. When she handed his phone back to him, their hands touched.

Merriman got tingly and warm in spite of the cool air. He wanted to bend over and kiss the tears out of those beautiful honey-colored eyes.

Why not? he thought. But he didn't. He didn't want to kiss her the first time in this space so crowded it seemed like a cramped zoo. So he restrained himself into merely leaning closer.

"I'm so glad they found him," she whispered. "I only wish he was coming with them."

"Everything's going to be fine," he promised. "Nothing's going to go wrong—"

"Wrong!" the parrot suddenly screamed. "Wrong! Wrong! Wrong!"

EMERSON WAS an excellent driver, but she let Eli take the driver's seat. He was physically stronger than she was, and if the steering wheel needed to be wrenched in an emergency, he had more muscle.

But as he backed the Volkswagen out of the garage, a

new clash of emotions shook Emerson. She felt fear and regret at deserting the house. Would this be the last time she saw it?

It had been her home since she was a little girl. She knew its every corner, scratch and scar. Every ornament, lovingly collected over the years. Every dish in the cupboards, every rug, towel, sheet, book—

She gritted her teeth and refused to think about the books, which would certainly be drenched, probably ruined.

Yet for all her sense of loss about leaving, she knew they must. To stay was dangerous. But it was dangerous, too, to go. Part of the highway was only three feet above sea level. One bad surge could bring disaster.

The wind shook and rattled the small van. Water coursed down the windshield in blurring sheets. Eli's face was tense, his hands tight on the wheel.

"Have you ever driven in anything like this before?" Emerson asked, her hands clenched in her lap.

He nodded. "I stayed just ahead of a hurricane in the Caribbean. It was just as bad. Maybe worse."

He flicked on the radio, tuned to the weather station. The hurricane, said the newscaster, seemed stalled again. The eye was poised sixty miles from the Lower Keys, and the storm might change course, hurling across the Gulf of Mexico without coming any nearer Florida. No one was sure.

"That's good," Eli said. "This might give us the break we need."

Emerson nodded, but they were still negotiating the narrow asphalt road. She didn't know what the highway would be like when they reached it. Probably still bumper to bumper and moving sluggishly.

Suddenly, Eli braked. The van stopped so abruptly that Emerson lurched against her seat belt, and Eli flung his arm in front of her to keep her from being thrown farther.

"What?" she cried.

"That metal bridge that crosses the gully. It's out." He stared through the watery windshield. So did Emerson, but she couldn't see what he saw, and his words didn't register.

"A tree fell on it."

Then she saw, and she felt sick. The bridge was small, hardly twelve feet in length. It was made of a kind of rusty steel grating. She'd rattled across it thousands of times without giving it a second thought.

But a huge tabebuia tree had crashed down on it with such force the bridge had buckled in the middle. It had wrenched loose from one of its concrete pilings. Its far edges tipped up at a precarious angle.

The ditch swirled with rushing water, and now the water flooded over the bent part of bridge, pinning the trunk of the tree across it.

Eli swore. Emerson wanted to rage and swear herself, but she could only look at the uprooted tree pressing against the sagging metal. "It's going to give way, isn't it?" she said hopelessly.

"We can't cross it," he said.

Another tabebuia leaned at a dangerous angle toward the bridge. It, too, might topple at any moment.

There was a grove of tabebuia trees, and her grandfather had especially loved them for their size and strength and their yellow flowers. *The Captain will hate losing these trees,* she thought numbly.

Eli hit the steering wheel with the flat of his hand in anger. "Is there another road out of here?"

Numbly she shook her head. "No."

Then she turned to look at him, feeling light-headed and unreal. She said, "We're trapped. We'll have to ride out the storm. Here. At Mandevilla."

CHAPTER EIGHT

ELI DROVE BACK to the house inwardly seething that Roth had planned only one way out of Mandevilla. But his concern for Emerson was greater than his anger at the old man. She'd suffered an onslaught of emotional blows today. The toll was starting to show.

He parked the truck and together they unloaded it. They did it in silence. She hadn't spoken since she'd said they'd have to ride out the storm.

He said, "You said your grandfather built this house to last. It seems solid—damn solid."

"It is." She didn't say it with great conviction.

But then, as she hauled her suitcase inside, she seemed to snap back to herself. "If the storm moves into the Gulf and doesn't get any worse than this, we'll be fine." She paused by the light switch and flicked it. Illumination flooded the kitchen.

She set down the suitcase, went to the sink and turned on the faucet. Water flowed. "Still electricity and water," she murmured almost to herself.

He set down the box with emergency supplies and came to her side. "Why don't you make us some coffee? You should eat, too. I'll finish unloading the car."

"Right." She sighed. "And maybe it's best that I'm here. I can get right to the Captain as soon as it's over. That'll be good for him. And Nana will be happy he's got family with a van."

She lifted her eyes to his. "But I'm sorry you got trapped here. I'm…terribly sorry."

He settled his hands on her shoulders. She wore a turquoise-blue T-shirt that set off her startling eyes, and a short yellow slicker that set off her dark hair.

Her hair was tousled and still damp. He was tempted to smooth it, run his hands over it, but he'd gone too far already, even touching her as he did.

"Don't apologize. You didn't ask me to stay. You aren't responsible."

But you are, he thought. *I didn't stay here for Nathan Roth. I stayed for you.*

"I'll make the coffee," she said, stepping back from him.

WHEN HE'D UNLOADED the Volkswagen, the last things he brought in were the paintings. "Where do you want these?"

"In the hurricane room," Emerson said. "Down the hall, next to the sitting room."

He carried the paintings out of the kitchen, and she wondered what he'd think when he saw the hurricane room. The whole house stood as sturdy as any in the Keys, but the hurricane room had been doubly reinforced.

It had its own half bath with a chemical toilet, a front door, a back door and even a trapdoor in the ceiling. It had shelves of food and water, a battery-powered radio, a toolbox, flashlights, lanterns, a propane stove…and a double bed.

The bed had been for the Captain and Nana, of course. Emerson and Claire had sleeping bags and air mattresses. But Emerson had insisted Claire take those in case their party got marooned and had to share a room somewhere.

She hoped the bed didn't give Eli any ideas.

He strolled into the kitchen. "Odd room," he said. He looked her up and down, and her blood stirred with awareness of him.

Emerson pretended to concentrate on making peanut butter sandwiches. "This isn't much," she murmured. "But I want to keep the refrigerator shut as much as possible. If the electricity goes off—"

"I understand. There's a little fridge in the hurricane room, too. What's in it?"

"Staples. Eggs. Cheese. Some frozen food. Ice. Claire changes it every so often so nothing petrifies. Have a seat."

He sat. "Your grandfather thought ahead."

She set down his plate and a mug of coffee. "He tried to. Hurricanes bring tornadoes. It'd be a safe place in a tornado. But…"

She didn't finish the sentence. She took her own plate and coffee and sat across from him.

"But against a hurricane surge, it wouldn't help much," he said.

"Against a surge *nothing* would help much," she countered. She bit into her sandwich. It seemed as tasteless as cardboard.

"What about your grandfather? How safe is he in Key West?"

She pushed the sandwich aside and sipped her coffee instead. It felt like heaven going down. She held the mug in both hands and gazed at him over the rim, as steady a look as she could muster.

"He's probably safer there than here. The shelter's a long way from the water. We're right on it."

"Hurricanes go in categories from one to five. How safe's the shelter?"

This question unsettled Emerson, but she tried not to show it. "No shelter in the Keys is safe beyond a second category."

"But when this storm was upgraded, it had already gone to three."

"I know."

"So what about Merriman and Claire and your grandmother?"

"They need to make it to the mainland, then get inland. A lot of people pick Orlando. I decided Fort Myers would be an easier trip for the Captain and Nana. And the route wouldn't be as crowded."

"You're more worried about your family than yourself, aren't you?"

"Yes," she said truthfully. "I am."

On the counter, a small radio droned the news. All along the storm's course had been wobbly and erratic, its strength increasing and decreasing and increasing again. Now it was jogging back and forth uncertainly. The winds in the Keys had gusted to ninety, but now were slowing to the fifties.

Outside, the wind thundered and keened.

CLAIRE TRIED TO KEEP her grandmother comfortable and the pets calm.

With Nana, she succeeded. Nana would wake, look about in confusion and then doze again. Sometimes she asked where the Captain was, and Claire always assured her that he was safe, following them with Emerson.

This, Claire knew, was not the whole truth, because Emerson had to leave the Captain in Key West. But Claire did not want to upset Nana. Now the older woman had awakened, muttering about the noise. The wind howled, and from time to time, it gathered such force it roared and shook the truck.

Claire unfastened her seat belt and turned around so she could hold her grandmother's hand.

Merriman tossed her a concerned glance. "You shouldn't do that. Keep your seat belt on. I can barely keep on the road when the wind gusts."

"I'm sorry. But she needs me. I'll put it back on when she naps again."

Claire was trying to soothe the animals, as well. Bunbury and Bruiser were in pill-induced peace.

But Fang grew more frantic by the mile. Earlier Claire

had shushed him by singing to him and reaching through the bars to stroke him, but these ploys didn't work any longer.

In Grassy Key another traffic jam stopped the car, and she gave up, climbed into the back seat and gave Fang another of the precious tranquilizers. It was a struggle, for Fang hated pills.

"Claire, get up here, please," Merriman pleaded from the front seat. "The traffic's starting to move."

"Move!" squalled the parrot.

"Oh, dear," said Claire. But she managed to get Fang to swallow. She climbed awkwardly into the front seat.

"Buckle up," Merriman told her.

She did, but the parrot kept up its caterwauling. "Move! Move!"

"Don't they make tranquilizers for parrots?" Merriman asked out of the side of his mouth.

"He shouldn't be in a cage," Claire apologized. "I had a carrier ordered for him, but I didn't order it soon enough. And my vet said if I needed to tranquilize him to try chamomile in his water. But—" she grimaced "—it doesn't seem to work."

"No," Merriman said, something close to despair in his voice. "It doesn't."

But the parrot soon went into another of his silent sulks. Fang grew quieter. He stopped scratching to escape and let out only an occasional whimper. Finally he lay down.

The traffic continued to inch along.

Claire barely heard the radio anymore. It endlessly repeated itself. The hurricane might hit the Keys straight on. It might not. Its winds might grow weaker. Or stronger.

The announcer's words turned into background noise, meaningless. So had the wail and thump of the wind. Twice Claire had tried to phone Emerson, but could get no answer. Neither had Merriman been able to reach Eli Garner.

Now Claire dialed again, but still could not connect.

"I hope she's not having trouble." She couldn't keep the quaver out of her voice.

He reached over, took her hand and squeezed it. "She's fine. The storm's screwed up phone reception, that's all. Probably a tower down."

She looked down at their linked hands and felt a glow of tenderness. He was such a kind man, so good, so patient. But he was worried, she could tell. He stared out the streaming windshield with the lined forehead she'd grown so familiar with, his eyes straining to see as far as possible.

He was an excellent driver. Even when the wind threatened to knock the truck off course, he held it steady.

"We're almost through the Middle Keys," she said. "Almost halfway to the mainland."

"Does that make us any safer?"

"It puts us farther from the hurricane...for now."

He nodded but without conviction. They both knew if the hurricane came rushing their way it would overtake them easily. But she had faith that Merriman would somehow keep them safe.

His hair hung in his eyes, and she had an impulse to stroke it into place. She was not used to having such feelings, but he really did seem heroic to her.

"I can't thank you enough," she said. "I could never have done this alone. Emerson could have driven. She's fearless about these things. I'm not."

"You're good at what you do," he said with a sidelong glance. "You're the nurse and the zookeeper and guide, and you keep me going."

She smiled, but it quickly faded. "I just hope Em's all right."

"She's with Eli. He's tough, he's resourceful and he's not afraid of the devil himself."

Claire felt a bit better. "Sounds like Emerson."

He tossed her an amused look. "See? Made for each other. They'll probably find a way to beat us to Fort Myers."

EMERSON RINSED off the dishes. Since there was still hot water she decided to take a quick shower.

"Sounds good." Eli said.

"You can, too," she told him. "There's a full bathroom off the sitting room. But we'd better be fast. I don't know how long the lights or water will hold."

"Right. We'll have to make it a quickie." He gave her a one-cornered smile.

She forced herself to ignore it. "Then get on with it. And please don't go upstairs. I'd rather you didn't. I'm declaring it off-limits."

He shook his head ruefully, but his smile stayed in place. "It wasn't before."

"Before, you weren't staying." Before, he would have had no time to snoop. There were things upstairs that she didn't want seen.

"Still hiding things from me, Em? After all we've been through? I'm hurt."

"I'm sure your skin is thicker than that." She turned and left him.

As she ran up the stairs, she realized he'd called her "Em" for the first time. She should have told him not to. She let only people she loved call her that.

It doesn't matter. I've got bigger problems than nicknames, she thought, switching on the bathroom light. But she warned herself not to let her guard down. He might pretend to be a pussycat, but at heart he was a panther.

Emerson stripped with nervous speed. What she yearned for was a bubble bath, long and leisurely. She wouldn't chance it, though. She threw herself a cursory glance in the mirror on the back of the door.

Her body was usually marred only by bikini lines. Now

her skin was flecked and patched with bruises, so many that she couldn't remember where most had come from.

She wondered if Eli was as bruised. She had a sudden image of him, stripped, like her.

She tried to block the mental picture, but it was too compelling. He was a well-built man. Broad shoulders, narrow hips, flat belly—she knew he'd be lean and muscular—

Stop! Emerson ordered herself, stepping into the shower stall. She turned on the water, quickly soaped herself, and just as quickly rinsed. It felt wonderful, and she hated to hurry, but she did. She shampooed her hair, grateful that the water stayed on while she sluiced out the suds.

She dried herself, then wrapped one towel around her torso and another around her hair. Her body tingled and glowed with warmth.

The towels downstairs were the same color as these, mocha brown. Did Eli now have one around his waist, the only thing covering him?

Stop it!

She began to blow-dry her hair, telling herself that this was no time to be thinking of sex, even if she was marooned with a highly sexy man. If the storm did its worst, she could be *dead* in the next twenty-four hours.

But sex crossed her mind anyway. She realized her experience with it was limited, and mediocre. She had been celibate for over two years. Her last affair, with Jason, had endured a year and a half.

Jason was a New York yacht broker. He was handsome, witty, athletic and, like her, he loved the sea. She'd stayed with him when she was in New York, and she had been completely faithful. He had not. When she found out, she broke up with him.

In truth, she wasn't hurt that much. Their relationship had little depth and wasn't gaining any. As a lover he was competent, but predictable. In fact, she couldn't clearly remember the last time they'd had sex, because each time was exactly like every other time. She was sure Eli wouldn't be so—

Stop it!

Sternly she forbade herself from putting on lotion or perfume or anything that might hint to Eli that she wanted him to come hither. No makeup, not even lipstick. No alluring clothes, either. Back into the same underwear, the same plain black jeans and aqua T-shirt. She gathered her hair into a ponytail, not a saucy one, but demure, unremarkable.

I look like I'm going out to scrub the garbage cans, she thought cheerlessly.

She went downstairs to join him, resolved to keep her mind on her family's welfare.

ELI SAT IN the living room, listening to the rumble and shriek of the wind. He pretended to leaf through an art book, but he'd situated himself so he could see Emerson when she came from upstairs.

He hadn't bothered to dig in his suitcase for fresh clothing. He wore the same blue jeans and tan shirt. Under the clothes, his body felt restless and lively from the shower. He'd needed a hot shower, but he'd ended it with a long blast of icy cold water.

Knowing Emerson was naked upstairs, probably doing something wonderful like stroking soap across her breasts was too arousing. As he'd dried himself on the mocha-colored Turkish towel, he imagined her doing the same, up and down her body, touching all the places he'd like to touch.

Eli'd told himself if he slept with her, he'd compromise his assignment or compromise her, and he didn't relish doing either. He admonished himself to be a gentleman. He'd come to Mandevilla to do a story that could hurt her. He had no right to use her, adding insult to injury.

His brain understood this perfectly, but his body did not. Hell, he and Emerson could *die* here. Then what difference would it make if they had sex? Of course, if they made love and then *didn't* die, he could be in a nasty dilemma. He had to remember that he was the reporter and she was the quarry. It was information he needed from her, not sexual satisfaction.

But his blood quickened when he saw her descending, one hand on the polished banister. She carried the same flashlight she'd taken upstairs, just in case. She moved slowly, her head high, as if she was reluctant to join him. She kept an aloof expression.

It didn't matter. His chest tightened and his pulses hammered. Did she wear those black jeans to emphasize the length of her legs? Did she understand how that T-shirt hinted with maddening subtlety at the breasts beneath? How that color set off her exotic eyes and dark hair? She'd pulled her hair back—was it to emphasize her face?

Or, ironically, was she trying to play down her looks? She should know such a thing wasn't possible.

"Well, we made it." His voice came out more gruffly than he'd intended. "We got clean without the roof flying off. We didn't get sucked naked into the maelstrom."

"So far, so good." Her tone was cool.

"And what do we do now? Sit and stare at each other?" *I could stare at you a long time,* he thought.

"No. We sit and stare at the weather channel," she said, switching on the television, "if we can get any reception."

But the screen showed only flickering specks of light. "Damn," said Emerson from between her teeth. "I look for a hurricane and get snow."

"The radio works. Nothing's changed that much. The storm's still stalled."

In truth, Eli was glad the TV wasn't working. He'd sat through such emergencies before, trapped in a hotel room staring at the same weather map and watching the same blurry footage rerun dozens of times.

Emerson switched off the set, put her hand on her hip

and sighed. When she sighed, her breasts heaved, a fascinating phenomenon.

"Amuse yourself as best you can," she said. "I'm going back upstairs. Claire and I didn't have time to do all we should have."

He leaned back, draping his arm along the top of the sofa. "Such as?"

"Pack the fragile things in dresser drawers. Cover what I can. In case the roof leaks."

At that moment, the wind gusted, slamming into the house. The walls shivered and the stained-glass fixture swayed overhead. Then the lights flickered and went out. The room, its windows shuttered, plunged into darkness.

Emerson swore a short, passionate oath and flicked on the flashlight. "I'll get the lanterns from the hurricane room."

"I'll help." He'd seen them lined on a shelf, at least half a dozen of them. He stayed close to her side as she made her way down the hall and into the room.

She switched on two of the lanterns. He gathered up the other four. She clicked off her flashlight and stuck it in her rear pocket. Tucking the battery radio under her arm, she carried the two lanterns back to the living room and set one on the mantel, the other on the coffee table.

They gave off a small, deceptively warm glow, but most of the room remained shadowy. She turned on the little radio and placed it, too, on the mantel. It crackled, then the announcer's voice came on in a tinny drone.

"One lantern for the kitchen?" Eli asked.

She nodded, and they set one in the middle of the kitchen table, but it couldn't really illuminate the room. As soon as Emerson stepped back from it, her features were obscured by darkness.

"Where else?" he asked.

"One in the hallway, in case we have to move that

way fast. One on the stairs. I'll take the last one upstairs with me.''

"You sure you want to go up there in the dark? That last gust was bad, and the next could be worse.''

"I'm sure," she said, taking another lantern from him to set on the stairs. She fumbled slightly, and their hands brushed. Eli felt more electricity run through him than was coursing through all the batteries she'd switched on.

She put one halfway down the hall. They were old lanterns, little more than glorified flashlights and must have been bought a decade ago. She took the last and climbed the stairs.

He watched the light ascend, going farther away. It made her into a mysterious silhouette, faintly outlined. Then she disappeared into one of the rooms.

He stood at the bottom of the stairs, his hands clenched into fists. His heart beat hard, too hard. He didn't like having her up there alone. He fought the urge to stalk after her and bear her back down, even if she flailed and kicked.

EMERSON FELT LIKE the heroine in a gothic novel, carrying her light up the dark stairs while outside the storm raged.

She went into her grandparents' bedroom first. She put a matching pair of small Tiffany bedside lamps into the cedar chest, along with an antique porcelain clock. A ceramic sculpture of a peacock went into a dresser drawer. It had been created for Nana as a special gift by a renowned Spanish artist.

A group of family pictures in gold frames went into a second drawer. A velvet box of costume jewelry went into a third, along with a set of antique etchings.

She knew harder work faced her in Claire's room, for Claire loved to keep things. She had a large collection of china dogs and cats, half a hundred framed snapshots, a curio cabinet of fanciful blown-glass animals, especially parrots.

Emerson packed them all away as safely as she could, glad to stay busy. The whole time the hurricane shutters creaked and rattled, and the window glass seemed to shake. From overhead came strange crackling noises, as if goblins were ripping up the shingles.

Yet Emerson felt safer up here alone than downstairs with Eli. He made her feel vulnerable and prickly and a bit giddy—she who *never* felt that way about a man. He looked at her as if he looked hard enough, he would steal her soul.

No, she felt more secure here, even if the roof threatened to fly off. She finished Claire's room and went into the studio, where it was easy to tuck things into safer places. The studio was always kept in the most precise order, sparely furnished, every object in its assigned place.

She put away the ceramic jars of brushes, the primed canvases, the case of oil paint tubes. This, she knew, was the room Eli would most like to investigate. Merriman had seen only what she'd wanted him to see. She had hidden things away, certain things that would raise suspicions.

She faced her own room last. It was as orderly as the studio. Unlike Claire, Emerson did not surround herself with sentimental objects. The place was stylish and uncluttered. She had long ago trained herself not to get attached to things. She kept her real and her emotional baggage to a minimum.

Everything here was sleek, modern and impersonal. Everything except the figurine of Ganesh, which she'd bought when her father had died and she'd taken over his job. Ganesh symbolized many things, including success in new undertakings.

The figurine had spoken to her in a way that she didn't fully understand and perhaps was fearful of trying. It was unsettling to remember that an almost identical image of Ganesh was tattooed on Eli's arm.

Her figurine was of white porcelain. She got out all her

silk scarves and made ready to wrap him, when she heard Eli's voice calling her from the top of the stairs.

"Emerson! Em? Where are you?"

She rushed to the door, flung it open and turned the lantern's beam on him. He squinted against its glare.

"What do you want?" she demanded. "I told you not to come up here."

"You've been up here an hour. The storm's changing. They think it's going to hit hard. The winds could go up to 125 miles an hour. You're on the side of the house where one window's blown in already. Besides, I got through to—"

A blast jolted the house. She heard a gigantic ripping sound directly overhead. She dropped the light, braced herself with both hands against the sides of the door frame and flinched, squeezing her eyes shut.

"Come *on!*" he yelled.

She forced herself to open her eyes. At the foot of the stairs, his figure was shadowy behind his light. "I have to get something," she said.

"Get it and get the hell out of there."

She snatched up the lantern, which still worked, and swung its beam back in the room. The figurine stood poised on the dresser, surrounded by the rainbow of scarves.

But the light caught something else: a ghostly glistening falling through the air. She focused the beam on it and muttered a curse. "The ceiling's leaking."

He was upstairs now, standing in her doorway. "You're lucky you've still got a roof."

"It's leaking on my bed," she protested in irritation. "I have to move it."

"Are you crazy?"

"It's an expensive bed. I just bought it," she retorted. "The bedspread alone was—"

"To hell with your bedspread."

She went to the bed's far side and began pushing anyway. "Go get me a bucket or something to catch the rain," she ordered.

"You are the most stubborn woman—" he complained, but he moved quickly to her side. He was more powerful than she, and with two strong heaves, he'd shoved the bed out of the thin, steady drip.

He grabbed her by the elbow. "Get out of here. Hear those shutters? That window could go next."

She struggled to tug free. "I told you—I have to get something."

"Hurry up, or I'll throw you over my shoulder and *carry* you downstairs."

He freed her long enough so she could grab her precious figurine and the scarves. Then he seized her arm again and hauled her toward the door and down the stairs.

At the bottom, he drew her into kitchen doorway. She knew a beam ran overhead there, so it was a more secure spot than the open room, and he understood that. When the gusting slowed, he stared down at the figurine in the crook of her arm. He frowned in disbelief.

"What's that?"

"My Ganesh," she said defiantly. "I'm wrapping him up and putting him in the linen drawer."

She moved to the couch, sat down and began to wrap the figure in the silks. Eli stood, shaking his head.

"Then," she vowed, "I'm going up there with a bucket. The library's already ruined. I won't have my room wrecked."

"A bucket's not going to help. Forget it."

He was right, of course. She was ready to weep with frustration, but she clamped her lips together. She finished wrapping Ganesh, then rose and went to the hall linen cupboard. She gently nestled him among Nana's tablecloths.

Then she came back to the living room and threw herself on the couch, hugging her knees. She realized she was exhausted, emotionally and physically. Her pulses hammered, and she was out of breath.

Eli stood, leaning one elbow on the mantel and staring at her. The lantern's glow highlighted his cheekbones and square jaw.

"Listen." He nodded toward the radio.

Emerson again became conscious of the announcer's crackling voice. "Now that the storm is moving again, its strength is intensifying.

"The director of the Center has stated, 'We're deeply concerned that the Keys could be inundated with water and a number of lives will be lost. All stragglers are urged to take shelter immediately.'

"In Miami…"

Emerson hugged her knees more tightly, because she suddenly felt shaky. But she forced her voice to be chipper, almost flippant. "Well, that's not heartening, is it?"

"No." He came and sat at the other end of the couch.

"I tried to get through to Dr. Kim while I was upstairs. I couldn't. I tried to reach Claire. I couldn't."

"I got through to Merriman."

Stricken, Emerson turned to him. "You did? Why didn't you tell me?"

"I was starting to when the gust hit."

"Oh, Lord, how far are they?"

"He said it's been hard going, but they're almost to Plantation Key. They should get to a mainland highway in a few hours."

"Thank God." But if Claire and Nana were near safety, the Captain, in Key West, was not. And he was so elderly and getting so frail—was he frightened? Did he understand what had happened? She gnawed at her thumbnail.

Eli said, "I told Merriman we can't get to Fort Myers."

"You *told* him? That we're trapped?"

His face was expressionless. "We are, aren't we?"

"Oh, my God. Will he tell Claire? It'll kill her if she knows."

"I don't know what he'll say. He'll try to do the right thing."

"She'll worry herself to bits if she hears these damn weather reports—"

"Em, she's *going* to hear them. They can't stop listening. They've got to keep track of the storm, too. They're not in the clear yet."

Emerson, already tormented over her grandfather, couldn't bear to think about her tenderhearted sister. Or what Nana would do if she knew that the Captain was in danger.

Emerson put her face in her hands and began to weep.

Eli moved next to her, put his arms around her, drew her to him. "Come here," he said. "Come here, love."

CHAPTER NINE

ELI PULLED HER CLOSE, burying his face in her hair. He splayed one hand against her back, feeling the tension that knotted her body.

She'd been through hell this day. She would face more hell in the coming hours. She wanted her family, but all she had was him.

Eli wasn't used to feeling inadequate. He wasn't used to giving comfort, and instinctively he knew she wasn't used to taking it. She wept for a full minute, not hysterically, but with a kind of desperation that racked him.

Then she pushed away from his chest, but didn't draw back completely. She wiped her tears with the back of her hand. The gesture was angry, and he guessed that her anger was at herself.

"I didn't mean to do that," she said. "I don't intend to do it again."

"It's okay."

She gave an abashed shrug. "I felt so powerless. I don't like it. I—I'm not used to it."

"Control freak?"

"Absolutely." She lifted her chin. "And so are you, I think."

"To a point," he admitted.

Even in the dim light, he could see a spark of challenge return to her eyes. "What point?"

"Being in danger means precisely that—not being in

control. So you go with the flow and wait, hoping for an advantage, a break.''

She studied his face. "I've read about you. You *like* danger.''

It was his turn to shrug. "It gets the adrenaline pumping.''

"It's a high for you? That's the attraction?''

"I didn't say I liked it. I'm used to it. And I count on luck.''

Her mouth took on a skeptical quirk. "Nobody can count on luck. That's why it's luck. Chance is all it is.''

He shook his head. "My first dicey assignment was tracing stolen paintings to a drug dealer in Colombia. On a street in Bogotá, an old man called out to me, a fortune-teller. He said he could see my aura, and it wasn't like other people's.''

"Oh, really," she muttered and tried to draw farther away.

He kept her where she was. "Really. He said I'd be in danger many times. But I was a man of uncommon luck. I'd live to my nineties and die peacefully in bed.''

"And you believe that? The last thing you seem is gullible.''

"I'd say so far he's been right. I've been in some tight spots.''

"I know, I know. Nearly killed in Yucatán. Caught in a crossfire in Baghdad. You're crazy, you know.''

"Maybe. But I'm also lucky. So stick close to me. Maybe the luck'll rub off.''

"And maybe it'll run out. Besides, I'm not worried about me. I'm worried about my grandfather and Nana and my sister.''

She had him there. He had learned to accept situations that were dangerous to himself, times when he wasn't in control. But he'd never been able to give up control of his emotions. He didn't want to care too much about people; it would give them power over him.

She was fearless in her love of her family. It made her brave, but God, it made her vulnerable.

CLAIRE HAD BRIGHTENED when Merriman's cell phone rang. But she'd grown alarmed as she watched his face go taut with concern. He'd said almost nothing, just listened.

As he'd ended the connection, she'd stolen a glance into the back seat. Nana had nodded off. Both dogs dozed. The parrot was quiet. Claire leaned toward Merriman. "What's wrong? Something's wrong. What?"

He'd told her. Emerson couldn't get out of Mandevilla. The bridge was out. A tree had come down on it.

The words had hit Claire like physical blows. She was still stunned. The car was stalled by the traffic again. She could only sit, dumbstruck, clinging to Merriman's hand. Emerson and Eli stranded at Mandevilla?

In her mind she could see the bridge, the rusty old clattering thing they had all taken for granted. She saw the stand of trees next to the bridge. Once Nana had told the Captain she worried about the trees. "What if one falls?" she'd asked, but the Captain had pooh-poohed the idea.

It numbed Claire to realize that Emerson was cut off from escape by exactly what Nana had feared. Emerson and Eli, too. The radio kept repeating its latest bulletin as if calling down an evil spell on the Lower Keys. The storm, growing in fury, was headed straight for them.

Straight for the Lower Keys. Straight for the Lower Keys.

"Are you all right?" Merriman asked. "Claire?"

Tears rose in her eyes, but she blinked them back fiercely. *I can't cry. I have to be strong. Merriman can't bear all the burdens. I have to be strong for him and Nana. Emerson would want that.*

So she bit her lip, hard.

Merriman squeezed her hand. "Honey," he said, "the storm might veer again. They might be fine."

She nodded, her throat choked. She could not speak. But she did not cry. She gripped his hand more tightly and said a silent prayer for Emerson and Eli, and for the Captain caught in Key West, separated from all he knew and loved.

AT MANDEVILLA Eli listened to the huge sound of the storm and the small, rasping one of the radio. Miami was being ordered to evacuate. There were rumors of water spouts hurling around the Tortugas.

Emerson fidgeted, then gave Eli a long look of scrutiny. "I haven't seen you try to phone anybody except Merriman."

"I phoned my editor. Told him I was riding out the storm."

"Your editor? That's all? Don't you have family somewhere, wondering if you're all right?"

The answer to that was simple. "No."

Her gaze stayed steady. "You know almost everything about my family. What about yours?"

He didn't like such conversations. "Not much to tell."

She gave a laugh edged with bitterness. "My family's privacy doesn't exist. But yours is sacred. Is that it?"

Okay, he thought. *Touché.* He rationalized that if he opened up to her, she might do the same to him. "I was an only child. My mother left us when I was six. My father was never around much."

Her expression softened. "What did he do?"

"The same thing I do. Exactly. He died on assignment to Africa. Dengue fever. I was eleven."

She looked stricken. "Good grief. Who raised you? Who took care of you?"

He made his tone one of scientific detachment. "My aunt moved in. And there'd always been our housekeeper. Tonya. I was off at boarding school a lot. Tonya got married right after I went to college. She moved to Buffalo. My aunt died the same year.''

"Were you close to your aunt?''

"No.''

"Why not?''

He almost snorted with derision. "She didn't much like kids. She loved living in my father's apartment. She didn't love that I was part of the deal.''

"What about the housekeeper?''

"Tonya? Tonya was good. Yeah, I liked Tonya.''

"Did you stay in touch with her?''

A sore point— Eli felt an unfamiliar sensation, the pinch of guilt. Emerson had zeroed in on him again. He said, "She had a new husband, a houseful of stepkids. She had a different life then. So did I.''

He was shamed by the truth, which was that he'd felt betrayed by Tonya's leaving. She'd been the one dependable person in his life. She alone seemed to love him unconditionally. But when she left, he'd felt jealous and abandoned. She'd written him, always sent him birthday and Christmas cards.

He'd answered brusquely at first, then not at all. Let her have her new family. What did he care? He didn't need her. He didn't need anybody.

Emerson looked at him even more curiously. "What about your mother? Is she still alive? Do you know where she is?''

"Hawaii. She's married to a plastic surgeon. I've heard he keeps her looking half her age. She doesn't want people to know she's got a son who's past thirty. That's fine with me.''

"You're almost like an orphan. Privileged, but an orphan.''

It was true. They could put his picture in the dictionary to illustrate the word *loner*. He didn't care. He got close to stories, not people.

Emerson said, "So you've essentially got no family? That's sad."

She said it matter-of-factly, without pity. But she laid her head on his shoulder. It was as if she understood what it was like to be him, to be too strong for one's own good. He thought she would know because she was the same way herself.

EMERSON SAT, nestled against Eli for a long time. The wind rumbled and roared like an insane pipe organ. The rain hammered down. Sometimes the house shuddered, as if tired of being beaten.

She was worried sick about the Captain. And about Nana and Claire. And about the house, hoping it would stand, so her family could all come home again.

As for herself, she was resigned to danger and a strange calm filled her. She was almost amused by the irony. If the storm swept her away, it would also take the man who was her family's greatest threat.

She'd known from the start that she and Eli were opponents. What she hadn't known was that only a rival truly appreciates a rival's strengths. In terms of physical bravery, he was tougher, more seasoned than she was.

Emotionally, he was more armored. Yet, as Emerson rested against him, she found herself feeling strangely sad for him. He was smart, courageous, aggressive and his past was rich with adventure and success.

But he was a shell, empty of emotion.

He would make love to her in a minute if she gave him the slightest encouragement. She knew that. But she gave no sign. Even the most attractive enemy was an enemy still. Yet it was good to reach this truce, to sit together, his arm about her, her head on his shoulder.

The radio snapped with static, its words sputtering on. The hurricane was still heading toward the Lower Keys. Its speed had picked up. The winds were a hundred miles an hour. Its outer ring was striking the Middle Keys. Reports conflicted about how hard.

Thank God that Claire and Nana are past the Middle Keys by now. Thank God it's not hitting Key West, where the Captain's helpless and trapped.

She sighed with futility.

Eli's arm tightened around her. "Scared?" He nuzzled her hair.

Resist him, she warned herself. "I'm here and I'm stuck," she said. "There's nothing to be done. What happens, happens."

But she didn't move away from his caressing.

Eli murmured, "I don't think it's good for us to just sit here, waiting."

Her nerves prickled. She raised her head from his shoulder and gave him a critical look. "What should we do? Go outside? Have a game of badminton? It's a little windy, but I'm willing to try if you are."

"Cute. What I had in mind was cards. I saw a deck in the hurricane room."

She frowned in suspicion. "Cards?"

"Something to occupy your mind. Or can't you play?"

"I can play." That was an understatement. The Captain had started teaching her to play when she was six, simple games like casino and cribbage. By sixteen she had poker down to a science.

"Fine," he said, drawing away and rising. "I'll get 'em. And do you have anything in this house to drink? A beer? A glass of wine? Anything?"

She was surprised at how empty the room seemed when he was gone. The couch seemed lonesome. Snuggling against him had been more comforting than she'd realized. And warm, deliciously warm.

She slipped from the couch and into the kitchen. There was always champagne in the refrigerator for the Captain.

She was at the kitchen counter, uncorking a bottle, when Eli came back.

"Let's sit on the floor," he called to her. "That couch is uncomfortable."

"It's not uncomfortable," she said, puzzled. She got two champagne glasses and carried them into the living room.

He'd lowered himself to the Persian rug and sat cross-legged. "Sitting that close to you on that couch is not comfortable for a red-blooded man. He can think of nothing except getting you horizontal on it. The floor. Please."

"Oh, all right." She set the bottle and glasses on the coffee table and lowered herself to the floor across from him. She and Claire had played games on this carpet a thousand times. Now the wind wailed in the chimney like a tortured ghost.

He looked at the champagne in surprise. "Dom Pérignon? Good grief. Does this mean you like me, after all?"

"It means that this isn't the sort of night to be saving the good wine for the future. Carpe diem."

She filled the glasses. "Carpe diem, indeed," he repeated. "Let's seize the day. Except it's getting toward night."

"Whatever," she said, handing him his glass. She touched hers against it. "To survival. The Captain's and Nana's and Claire's and Merriman's and the whole menagerie."

"You're leaving out us."

"And us," she added.

They both sipped. "Good girl," he said with an approving nod. "Classy move, this."

The lantern light made his features look more sharply sculpted. His hair hung over his forehead, blacker than the shadows behind him. He was a handsome man in his way, the sort whose face was not merely good-looking, but interesting.

He set aside his drink and began to shuffle the cards.

Then he handed them to her. "You first. Dealer's choice. What's your game?"

"Poker," she said without hesitation. She reshuffled as expertly as a magician. "Five card draw."

He cocked an eyebrow ruefully. "I expected as much. No lady's games for you."

She reached into a basket beside the fireplace and pulled out a box of safety matches. She spilled them on the rug and divided them into two equal piles. She pushed one heap toward him. "Our stakes."

"Ah, at last. I'm filthy rich."

"You won't be for long. I'm going to take you to the cleaners." She threw a match down between them. "Ante up."

She beat him four hands in a row.

"I think you cheat," he said, frowning at his latest hand.

"I know when to hold them and know when to fold them," she said. She beat him again and laughed, before taking a long drink of champagne to celebrate.

"Poker isn't really my game," he grumbled.

"Then what is?"

"Solitaire," he said. "I was an only child, remember?"

"Oh." Somehow that saddened her a bit. In her mind's eye she saw a lean young boy, sitting alone, playing a lonely card game. She took another sip of champagne to cheer herself.

At last he won a hand. "Thank God," he said. "You were destroying my masculine pride."

"I doubt that's possible. The champagne sparkled coolly when it went down, but it was also warming and soothing her. She refilled both their glasses.

ELI WATCHED HER with interest. She seemed the sort who would be able to hold her liquor, but clearly the champagne was hitting her. He'd read women's hormones made their reaction to alcohol less consistent than men's. Maybe so.

But he suspected there was more to Emerson's tipsiness than that. She'd been on edge all day, her resistance was down, and she hadn't eaten anything for hours.

He was a fine poker player, the best card shark in boarding school, college, or any bunch of reporters. But he let her win most of the time because it made her happy. God knew she'd had little enough happiness today, and she deserved some.

And if she got a little wasted, it would be good for her. She could do nothing more to help her family or herself. Worry was worthless and would only exhaust her. If he could get her to open a second bottle of champagne, she might even sleep.

Besides, he liked seeing her looser, her cheeks growing bright again.

He told himself that a little too much wine would do her more good than harm and that he wouldn't take advantage of her.

No, he would not.

He certainly would not.

He absolutely would do no such thing.

But he could not resist pushing for an advantage. He'd start by going for just a small one. "Let's make this more interesting. Let's raise the odds."

Instantly she was on guard. "What do you mean? If you're going to suggest strip poker, the answer is *no*. Emphatically."

He affected an air of wounded innocence. "I wasn't. Let's just say that the loser has to answer a personal question—"

He saw her wariness growing and held up his hand to quell it. "No, I don't mean about your family or your grandfather's work or anything in that line. Just personal, you know. Like we're just two normal people getting to know each other better."

She looked hesitant. He said, "Look. I'll make it retro-active. I lost the last hand. Ask me a personal question."

She seemed to mull it over. She was lying on her stomach now, propped on her elbows. At last she said, "What's your earliest memory?"

An odd question. He grinned sheepishly. "Trying to set the bathroom door on fire."

"What?" She looked horrified. "How old were you?"

"Two and a half, I guess."

"Why did you want to set the door on fire?"

"I don't know. Because it was there."

"What did you do?"

"I heard my father in the bathroom in the morning when I woke up. I climbed out of my crib. My mother smoked. She'd left a book of matches on the coffee table. I took them and sat down in front of the bathroom door. I actually got a match lit."

"And *then?*"

"My father opened the door, saw me, took away the matches and carried me to my room. He said, 'Go back to bed, Eli.' Later I heard him yelling at my mother. Then the memory just…fades to black."

Emerson still looked stunned. "Goodness—were you acting out some deep, inner hostility? A—an Oedipus complex?"

He shook his head. "No. I probably saw a cartoon or something. Want to deal?"

"If you were my child, I'd have been worried." She dealt the cards, and again he let her win. "Damn!" he said with false irritation. "Okay. Ask away."

She sipped her champagne thoughtfully. "Did your parents argue a lot?"

"Only when they were speaking to each other."

"Did it bother you?"

He was allowing her free questions, but what the hell. If he was cooperative, she might be, too. "It was…

unsettling," he admitted. "But it was also usual. It was how things were. Kids are more adaptable than people think."

She slid the deck to him. He shuffled and dealt, and this time she won fair and square. All the better. He made a helpless gesture. "Got me again. Fire away."

"When your mother left, were you sad? Angry? How did you feel?"

Damn. He wished she'd get off the childhood questions. He drew a deep breath from between his teeth before he spoke. "Sad. Angry. Confused. Relieved."

"*Relieved?*"

"I don't think she should have had a kid. I don't think she wanted a kid. She wasn't patient. She wasn't interested."

Emerson looked outraged. "Was she abusive? Neglectful?"

"No. Not that. Just not interested."

He remembered his mother, a cool, slim blonde. She didn't like being touched. *Don't climb on me, Eli. You're messing my hair. Don't hang on my dress. You're wrinkling me.* He'd go to Tonya instead, who let him help make cookies, who hugged him even when he was dirty or dusted with flour or sticky with candy.

"I don't remember her all that well," he lied. In truth, he wished he remembered her less clearly. "My deal."

They played and he won, three jacks to her pair of nines. "My turn," he said. He, too, was stretched out now. He put his chin on his fist and studied her. He would start simply.

"I've heard," he said, "the woman can't name all the boyfriends she's had. But she can name every cat she ever owned. True?"

She thought about it for a moment, then laughed. "My God, it *is*! I'd never realized it. And with Claire, we've had about a thousand cats— There was Boots, Freddie, Gideon,

Dinah, Snoopy, Spider, Willy, Rio, Pilgrim, Podkane, Chewbacca— Oh, you really don't want to hear them all. It'd take till dawn.''

"What about the boyfriends?"

"Oh." Her smile faded. "Well, a lot of them weren't anything special. Just a few dates. They sort of blur together…."

"How many special ones?"

Her expression grew reluctant. "Maybe…four?"

"And you can name them?"

She took another drink of champagne to fortify herself. "Martin. Russ. Lars." She stared down at the rug. "Jason."

He knew about Jason, of course. The detectives had uncovered that story. A yacht broker. Successful, bright, but obviously too limited for a woman like Emerson. He didn't know who the other men were, and was surprised to find he resented them. Especially Lars, who was probably a muscle-bound ski instructor with golden hair and a smile like a toothpaste ad.

She took the cards, antied and began to deal. "I think I'll change to seven card stud."

He let her win. True to form, she had a whole flotilla of killer questions.

"How'd you feel about your father? Did you love him? Miss him when he was away? Why'd you follow in his footsteps? You lost him when you were very young. How'd that affect you?

When she asked personal questions, they were damn personal. He hated discussing this sort of stuff. But he didn't let it show. Instead, he picked up his empty glass and gently shook it.

"If I had one more drink, I might face answering that."

She took the bait. "I hope you're not getting smashed."

She went to the kitchen. He heard the pop of a second champagne cork.

This tickled his sense of irony. But it also tweaked his conscience—slightly.

I SHOULDN'T BE doing this, Emerson thought, carrying the second bottle of champagne into the living room.

She was not a drinker. Two glasses of wine were her usual limit. But the wind rocked the house; it banged the shutters and yowled in the chimney, and it seemed to scream *Nothing is usual. Nothing.*

So she sat down and refilled their glasses. She tried to keep focused on their conversation and not on the fact that the house might cave in on them at any moment.

"I asked afout your fovver," she said, then corrected herself. "About your father."

"To my father," he said, clicking his glass against hers. "Did I love him? I guess. He wasn't home often. But when he was, he seemed larger than life."

"A mythic figure."

"Exactly. Did I miss him when he was gone? No. I think I was used to it. Why'd I go into the same field? I liked it. I read his articles, his books. He knew strange things. Interesting things. He had adventures. Seemed like a good life to me. Whose deal is it?"

Emerson frowned. "I don't remember…."

"Mine, I think. Five card draw." She looked at her cards and fought against making a face. She threw away three and asked for new ones. He stood pat and beat her so thoroughly that she had to fight back a grimace.

"My question," he asked. "What about your parents? Your mother?"

Emerson's faint buzz of relaxation vanished. "Our mother? An accident, when we were little girls. A tire blew. She hit a bridge railing. She died instantly. Claire was with her. Claire wasn't even scratched. But I think that's why she's afraid to drive. She remembers. Not well. But she remembers."

He looked at her with a kindness she found disturbing.
"How old was she?"

"Four."

"And you?"

"Seven."

"And you came here to live. To Mandevilla?"

"Yes."

"Where'd you live before that?"

"Not that far away. Miami."

"Did you like it here?" he asked. "Or feel uprooted?"

"I *loved* it here," Emerson said with passion. "It was a
magic place. It still is."

She listened to the drumming of the wind, to its dirge in
the chimney. The radio was fading out, growing dim. She
should change the batteries. But suddenly she was tired, and
she didn't want to hear more bad news.

She shut her eyes. "This will always be a magic place.
It will always stand. It'll make it through this."

She had to believe that. She had to. She heard a rustle
of movement, sensed Eli's warmth next to her. "Falling
asleep, Em?"

The words were warm in her ear.

"Maybe," she whispered.

He put his arm around her shoulder, moved so that she
could lean against him. How many times had she leaned
on him today? She'd lost count. She only knew she'd come
to depend on him.

"Sleep, love," he breathed. "You need it."

She snuggled against the hardness of his shoulder and
slipped into dreamless sleep.

CHAPTER TEN

NORMALLY Merriman would have thought the Kumfy Korner Motel was a dump. Its cluster of aging units had once been painted pink, but time had stained them mildew green.

Yet to Merriman, after over eight hours of driving, the place looked as posh as a sultan's palace. Its skimpy little parking lot was jammed with cars, vans and trucks. A chorus of mismatched barks and yaps rose from different units. The Kumfy Korner was one of the few motels that accepted multiple pets.

Merriman slogged to the office to register and found a crabby teenager behind the counter. She had blue hair, a gold ring in her nostril and wore a T-shirt with a vampire bat on it.

"Two rooms for Roth," Merriman said. "We have reservations."

"You're late," the girl said sourly. "Another half hour, and I'da given your rooms to somebody else. You were s'posed to be here by five o'clock."

Merriman didn't like being scolded, especially by a sour-faced child with blue hair and a nose ring. "I've been in a four-hundred-mile-long traffic jam," he snarled. "We're trying to get away from a hurricane."

"Well, duh," said the girl. "Like, who isn't?"

She stared for several millennia at her computer. "You got *four* pets? That's a four-hundred-dollar deposit, plus fifty dollars unrefundable."

"Fifty dollars *unrefundable?*" Merriman was incredulous.

"Parrots cost extra," she informed him. "On account they tend to yell."

Merriman couldn't argue with that. His head rang with the parrot's noise. He sighed and gave Vampira his credit card.

"You're just lucky I kept both rooms for you," the girl said. "I coulda rented 'em a dozen times over for twice the price. If I was manager, I woulda. People should be on time."

Merriman resisted the desire to bound across the counter and seize her by her grubby throat. He filled out the forms while she snapped her gum and picked at her black nail polish. She threw the keys on the counter and he snatched them up. "Is there any place to get food around—"

"No," she sneered. "The coffee shop closed an hour ago. If you'd been on time, you'd've made it. Maybe something's left in the vendin' machine. But I wouldn't count on it."

He stalked back through the drizzling rain to the truck. He was tired, he ached, and in the course of four hundred miles, he'd developed a serious case of parrot hatred.

But something melted in him when he opened the door and saw Claire's pale, questioning face. "It's okay," he assured her. "We've got the rooms on the end."

"Thank heaven," Claire said. "I'll take Nana and the pets. You can have the other room to yourself. You've been crammed in here with us for hours."

Something chivalric stirred in his soul. "I'll take the cabin on the end. And I'll keep the parrot. If he gets loud, he'll disturb your grandmother—"

"But—" Claire tried to protest.

"I insist. You and she need a decent night's rest."

"But—"

"Rest!" croaked the parrot. He was hoarse by now. "Night's rest!"

"See?" Merriman said. And now he knew he must be in love. Only love could make him volunteer to spend the night with this winged fiend from hell.

He put the truck in gear to drive the short distance to the sad-looking units. "You must have had to pay for the rooms," Claire said. "I'll reimburse you."

"There's plenty of time for that. Don't worry about it."

Nana spoke for the first time in a long while. "Where are we? This is so…confusing. Claire, where's the Captain? Is he all right? Where's Emerson?"

Claire gave Merriman a guilty look. "Everything's fine, Nana," she said softly. "You know Emerson. She won't let anything bad happen."

"Don't you worry, Mrs. Roth," Merriman assured her. "Everything's going to be fine." He parked, got out and helped Claire get Nana out of the truck.

He swept the older woman up into his arms and carried her inside the bungalow. He'd made it. He'd gotten his little party to safety.

He wondered how in hell Eli was doing.

ELI LAY ON THE COUCH with Emerson in his arms. He'd half hoped that the champagne would make her amorous. It had only made her sleepy. Maybe that was the safest thing for both of them.

He'd lifted her to the big couch, marveling how light her sleeping body seemed. In the storm, she'd surprised him with her physical strength, and he expected her to carry more muscle on her slim body.

Maybe it wasn't muscle that gave her strength, but something less tangible, like willpower. Or character. But now her body itself was exhausted, and maybe her spirit, too, needed rest.

He realized that he was tired, as well. The couch was

wide, and he stretched out beside her. He drew back slightly, though, so he could study her face as long as he liked.

She was a beauty, and even in sleep, those eyes fascinated him. They were her heritage from Lela Roth, beautiful Middle Eastern eyes with thick black lashes. The lids were naturally shadowed; she needed no cosmetic to do it for her.

He could not resist raising his hand and tracing his fingertip lightly along the curve of her lips, first the upper, then the lower. She stirred, just barely. She moved her hand so that it rested against his.

For the first time he noticed the number of bruises on her arm. When he'd stripped to shower, he'd seen bruises all over his body. He wondered if she was the same. Of course. She had to be. She probably ached like hell.

She hadn't complained of it. Not once. He ran his knuckles along the silky, swept-back hair. She smelled enticingly of soap and shampoo. He was tempted to let his hand move up and down her side, to feel the curves of her body.

But he resisted. He'd taken enough liberties. He lay his head on the pillow beside hers. His breath mingled with hers. His arm was around her in an innocent embrace. He dozed and sometimes in his sleep, he nuzzled her.

CLAIRE MADE NANA as comfortable as possible, while Merriman lugged in the dog crates, the cat carrier, the baggage and the supplies. He carried the parrot to his own room. He came back as Claire was looking up the number of a physician whose name Dr. Kim had given her.

Merriman took Bunbury from his carrier. The cat looked hungover and moody. While Claire tried to reach the doctor, Merriman let the dogs out of their crates, snapped on their leashes and took them out to walk in the rain. The man was as tireless as he was thoughtful, Claire mused.

She looked at the closed door and missed him already.

She dialed the number twice, got no answer, not even from a machine. But on the third try, a man *did* answer. His voice had the rasp of age, but it was hearty.

"Dr. Jack Swenson here. Thought I heard the phone ring. Was in my workshop."

Claire apologized, then haltingly explained who she was, that Dr. Kim had told her to call, and tried to explain what had happened to her grandmother.

"She—she had a shock. She got word her mother is dying. On top of the evacuation, the news upset her very much. Then a window broke in the room where she was sitting. Her cheek was cut. Dr. Kim dressed it, but he wanted someone here to see her. She was sedated and she's still groggy. He said that—that maybe you—I—we could bring her over if it was all right—"

The strong voice almost boomed. "If Willard Kim wants me to see her, I'll see her. I owe my life to that son of a gun. Back when we were medics in 'Nam. Don't move her anymore. I imagine she's spent enough time in a car for one day. Where are you? I'll be right over."

Claire told him, then added, "There's more, Dr. Swenson. My—my sister and grandfather were supposed to follow us in the other car. But there was trouble. They're—they're trapped, my grandfather in Key West and my sister at our house. They can't leave the Keys. My grandmother doesn't know yet. I don't know if I should tell her—"

"Little lady, you're coping with a whole herd of problems, aren't you? You let me get over there and have a look-see, then we'll figure out what to do. Don't you fret, honey. Old Doc'll be there in two shakes of a lamb's tail."

Claire was overwhelmed by the man's generosity. Tears stung her eyes, but she blinked them back. She had to stay strong.

When Merriman returned, he looked at her through his dripping hair. "Did you get hold of the doctor?"

"Yes…and he sounds very nice. He's coming right over. But Merriman, you're soaked. I'll get you a towel."

"I'm okay," he said, kicking off his wet shoes.

"Give me that jacket," she said. "I'll hang it in the shower for you."

He let her help him strip off the jacket. She arranged it on a hanger and put it in the shower to drip. She came back with a towel. "Sit down. I'll dry your hair."

"You don't need to do that," he said, with the rueful smile that made his forehead wrinkle. "You don't have to fuss about me."

"After all you've done for us today?" she asked. She cajoled him into sitting in a rickety desk chair and letting her towel dry his hair. She liked fussing over him. She loved it.

DR. SWENSON was a tall, barrel-chested man with a gray walrus mustache and bushy eyebrows. He pumped Claire's hand and then Merriman's. "You the man of the family?"

Merriman, taken aback, saw Claire's face grow rosy with embarrassment. "Er…no. No relation. Just…an acquaintance. I'm—uh—staying in the next unit."

"A friend," Claire amended with feeling. "He drove us. We'd have never made it without him."

Merriman felt his own face grow hot.

"Hmm," Dr. Swenson said, looking them both over. He smiled, as if to himself.

Fang and Bruiser sniffed at him with mild interest, as if they knew he was a friend, and Bunbury rubbed against his pant leg. "And you transported a menagerie. Must have been quite a trip. And your grandmother?"

"She's in the bathroom, freshening up," Claire said. "She's still a bit woozy from her medication. But she's coming out of it."

"And she doesn't know her husband and your sister are still in the Keys? That they can't leave?"

"No. She doesn't." Claire's face went sad. Merriman saw that more lying was going to be hard on her. He began to understand what a burden of secrecy weighed on the family, and how it oppressed her.

Dr. Swenson patted her shoulder and nodded toward the television set on the dresser. "I'm surprised you haven't got that on, tracking the storm."

"It's not working," Merriman said.

"Maybe it's best," Claire said. "It would only worry Nana more."

Swenson nodded. "It's possible. Now, you say your grandmother had bad news right before this trip. Her mother is dying?"

"Yes." Claire cast a nervous glance at the bathroom door. "I mean, her mother's very elderly. It's not altogether a shock. Still, Nana hasn't seen her mother in years—they live on different continents. And her mother's refused to communicate with her. So that makes it doubly hard on her...."

"I think I understand," Swenson said. "Your grandmother knows there'll be no reconciliation. And her mother's in…Europe?"

"No. Algiers. It's where she was born. She went back there after her husband died. They'd lived in Paris for years. But she didn't really like the West."

Swenson pursed his lips. "Cultural differences."

"Yes. It's very sad. Because my grandmother never stopped loving her. Not really."

Merriman studied Claire's troubled face. She had just revealed more about her family in two minutes than she had in the past two days. Did she even realize she had done so?

Swenson shook his head. "It's never easy to lose a parent, no matter how old you are. I know. From experience." He put his hand on Claire's shoulder, and she looked away, blinking fast.

The bathroom door swung open, and Lela Roth hobbled out, her gait unsteady. Her face was pallid, her eyes still a bit dazed, but she somehow maintained her dignity.

She sat down in the armchair, an elderly plaid thing that clashed with the beds' mismatched floral bedspreads.

"Forgive me," Lela said to him. "I am still fatigued."

"You've had a long and harrowing journey," the big man said kindly. "I'm Dr. Jack Swenson, an old friend of Dr. Kim. He asked me to look in on you."

"And I am Lela Roth. I would offer to shake your hand, but I have, as you see, the arthritis." She held up one knotted hand.

"I'm sympathetic," he smiled. "I have it in my knees." He turned to Claire and Merriman. "Could I have a few moments alone with Mrs. Roth? I'd like to examine her, talk with her a bit."

"Certainly," Claire said, then looked up at Merriman. "Would you mind if I came to your room for a little while?"

Would he mind? He almost moaned with pleasure at the thought.

"I'll get your jacket," she said.

She ducked into the bathroom and returned with his jacket. She slipped into her raincoat, and together they darted outside.

The rain had become a mere drizzle, and Merriman prayed that this was a good omen. The parrot grumbled hoarsely when they came in. Merriman switched on the light, and he and Claire stood awkwardly in the entryway.

His room was even shoddier than the women's, and someone had kicked a hole in the wall next to one of the twin beds. He was suddenly far too conscious of those beds. This room had no armchair, and the beds were the only place to sit.

He helped her off with her coat, then gestured for her to sit on the bed that looked least lumpy. He stripped off his jacket, hung it in the tiny bathroom, then sat on the opposite bed.

He made a helpless gesture. "I'm sorry I can't offer you anything. The vending machines are sold out. Can't even get a cup of bad coffee."

She pushed back a smooth strand of hair and looked chagrined. "This really isn't a nice place. I'm sorry you're stuck here."

He wanted to tell her that any place she was in was as fine as a palace to him, but he wasn't good at saying such things. So he shrugged. "I've been in worse, believe me."

She spread her hands out in a helpless gesture. They were scraped from when she'd helped him move the fallen branch. He wanted to take them and kiss them repeatedly.

She said, "This was the only place that Emerson could find on short notice that would take all our animals. This would have been our room. Hers and mine and the animals."

A charged silence fell between them. The only sound was the parrot, kicking seeds out of his feeder and making a low, gargling noise.

"I—I," she stammered, "I wonder what the doctor's going to tell us to say to Nana about Emerson and the Captain and Eli."

"I don't know." *I wish I did. I wish I could carry the weight of all this for you.*

"Maybe it's good Emerson's at Mandevilla," she said pensively. "She can get to the Captain as soon as the storm passes. He gets…confused, sometimes. Maybe this trip would have been too hard on him. At least he's near home. And she's close to him. That makes me feel better."

Merriman locked his hands together between his knees. There was something he had to say.

"You told the doctor that your great-grandmother was from Algiers. I don't think anybody's ever been sure about that. It was one of the things Eli wanted to know. I never heard that Lela—that your Nana—was estranged from her mother. I'm not sure Eli knows that, either. Don't worry. He won't hear it from me."

Her hand flew to her mouth as if she could trap the words that had already escaped. She was clearly upset with herself. "I didn't *think*. I just wanted the doctor to understand— I didn't mean to—"

"It's all right. I'm not a reporter. I don't look for secrets. I don't tell them."

She leaned toward him earnestly. "But he's your partner."

"No," he said. "He's just a guy I got assigned to work with."

"But you must have signed a contract to work on this article."

"There are things more important than articles."

She stared into his eyes until he felt dizzy with it. She leaned closer still, her voice breathy with disbelief. "You'd do that for *us?*"

"No," he said, bending forward until his mouth nearly touched hers. "I'd do it for you."

He took a deep breath. He was going to do it. He knew. He was going to kiss her. And she was going to let him.

But at that second a robust knock shook the door, and Dr. Swenson's voice rumbled out good-naturedly. "Miss Roth? I'd like to talk to you about your grandmother."

EMERSON STIRRED DOZILY. Outside the storm still hammered and howled, but in her sleepiness, she could almost ignore it—she felt safe nestled against the strength of the man beside her. His arm held her protectively close.

The couch was soft, and he was warm and solid. His even breath stirred her hair, and his face lay against her throat.

She sighed and snuggled closer.

What? she thought in confusion. *What?*

It couldn't be *Eli* she was lying entwined with so intimately, so cozily.

Obviously she was dreaming. Tentatively she let her hand move to rest on his chest. For a chest in a dream, it seemed very solid, and she could feel the beat of his heart.

His scent, clean and soapy, filled her nostrils. Whether he was a dream or real, he smelled nice. He, too, stirred, drawing her closer. His jaw, slightly stubbled, tickled her neck, and he gave a low sigh in her ear.

She moved her hand higher. His shirt collar was open, and her fingertips touched his bare flesh, felt the ridge of his collarbone. His hand moved just under the back of her shirt, making her flesh tingle.

She was becoming certain this wasn't a dream, but she wanted it to be, and she didn't want to wake from it. But now, in the background, she could hear the radio staticky and dim.

Its batteries must be running down. She should change them. She needed news of the storm. But she didn't want news. She wanted to shut out the reality of the hurricane. She wanted to shut out so many things....

"Em?" Eli said her name softly. "Are you awake?"

"I...don't know," she said, her fingers still curved against his collar bone. "I didn't mean to fall asleep."

He laughed low in his throat. "You were exhausted. And the champagne hit you."

"Mmm." She remembered now. She *had* felt a little tiddly. In truth, she still did. Slightly abuzz and languid and blessedly insulated from anxiety.

She tried to make a joke of it. "I didn't put a lampshade on my head or anything, did I?"

"No. You just nodded off. So did I."

Emerson knew she should disentangle herself from him, but she couldn't, not yet. He'd begun to stroke her back under her shirt, slowly, gently. It felt lovely.

He moved his mouth closer to her ear. He kissed it lightly. Then more lingeringly. That, too, felt lovely.

"Your ponytail came loose," he murmured. "I'm glad. I like your hair when it's free."

He lifted a heavy lock of it and pressed his lips against the pulse in her throat. He laced his fingers through her hair, and kissed the edge of her jaw.

She was losing herself in a world of feeling, and it was delicious. She turned her face to meet his, and his lips closed over hers, gently at first, then more ardently. He had a warm, artful mouth; it made wonderful moves against hers, some subtle, some bold. She shut her eyes more tightly so she could experience the sensation more completely, melt into it.

She wound her arms around his neck to kiss him back. He gave a small gasp of pleasure and shifted so that the full length of his body pressed against hers.

The sturdy plane of his chest bore down on the softness of her breasts, making them throb with growing excitement. His groin was thrust against hers, and she wanted to be closer to him still, closer all over.

She wanted to forget everything but this dark universe of needing to touch and be touched. He drew away, his upper body braced above hers, breathing hard.

Then he bowed his head and kissed the hollow of her throat, then with maddeningly slow deliberation moved to her breasts. He cupped his hand around one, and pressed his mouth over the other. She felt the heat and moistness of his mouth through the cloth of her shirt.

She moved beneath him with yearning urgency. She was in a spell and letting it take her.

Eli's cell phone rang. It rang three times before it really registered on either of them. Reality came crashing back. Emerson pushed away from him desperately. "Maybe it's Merriman. Maybe it's Dr. Kim. Answer it, answer it—"

With a harsh sigh, he heaved himself to a sitting position

and groped for the phone, which had fallen to the floor. He took a deep breath and pressed the talk button. "Eli Garner here," he said from between his teeth.

Emerson stared at him in a wild mix of concern and embarrassment. For a few moments she had been thoughtless to the point of abandonment. Her heart thudded, and she ran her hands through her hair, trying to smooth it.

She could see the clear evidence of Eli's arousal and turned away. She wasn't priggish, but she wasn't proud of herself.

"Okay," she heard him say. "Good. What did he say? Okay. That's probably right. Is Claire there?"

Emerson whipped her head back to face Eli again. "Merriman?" she mouthed.

He nodded and covered the mouthpiece. "They made it. They're in Fort Myers. The doctor's seen your grandmother. He thinks she'll be fine."

He spoke into the phone again. "Listen carefully. Can you talk freely in front of Claire? Good. She knows how bad the forecast is? All right. Key West? No. We've heard nothing about it. The wind's blowing like hell here. We might have lost a piece of the roof, but Emerson's fine, I'm fine. Our radio's going out. What? Okay. Let me tell Emerson."

Again he covered the mouthpiece. He leaned toward Emerson, his face somber. "Claire wants to talk to you. She knows it's bad here."

She nodded. She didn't want to lie to Claire, but she didn't want to make her crazy with worry, either.

"All right, Merriman. Put Claire on." He gave the phone to Emerson.

Emerson's hand shook. So did her voice. "Claire? You made it?"

Claire's voice quavered, too. "Yes. Oh, Em, sometimes the car shook like it was going to blow away. But Merriman got us through. A doctor came. He looked at Nana. He thinks she's going to be just fine, but she's very anxious. He thinks we should wait to tell her about the Captain. And about your not being able to get out of Mandevilla. So…we lied.''

Emerson winced. Claire said, ''She's dozing off again. We told her that you made it as far as the Upper Keys. That you're safe there. Oh, God, Em, I hope it doesn't turn out to be a complete lie. Are you safe so far? Is it bad?''

Emerson steeled herself. ''Fine so far. Not really that bad. You know how well this place is built.''

''You'll get the Captain as soon as you can?''

''Absolutely.''

''Give him my love and a kiss and tell him I can't wait to see him, and neither can Nana.'' The signal was growing weaker, breaking up.

''Will do. Kiss Nana for me.''

''I love you, Em.''

''I love you, too. Take good care of Nana. I know you will.''

But there was no answer. The line had gone dead.

Emerson punched the End button and numbly handed the phone back to Eli. She put her elbows on her knees and her face in her hands. She wanted everyone safe again at Mandevilla, the way things were supposed to be.

''Emerson?''

Concern vibrated in Eli's voice. She straightened, tossed her hair and said, ''I'm just relieved they made it. I need to get some batteries for the radio. It's running down. I can barely hear it.''

She rose, but he rose, too, taking her hand.

She tried to pull away because she was angry with him and with herself for those moments of heedless desire. She started to say something sharp, but he cut her off, ''Listen. It's changing. It's coming.''

He'd said it loudly because the sound of the wind had

suddenly risen, beating against the house with a deafening, unending roll of thunder. The walls began to shake.

Somewhere in the house a window burst, and then another.

Eli practically knocked her to the floor, and before she could protest, he was on top of her, screaming, ''Stay down! Stay down!''

Then there was a gigantic noise as if the sky itself was exploding, and Emerson clung to him, wondering if these were the last seconds of her life.

CHAPTER ELEVEN

To Eli, it sounded as if a thousand freight trains roared and rumbled overhead. Wind jackhammered the whole house. Plaster cracked off the walls, it fell from the ceilings. Emerson screamed, and he tried to shield her body with his own.

A window in the living room shattered. A stiff blast of air burst through the room, spraying glass and splinters.

The white drapes blew off, rod and all, dancing like insane ghosts across the room until the rain pasted them to the wall. Objects became airborne, smashing into walls and the fireplace. It was as if a thousand angry poltergeists had invaded the house.

The radio rose as if by magic from the mantel and zoomed away like a thing bewitched. The lanterns blew from their places, crashing and plunging the room into darkness.

Water came driving into the room, hurtling through the broken window, filling the air with spray. Eli could smell salt in it and taste salt on his lips.

Had the sea risen that close to the house? The little radio had warned of surges. How high a surge would it take to bring the gulf to the very door of the house? Fifteen feet? Ten? A mere five?

A sound like an enormous cannon made his ears ring, and the whole house shuddered as if struck by an enormous mallet. "The garage doors!" Emerson cried. "They blew out!"

Eli kept his head down, gritted his teeth and swore. The air whirled with wind and wetness, and again he tasted salt. He wanted light. He also wanted to get himself and Emerson out of this room. But where?

If a surge came, if water gushed under the doors and up through the floorboards, he needed to get her higher—to the second floor? But if the wind sucked the roof off the walls could bow until the beams collapsed and the second floor crashed down in ruins.

He lifted his head, shielding his eyes. He saw a gleam of light from the stairwell. That lantern still shone, though the kitchen, too, was dark, rattling and banging and clanging in the flurries of wind.

"I'm going to get the lantern," he shouted in Emerson's ear. "Then let's get to the hurricane room. I'm going to leave you alone, for just a minute."

"No, you're not." She seized him by his shirt front. "Where you go, I go."

"No," he argued, holding her down. "I'm going to try to stand. The floor's full of broken glass. If we try to crawl, we could get cut."

She still clutched his shirt. "No. Together. If we can hug the wall, we can make it. Let me up. You're squashing me."

He gave up. He pulled himself up into a crouch, then hoisted her up with him. He held her close. He could see, by the dim light in the stairwell, the drapes still flapping phantomlike against the wall.

"Okay," he shouted, "we're going to have to try to scuttle for the wall."

He tried to keep his balance and steady her, as well. They hunkered down like soldiers under fire. Emerson tottered once, went down on all fours, but quickly righted herself.

At last Eli rose to stand against the wall. Away from the direct blast from the window, it wasn't hard. He drew Emerson up, and holding her hand, together they inched along the wall, then sprinted for the stairwell.

Eli snatched up the lantern and let its beam sweep the room. "Oh, shit," he muttered. He saw what had broken through the window. A piece of wood like a fence post had impaled itself in the armchair with such force that the chair lay on its back like a stabbed corpse. The thing must have flown through the window like a spear. It would have killed a human.

"Ooh." Emerson's voice was quavery. The room lay in ruins, and the couch was starting to move, as if creeping backward from the wind.

He pulled at her hand. "Let's get the hell out of here."

But she didn't move. The destruction transfixed her, rooting her to the spot. He had to yank her along behind him.

The other lantern lay on its side in the hall, still glowing. He grabbed it up, then released Emerson's hand long enough to fumble at the door. He got it open, set the lights on the floor, hauled her inside and slammed the door shut.

She was panting and looked in shock. He shook her gently. "Are you all right? Em?"

"Nana's living room's a mess. She'll be sick when she sees it."

"Let Nana be glad if she still has a house standing by morning. It's you I'm worried about. Any cuts, splinters?"

She said nothing, only looked at her hands. She shook her head.

"That's a minor miracle."

She seemed to come back to herself. "You?"

"I think I'm all in one piece."

She wiped a strand of hair from her eyes. "I need something to drink." She moved the little refrigerator and opened it. "Do you want a cola?"

"I wish we'd brought the champagne." He wondered where the bottle was now. Probably blown out a back window and halfway to Bermuda.

"Cola? Or not?"

"Yes." He sat on the bed. There were several small chairs in the room. She handed him the can of soda and sat in the chair farthest from him.

The room, well insulated, dulled the noise of the storm to a mere roar. But he could still feel the house shivering. No plaster, though, had fallen in here. The ceiling looked sound and the walls unscathed.

"So," he said to Emerson. "How safe do you think this room is?"

She took a long drink, then said, "I have no idea. It depends on what happens, doesn't it?"

"I thought I tasted salt in the water that blew in."

"You did. That's why I want something to drink. To wash away the taste."

"Do you think a surge is coming?"

"I don't know. Probably. But that salt water could have blown in without a surge."

"Clear from the beach?"

"You've seen what the wind's doing. The rain's flying at us almost horizontally. It's coming off the Gulf, and the waves are high. Yes. I've seen it happen before."

She took another long pull from her drink.

"It wasn't this bad, though," he asked. "Right?"

"I've never seen it this bad. But it'd have to be a huge surge to come into the house, over twenty feet high. The Captain built on pillars just in case. That was before it was required by law."

"Great foresight," he said. "Barring a forty-foot tidal wave. And this room?"

"He planned it carefully. He wanted it to stand up to the worst storm that could come along. But already..." She frowned and shook her head.

Eli said, "But already what?"

"Already I've seen things happen to the house I wouldn't believe. But that's my fault. Not his."

Eli shot her a look of disbelief. "Your fault? How in hell could it be your fault?"

"I should have kept the place up better. This climate's hard on houses. I should have had stronger shutters made. I should have had the trees trimmed. I should have made sure the bridge was stronger. I should have cut down the tabebuia trees. No, he'd have hated that. I should have moved the bridge, just rerouted the road...."

He leaned forward, elbows on his knees. "You should have done this, you should have done that. If we're talking *should* here, why should everything rest on your shoulders?"

He saw her expression go from broody to guarded and knew she wouldn't answer.

But then her face suddenly brightened. "You know what? We've got another radio in here. A teeny one. I got it as a premium from the bank. You need earphones, but at least we can get the news."

She jumped up and rummaged among the shelves until she found it, the sort of combination radio and CD player that walkers and joggers wore.

He watched as she checked the batteries, put on the earphones and got the station she wanted. She listened, and as she did, the brightness died out of her face.

He went to her. "Em?"

Her eyes looked into his, and they seemed full of unfathomable emotions. "Key West. They're saying it's getting hit. The Captain—"

"Emerson," Eli said as kindly as he could, "he's probably safer than you are."

Her answer amazed and perplexed him. "I'm not important."

How could she say such a thing? How could she think it? To him, she'd become more important than he cared to admit.

NANA SLEPT. Claire sat propped up on the other bed with her legs stretched out. Bunbury lay in her lap, worriedly kneading her thigh. Fang was curled up next to her, his head on her other knee.

Bruiser, calmer, lay on the floor by Nana's bed. Claire tried to read the book she had brought, but had trouble concentrating. Next door, from time to time, she heard the harsh screech of the parrot.

Poor Merriman, she thought with a pang of guilt. He'd put up with so much. His room was even shabbier than hers and Nana's, and his television didn't work, either.

None in the whole motel did, she'd learned from the man in the unit on the other side. He'd knocked on the door in hopes of getting news from the Lower Keys; his car radio was out. He said none of the TVs in any of the units worked, and he sniffily theorized there was no television because the proprietor hadn't paid his cable bill.

This neighbor was a strange little man who wore a bad toupee and a SpongeBob SquarePants T-shirt. He had evacuated from the Lower Keys with his pets, a Vietnamese pot-bellied pig named Waldo and a ferret named Toots. He was moving farther north tomorrow to stay at his brother's acreage near Mount Dora.

Sometimes Claire could hear Waldo oinking and snuffling next door. The unit walls were thin, and she had unpleasant visions of the pig rooting through the plaster to come join her and Nana and to wallow in the kitty litter box.

A soft knock at the door startled her. Her heart leaped up in hope it was Merriman. Perhaps he had good news. Once an hour he went out to the truck and listened to the radio for a weather update.

She extricated herself from the pets and pattered to the door to open it. To her disappointment, it wasn't Merriman. It was Dr. Swenson, but she was glad to see the big man, so like a friendly graying bear.

Rain was falling hard again, and he stood with rivulets running down his slicker and dripping off the brim of his rain hat. Drops glistened on his big mustache.

"Dr. Swenson, how good to see you. Come in and dry off. I can't offer you much, but we have soft drinks in the cooler and some crackers and cheese spread."

He glanced over her shoulder. "Your grandmother's sleeping," he whispered. "I won't disturb her. But you mentioned you were short on pet tranquilizers. You may have to stay here several days. I brought you some substitutes. My wife's a herbalist."

His continuing kindness astonished her. "Why...thank you."

"My dear, I know how hard it is to travel with pets. We have a parrot ourselves, a Labrador and a Siamese cat. I'd never leave them behind if I had to evacuate. I described your situation and the animals to my wife. She says these are mild, but effective. There should be enough to last you."

He handed her a clear plastic bag. "She put them in separate envelopes and labeled them with directions. Some for the dogs, some for the cat. And some for the parrot."

Claire wanted to hug him. "Even the parrot?"

Swenson nodded. "He's an African green, right? Full-grown."

"Exactly. This is wonderful. He's been so nervous."

"Parrots hate hurricanes," Swenson said matter-of-factly. "Ours has been picking out his feathers. This helped him. I hope it'll help yours."

Claire stared at the bag as if it held a king's ransom in gold.

Swenson said, "Here I stand, letting the rain blow in. If you have any questions, feel free to call my wife or me at any time. I'll stop by tomorrow to check on things again. Good night."

He touched his hand to his dripping hat, smiled and

turned back toward his car. "Thank you again," Claire called after him. "Thanks so much."

He waved and got into the driver's seat. Claire, slightly damp from the blowing rain, closed the door and rebolted it. Nana stirred fitfully on the bed. "Claire? Who was that?"

Claire went and sat beside her. She showed Nana the envelopes and told her what Dr. Swenson had done.

"What a good man," Nana said with feeling. "When this is over, I want to give him a drawing. One of the good ones. The...older ones."

"That would be lovely." Claire smoothed Nana's hair.

Nana's brow creased in worry. "Are the Captain and Emerson still in Grassy Key? Any word from them?"

Guilt pinched Claire. "I talked to Emerson. She said they were doing fine. You know the Captain. He thinks storms were created expressly for his amusement."

Nana shook her head. "That man. That incredible character. I'm half-mad with worry, and he's probably *enjoying* himself." She said it as a criticism, but her voice was full of affection.

From next door, the parrot gave an insane scream.

Nana waved her hand hopelessly. "Mon dieu! That bird. Go give poor Merriman the pills for the thing. Or he will not sleep all night."

Another screech came, more ragged and prolonged than the first. "I don't want to leave you alone," Claire said.

"Leave me, leave me," Nana insisted. "I'll be fine. My hands are aching. All this rain. I'll crochet awhile. It usually helps."

Claire retrieved Nana's ball of crochet thread and hook from her suitcase. "I won't be long."

She put on her raincoat, dropped the bird tranquilizers into her pocket and kissed her grandmother. She unlocked the door and slipped outside. Squinting against the rain, she tapped on Merriman's door.

He opened it, smiled when he saw her and drew her quickly inside. He let go of her as he closed the door, but they were standing close and neither of them moved.

At the sight of her, the parrot began to cry pathetically in his ravished voice: "Pretty! Pretty! Pretty!"

Merriman gazed down at her. "Is that his name for you?"

She ducked her head, embarrassed. "Nana taught him that."

"She taught him the right thing, then. What brings you here? Is everything all right?"

Claire looked up at him with a grin that felt both shy and mischievous. "Dr. Swenson came by again. He brought us a present. Part of it's for you." She took the envelope from her pocket and handed it to him. "Some medicine to calm the parrot. Mrs. Swenson's a herbalist."

Merriman took the envelope, looking as if he might kiss it. "Dr. Swenson is the finest man on earth. We'll name our firstborn for him. Jack Swenson Merriman."

Claire blinked in shock. "Our what?"

"Our firstborn." He paused, frowning. "Unless she's a girl. What do you want to name her if she's a girl?"

Claire thought, *This isn't happening. I'm dreaming this.*

Merriman put his hands on her upper arms and bent nearer. "You haven't thought about it?"

She stared at him as if hypnotized, bound to him mystically and incapable of moving. She could only shake her head.

"Maybe," he said softly, "you'd better start."

She raised her face to meet his. He kissed her. She seemed to fly out of her body and into a different one, more alive and more exciting. She no longer heard the rain outside. She didn't hear the traffic from the highway. She didn't even hear the parrot, throwing a perfect fit of jealousy.

All she heard was the beating of her heart. And all she felt was the wonder of loving this man.

MERRIMAN FELT completely drunk with desire, but after much kissing, Claire pulled back, breathless and rosy. Her eyes were so languid he was struck speechless.

Her parted lips glistened, beckoning to his. But when he tried to take them again, she drew back even more. She was lovely. Rain gleamed in her amber-brown hair, made it curl about her face.

He became vaguely conscious that the parrot was thrashing furiously in its cage.

"He's going to hurt himself," she breathed. "We need to calm him."

Merriman nodded numbly. He needed calming down himself. My God, he'd just *proposed* to this woman.

EMERSON PERCHED on the lumpy bed, listening to the tiny radio through the earphones. She wasn't hungry, but she forced herself to nibble at a granola bar.

Eli sat on a camp chair, finishing his second cheese sandwich. "You should eat more than that. You're running on nothing but nerves."

She nodded, knowing he was right. She switched off the radio and tossed the earphones onto the bed.

"No news?" Eli's voice was sympathetic.

"The same thing again and again. There are no radio or television signals coming out of Key West. A few reporters are holed up at Emergency Operations, but all they can do is try to phone in reports. The one that got through doesn't know anything. But they play his stupid tape again and again about how wild the storm is. As if we didn't *know*."

Eli got up and rummaged in a cupboard. "At least you know there's still some communications open down there. And if E. Op. is still standing, the shelter probably is, too, so your grandfather should be fine."

"I just wish I could get through to Dr. Kim. And talk with the Captain. Tell him Nana and Claire are safe."

"And what would you tell him about yourself?"

"That I'm fine, and I'll see him as soon as possible."

Eli found two chocolate bars. He threw them on the bed beside her. "Eat those," he said. "That damn thing you're working on looks like birdseed. Maybe it's the parrot's food."

"You take one," she offered, but in truth, the sight of the chocolate bars made her mouth water. For the first time she realized how hollow her stomach felt.

"I'm fine. You need a sugar hit. Here, I'll unwrap it for you."

He sat beside her and began stripping away the paper cover, then the foil beneath it. He handed it to her. "Chocolate. Good for the female soul."

She took it and bit into it greedily. It tasted so luscious, she closed her eyes to savor its sweet richness.

"Em—" Eli's voice was calm, careful. "You said you'd like to talk with your grandfather. To tell him your grandmother and Claire are safe. So he's *not* deaf, is he?"

Her eyes snapped open. She had been stupidly careless, and he'd caught her. Yet he didn't look gloating or triumphant. His craggy face was almost sympathetic.

"I meant I wanted to hear his voice," she said a bit desperately. "That's all. And tell Dr. Kim to let him know we're all safe."

"Oh. It just came out wrong. Is that it?"

She took an aggressive bite out of the candy to give herself time to think. She swallowed and said, "That's exactly it. I'm tired. I'm stressed. You expect me to construct every sentence so it comes out perfect? Excuse me. I'm in the middle of a hurricane. I'm a little distracted."

He laughed and shook his head. "That's my Em. When in doubt, charge."

She gave him a sidelong glance of scorn. "Don't I have

enough trouble? Do I have to watch every word I say? Don't you ever let up?''

He smiled. "I'm a cad, eh?"

She wanted to tell him he was not merely a cad, he was a perfect cad. But she couldn't. He'd been too kind, too brave, too resourceful—and sometimes even gallant.

"You're all right when you're not being a reporter," she said and took another bite of chocolate.

"Ah, you *are* hungry," he said, and began to unwrap the second bar. She finished the first and took the second. "Thanks," she said grudgingly.

He put his elbow on his knee, rested his chin on his fist and watched her. "You're a bundle of paradoxes. You know that?"

Her nerves tingled with suspicion. "What do you mean?"

"You're beautiful. You're bright. You're full of spirit. And all you care about is your family."

"That's not true. I have a career. I'm a businesswoman."

"And a good one." He looked her up and down in a way that made her remember too clearly how seductive his mouth felt on hers, how caressingly his hands could move.

He added, "But it's a family business. So we're back to family again."

"Look," she said as levelly as she could. "I'm doing the job my father did. You're doing the job your father did. What's the difference?"

His expression turned to one of careful control. She'd struck a nerve, and it pleased her.

"The difference," he said, "is I do it for the love of the job."

"Not," she pointed out, "for love of your family."

"It wasn't much of a family."

"What about love?"

"There wasn't much of that, either."

"Then I'm sorry for you." She was surprised to find she meant it.

"And I'm sorry for you," he retorted. "Aren't you ever going to have a family of your own? What if your grandmother lives to be an old, old woman—like her mother? Will you still be her caregiver? Living with her, managing the estate?"

Emerson narrowed her eyes. "It's about more than business. It's about the paintings. The paintings are what are important."

"Ah," he said, sarcasm creeping into his tone. "The paintings. Is that why you said that you're not important?"

She leaned toward him, almost militantly. "The paintings belong to the ages. The paintings will outlive us all. They're immortal. I'm not. But I'm lucky enough to be connected with them. And I intend to see that their their legacy endures."

"Do you know how your eyes flash when you get passionate like that?"

She edged away uneasily. She *was* passionate on the subject of the paintings. Perhaps she shouldn't let her feelings show so openly. Especially while she clutched a last piece of melting chocolate. She probably seemed ridiculous to him.

"You ought to be able to understand," she said defensively. "Your field is art, too."

"Yes," he said, his eyes still on hers. "It is."

"Is it just a job to you?" she challenged. "You don't have any feelings about it?"

"Yes," he said, not shifting his gaze. "I have feelings. Strong ones."

"Well, there you are. Now let's change the subject." She popped the last of the chocolate into her mouth.

"All right," he said. He reached for her hand. She found herself unable to resist. Her breath stuck in her chest.

He said, "You've got chocolate on your fingers. It looks delicious."

He brought her hand to his mouth and licked a spot from the inside of her little finger. He did it lightly, but sensually, and her heart began to rap too swiftly, because her mind was saying *no, no, no,* but her heart was saying *yes, yes, yes.*

Then one by one, he sucked the tips of her fingers. His mouth was warm and provocative.

"Some people," he said, raising his head from her hand, "say chocolate is an aphrodisiac. They may be right. You've got some on the corner of your mouth."

Emerson parted her lips to protest, her free hand rising to rub away the chocolate, but he caught that hand, lacing his fingers between hers, and he delicately licked the corner of her mouth, then let his tongue glide over her lower lip.

Then he kissed her, long and fully, until her mind reeled, and all she could do was kiss him back.

CHAPTER TWELVE

REASON TOLD Eli it was unwise to make love to Emerson, but his testosterone told reason to take a flying leap. A hurricane threatened death, but sex was the very source of life, and he needed to warm himself at the core of its fire.

He and Emerson were still alive. He wanted her, and he was sure she wanted him. So he kissed her until he was inflamed with it, and kissing was not enough.

They lay on the bed, his legs entwining with hers, his mouth insatiable, his hands growing bolder and more avid. His heart pounded so loudly that he no longer heard the roar and crashes of the storm. *Good,* he thought fiercely, *drown the damn thing out.*

He wanted his pulses to pound harder than the fury from the sky. He wanted to lose himself in her until she subdued him, and his reckless power was spent.

He fondled her breasts with one hand, while the other groped urgently to undo her bra. It was at this point she pushed him away with such force that she almost knocked him off the bed, and his head hit the wall.

"Stop!" she cried. "Listen!"

Eli raised his head and stared at her, his skull throbbing. For a wobbly second, he saw two of her, then the twin images coalesced into one pale, strained face.

His ego plummeted like a stone down a well. She gripped his shoulder, as if forcing him to stay back. Her lips were swollen from the fervor of his kissing. "I'm sorry," he said. "I thought you liked it—"

She sat up, anxiety in every line of her body. "Listen," she repeated, her fingers tightening.

He listened, but all he heard was his own ragged breath and the blood drumming in his ears. He'd done it. He'd stirred up energy to quell the storm. He heard only a distant shutter banging and the faint rush of wind against the outer walls. That was all.

"It's gone quiet," she said. "We're in the eye of the storm."

She rose, snatching up the radio, clamping it onto the belt of her jeans, and headed for the door.

His haze of lust and disappointment cleared. He leaped to his feet and put his hand over hers to keep her from turning the knob. "You can't go outside. It isn't over."

"I'm *not* stupid enough to go outside." She jerked up her chin contemptuously. "I'm taking a look, that's all. Stand back."

Because he'd misread her signals so badly, he stood back. He followed her into the hallway. "Em? If I hurt you, I apologize. I never meant to. Or to offend you."

She didn't seem to listen. She had a lantern in one hand and trained its beam on the floor. It was strewn with debris. He saw fragments of a broken figurine, sheet music from the piano, the piano stool itself, broken into three pieces. Leaves, sticks and palm fronds lay mixed among the ruins of the household.

"Oh, this is dreadful," she said as if to herself. Glass crunched beneath her shoes, and Eli saw she had stepped on a small, framed photograph of herself as a child.

He bent to retrieve it, pulled it from the broken frame and shook away the fragments of glass. He tucked the picture into his shirt pocket, then followed her into the front room.

It was in shambles. The piano had been blown against the wall with such force it had punched halfway through it. The couch lay upside down, blocking the kitchen door. Paper and leaves and a muddle of trash littered the soaked carpet.

"They're just...things...." she said, as if convincing herself. "Just material things..."

He moved behind her. He wanted to touch her to show his regret. He didn't. He said, "Your house is strong. It's still standing." *Like you.*

"It's taken a lot of punishment," she almost whispered. *Again, like you.*

She knelt and picked up something. She stroked it. "Now this is sad."

A dead bird lay in the palm of her hand. It was a sparrow, half its feathers stripped away. Its head cocked at an unnatural angle, its neck broken.

She said, "I've heard it can rain so hard that the birds drown in the air. And that other birds get trapped in the eye and can't escape until the storm dies."

He nodded. He'd heard similar stories, about birds carried as far north as Canada. She set the bird down gently and stood. She moved to the broken window.

"Emerson, don't," he warned. "There's still wind. There are still things blowing out there."

"I want to see. I've never been in the eye of a hurricane before."

She stepped through the rubble to the westernmost window. Its shattered glass twinkled and winked across the floor like small, treacherous diamonds. The shutters, dashed to pieces, were a jagged string of rubble at the base of the far wall. The wooden window frame was buckling, and a fine mist blew through it.

"Be careful," Eli said.

She said nothing, but picked up a sodden ornamental pillow and swept it across the sill to clear away any broken glass. Then she dropped the pillow, leaned one hand on the sill and stared out.

She swore under her breath. He stepped beside her and looked where the beam from her light fell.

The poinciana trees stood like survivors of a forest fire, naked, broken and black in the mist. The palms, more supple, had fared better, but were tattered and had an air of exhaustion about them. The lawn was a wilderness of wreckage and broken limbs.

They could not see the edge of the Gulf. It was hidden in a moving curtain of spray.

"The Captain always loved those trees," Emerson said, looking at the stricken poincianas.

"New ones will get just as big." He didn't add, *But not in his lifetime.*

She probably thought the same thing, but didn't say it. Instead she looked up and gave a little gasp of surprise. "The moon! I see the moon!"

He followed her gaze. A stiff breeze blew, carrying cold drizzle, chilling his face and arms. Above them clouds drifted, but they did not obscure the whole sky. In places they broke, showing clear patches. He could see a silver crescent of moon, and here and there the ghostly twinkle of a star would appear, then fade.

Wonder was not an emotion Eli often experienced, but he felt it now. There was something mystical in that fragile sliver of moon, those spectral stars. For all their seeming frailty, they gave him a sense that the world might be battered but was still solid and that the universe was ruled by an order greater than the chaos of the storm.

Emerson kept staring up, the faint moonlight silvering her face. "I wonder how long it lasts? It being quiet, like this."

He shook his head, not knowing. Some hurricanes had large eyes, some small. The whole eye might pass over them, or only a fraction of it.

She slipped on her earphones and flicked the radio switch. Her brow furrowed in concern or frustration, he didn't know which. But then he saw a smile touch the corner of her lips. She was hearing something, and she liked what she heard.

"Key West was hit, but no surge," she said, clearly relieved. "Damage, but nothing major. They're saying our Key took the brunt of it."

"Good for us," Eli said sardonically. "Bully for our side."

He felt the wind stiffen and stepped back from the window. He had an eerie feeling that before long, they'd be taking the brunt again.

EMERSON LISTENED to the announcer at the National Weather Service repeat his message. "The top sustained winds in Key West remained near eighty miles per hour, but gusted to 120. A surge of almost four feet was contained by seawalls, but ten and a half inches of rain have caused minor flooding...."

She went weak with relief. With winds of that speed, the storm was still a category one, and the shelter in Key West was built to withstand up to category two. But the back side of the storm, the huge part on the other side of the eye was coming. It could be every bit as bad...or worse.

For what seemed the fiftieth time she dialed the number of the shelter in Key West, hoping to make it through. She'd been using Eli's satellite phone, more powerful than hers. She was amazed to hear a ring at the shelter's end.

A woman answered, sounding spent. "Monroe County Shelter, Zone One, Gloria Brinkley, Shelter Manager."

"Ms. Brinkley—is everyone there safe?"

"So far so good," she answered. "What can I do for you? We have to keep this short. A lot of people want to call in and out."

"If I could just talk to Dr. Kim, for only a moment. Please. It's urgent."

"Honey," she said wearily, "at this point, everything's urgent. But he's right here. Hold on."

Emerson couldn't believe her luck. Her pulses speeded.

"Dr. Will Kim here." His thin voice sounded sweet as music to her.

"Dr. Kim—it's Emerson. How's the Captain?"

"Emerson? Have you made it to Fort Myers?"

"No, no. A tree took out the bridge. We're riding out the storm here at Mandevilla."

"Good Lord, all of you? I heard it was bad there, and more coming fast."

"No, no," she said impatiently. "Nana and Claire got to Fort Myers. The photographer drove them. They're safe. Please, tell me about the Captain. How is he?"

"He's doing fine. Had chills for a while, but he's wrapped up in a blanket, fit as a fiddle. Tired, confused, but that's to be expected."

"You're keeping him incognito? Nobody but you knows it's him?"

"Yes, yes. But tell me, girl— Are you at Mandevilla all alone?"

"No, I'm with—with that reporter. Tell me more about the Captain."

"Emerson, I would but there's nothing more—"

The line went dead, and whether it was her connection that failed, or his, she didn't know. She stared at the silent phone in disappointment. A chill rippled over her, and she didn't realize it was from the window.

She felt Eli's hand on her shoulder, gentle, but urgent. "Em, let's get back in the room. It's coming. You can hear it."

She heard the familiar roar, like a fleet of jet planes bearing down on them, and nausea knotted her stomach. She brushed his hand away, but hurried down the littered hall to their cell of a room. She put the earphones back on, but the announcer was saying exactly what he said before. She switched off the radio and took off the earphones.

This time she didn't sit on the bed. She made a point of sitting in the camp chair. Eli sat on the bed. He gazed at her, his face impassive. "Your grandfather?"

"Dr. Kim said he's 'fit as a fiddle.'"

"Good. No ill effects from this morning?"

She shrugged tiredly. "Apparently n—"

Like a great fist the wind slammed into the house. The walls shook, the air quaked, and objects on the shelf danced and fell over. Emerson jumped in spite of herself.

She heard the ripping of wood, the smashing of glass. The rear of the storm had struck, and now the wind pounded from the other direction. Somewhere near another window exploded. She clamped her hands over her ears and squeezed her eyes shut.

She could barely stand the renewed rumbling of the storm, the sounds of fresh destruction. She had visions of every pane of glass shattered, the roof ripped away, and only the shell of the house standing, looking as if it had been bombed.

"Em? Em? Are you all right?"

She clenched both fists in her hair and bit her lower lip. Then she forced herself to raise her head, open her eyes. She let her hands drop back to her lap.

For the first time she realized he carried something, a colorful bundle. He held it toward her. "I checked on him. When you were on the phone. He's all right."

She recognized the rainbow of silk scarves. "My Ganesh?"

She took it, and with unsteady fingers stripped off the layers of silk. The china Ganesh was intact, not even chipped. She was so happy that she fought back tears.

"Why did you—why did you—" Her throat locked and she couldn't finish the question.

"I saw you wrap him up and put him in that drawer. The room had taken a beating, so I checked...."

It was ridiculous to let one intact possession nearly reduce her to tears. Yet in a house afflicted with so many broken things, the figurine's survival touched her deeply. She ran her fingertips over the smooth white curves.

She felt Eli watching her, so she struggled to keep her emotions under rein. He said, "I thought he might be safer in here."

Emerson nodded wordlessly and hugged the figure to her breast. She could hear things banging and crashing in other rooms.

Eli leaned forward, his elbows on his knees. "You acted as if you cared about him."

"I do," she managed to say.

"Mind if I ask why?"

She didn't want to talk about it now. Her feelings ran too high. "No. You tell me about the one on your arm. You go first."

He smiled. "It's a long story."

She stroked the elephant's trunk and listened to the thumping and yowling of the wind. "I'm in the mood to hear a long story," she said.

"Come sit by me again?" He patted the bed. "I'll behave."

She thought about it. A particularly strong gust hammered the house, and she winced as she heard another window break. It was better to be close to another human at a time like this; she could not deny it.

He moved so his back was against the wall, his legs stretched out on the bedspread. He gestured for her to join him. She rose, still cradling her Ganesh. She sat beside Eli, settling into the crook of his left arm.

He smiled at her. He showed her his right forearm. The figure on it was similar to her Ganesh, but not identical. Her figurine had six arms, his only four. Hers was ornate, his more stylized. But both images showed the god dancing joyously, balancing on one leg, the other foot in the air.

"Ahem," Eli said, close to her ear. "A speech. By me, Eli J. Garner. 'How I Got My Tattoo.'"

GOD, it was good to be holding her again.

But he could see she was wearing down, and he saw that his task was to comfort her by distracting her from the storm as much as possible.

"I got him in New Delhi," he said. "I got mugged near a temple. Beaten unconscious. By smugglers. The last thing I saw before things went black was Ganesh. He was part of the frieze on the temple. I thought, help me get out of this, big guy, and I'll wear your image for the rest of my life."

Her eyes widened in horror. "Beaten *unconscious?*"

He kept his tone nonchalant. "It happens now and then in my biz. But I didn't want to die, and I told Ganesh."

"Do you always entreat pagan gods?"

"Hey, I was passing out, and it made sense at the time. After I got out of the hospital, I hied me hence to a tattoo parlor and kept my promise. Look—if I flex my muscles, I can make his ears wiggle."

He showed her and was rewarded with a small laugh. "So I've gotten to like him," he said. "And if you're going to bring back a souvenir of India, what better? He promotes good judgment, good fortune and removes obstacles.

"He has big ears because he has the wisdom to listen. He has a big belly because he digests all kinds of experience. His trunk symbolizes both strength and subtlety. It can pick up a tree trunk—or a tack. He has a special significance to writers. A fine companion."

"Does yours have a mouse?" she asked, scrutinizing the tattoo more closely. "Mine does."

She pointed to the white china mouse crouched by Ganesh's stationary foot.

"Of course he has a mouse," he said, pretending to be affronted. He showed her. "There. He kind of blends into that lotus at the bottom."

"Ah," she said. "Better a blurry mouse than no mouse."

"That's exactly how I feel," he said.

"Did they catch the smugglers?"

"Yes. They got twenty years in the slammer. A museum got the stolen jewels. And I got my story. Also this."

He tapped the bridge of his nose, which was slightly irregular. "A busted schnoz. I've got a scar up here somewhere, but the hair hides it." He ran his forefinger along the top of his skull. "Want to feel it?"

"No, thanks." She edged away from him slightly.

He regretted the invitation. But he bent nearer to her. "Emerson, I'm sorry if I was out of line. I thought— I thought— You were as carried away as I was."

"I was." Her answer surprised him. "But it wasn't right. It was just…desperate. Selfish." She shook her head and wouldn't meet his eyes.

The word *selfish* also surprised him, unpleasantly so. He supposed it had been his usual attitude toward sex—selfish. So he didn't try to draw her closer again. Instead he touched his forefinger to the figurine's headdress. "I told you about my Ganesh," he said. "Tell me about yours."

So she told him. She chose her details carefully, because she could not reveal too much about the Captain. But she told Eli that her father had been born with a heart defect. Doctors had predicted that he would not see forty, but he lived to be forty-six.

She didn't tell Eli that her father had died on her twenty-second birthday. She hadn't celebrated her birthday since; she couldn't.

Eli raised an eyebrow in curiosity. "You were young, fresh out of college, right?"

"I suppose your detectives told you that."

He nodded, admitting it. "You went to Columbia. Graduated with honors in a double major, business and art history. Columbia's a long way from the Keys."

"It is. But it's where my father went," she said. "I wanted to go there, too. He could visit me whenever he came to New York. And I could learn about what I'd be dealing with, the New York art scene. Columbia was only half my education. My father was the other half."

"You knew he was training you to take his place?"

She turned to face him. "Don't think I was some sort of puppet or robot, programmed to imitate my father. I *wanted* to do what he did."

Again he tapped the figurine of Ganesh. "And what's this fellow got to do with it?"

She swallowed hard. But she told him how she'd found the figurine in an Indian shop in the Village on her first solo trip to handle the Captain's business.

"Why Ganesh?" asked Eli. "Some connection to your father?"

"No. I saw it sitting there, and it sort of spoke to me. I didn't know the symbolism, but maybe I felt it…a little. I felt it was what I needed at the time."

Eli frowned. "That was five years ago? In the summer?"

"August." She sighed. "The first week in August. I remember standing at a corner on Fifth Avenue one afternoon. A yellow leaf came drifting down. The first sign of autumn. I picked it up and looked at it and realized the season was changing. An odd thing to remember—one yellow leaf."

His frown deepened. "Emerson, five years ago in the first week of August, I was in New Delhi getting this tattoo of Ganesh. While you were half a world away, buying his statue."

Her muscles tensed, and she looked away, staring at the paintings leaning against the wall. "Just coincidence. A random chance."

He held out his arm and made the elephant ears wiggle again. "Think so?"

"Of course," she said, determined to stay sensible. "Ganesh is the most popular god in Hinduism. If you were in India, you were bound to see him. If I walked into an Indian store, I was certain to find him."

"Ahh," he said, his voice teasing. "But at the same time? And after a major crisis? Maybe it's synchronicity—a coincidence that has meaning."

"Absolutely not." Emerson folded her arms stubbornly and kept staring at the paintings.

"You're a true skeptic, aren't you?"

Up until this day she had believed she was. She didn't believe in charms or magic or omens or myths or anything of the sort. But today had shaken her in many ways.

She had never been sure why she had bought the Ganesh in the first place—it was unlike her. She had done it on an impulse, that was all.

"My family has always been interested in religious symbols," she rationalized. She began rewrapping the figurine in the scarves.

"Your grandfather's paintings are influenced by them, aren't they? Religious symbols? Sacred calligraphy?"

"Yes." Everyone in the art world knew that, Emerson thought, she was revealing no secret. She rose and placed the Ganesh in the small wall safe.

Eli watched her. "The time your grandfather spent in North Africa and Paris—it changed the way he saw things."

"Yes."

"And meeting your grandmother—that changed him, too."

She was about to make an evasive reply, but then a gale shook the house, top to bottom, making even the strong walls of the hurricane room shudder. Objects spilled off the shelves, the paintings fell over and Emerson lost her balance.

She stumbled and would have been hurled to the floor, but Eli seized her and pulled her against him on the bed. She clutched him and buried her face against his chest. She felt the strength in the arms that held her.

"Hang on," he ordered. "Hang on with all you've got."

CLAIRE SLIPPED BACK into the room she shared with Nana, the dogs and Bunbury, her heart still thudding hard in her chest.

Nana, sitting in the plaid armchair, her crochet hook working busily, gave her a shrewd look. "It took you a long time to give that young man the medicine for the parrot. But, at least, I do not hear the parrot."

"I—I wanted to make sure he was calmed down. And I—we—Mr. Merriman and I talked a bit." This was not the whole truth, and Claire, who was a poor liar, feared Nana would see.

Nana did. "There was more than talking, I would wager. I can see by your face. It shines like a beautiful lamp. You and this Merriman are falling in love."

Claire, embarrassed, peeled off her raincoat and hung it up to dry, playing for time.

Nana said. "I made a statement, *cherie*. You and your Merriman are falling in love."

Claire turned to her helplessly. "Oh, Nana, does it show that much?"

"Only like the sun at noon. Come, sit by me. He is a fine young man, I think. There is great kindness in him. Bravery, too."

Claire sat on the edge of the bed and took Nana's hand gently between her own. "It scares me."

"Of course," Nana said with a wry smile. "It should. It's very powerful."

"Powerful, yes," Claire said, shaking her head in confusion. "But is it possible? For something as important as love to happen so fast?"

Nana chuckled. Laying aside her crocheting, she reached out her other hand and stroked Claire's damp hair. "You ask me? The first time I saw your grandfather, I knew he was the one. And look at us. Over fifty years have passed. I love him just as much."

Claire felt a piercing guilt that Nana did not know the truth about the Captain and Emerson. She summoned all her willpower to hide it.

She must have been successful, for Nana went on. "I love him just as much—but differently. We are no longer the two hot-blooded young creatures we were then. But I think maybe the love is even better."

She patted Claire's cheek then laid her hand across her own heart. "So is it possible? Yes. When I met your grandfather, everything changed.

"The girl I had been was gone. Poof! Suddenly I was a woman who would walk through fire for love. Your grandfather was a man who would do the same. And we did."

Nana's face saddened slightly. "We walked through fire together. It hurt. There are scars. And yet, I would have died rather than live without him."

Again she touched Claire's face. "But you and your young man—you do not come from different worlds, as we did. It will not be as difficult."

Claire leaned toward her grandmother. "He says he loves me. But so soon after we've met? How can I believe it?"

"Tush," Nana said with a wave of dismissal. "Why ask about *believing?* You already know. You have faced great challenges together."

"Still…" Claire tried to protest but couldn't find the words.

Nana smiled, seeming to understand. "Difficulties compress ordinary time into something else. Just as pressure can turn coal into diamonds. In adversity, you see a person's true soul.''

''Do you really think so?''

Nana kissed her on the forehead. ''I know so, my love.''

ELI HELD EMERSON as tightly as he could. Roaring filled his ears and stunned his mind. The tumult of the storm vibrated deep in his bones. It rattled his heart and numbed his limbs.

The lanterns had tipped over, rolling back and forth across the floor, jerking the room into a drunken waltz of light and shadow. The bed shook, pitching and skipping like a mettlesome horse. He clutched Emerson and wondered, vaguely, why the bed didn't turn over, crash into the floor or a wall, or simply fly insanely around the room.

Eli no longer believed the house would stand. The roof would tear away, the rush of wind entering would implode the walls and bring them crashing down. The force could crush the hurricane room, but even if the room stood, he and Emerson would be trapped. If a gas line exploded, or somewhere, deep in the rubble, a fire began to smolder… He would not think about that. No.

Emerson's arms were locked around his neck, and his legs were tangled with hers in a desperate effort to stay connected. It seemed they spent an eternity that way, overwhelmed by the howl of the wind, dizzied by the crazy light, jolted by the bucking house.

And then, eternity began to end. The great noise lessened. It lowered to a growl, and the growl itself began to falter. The house's quaking changed to a shiver, and slowly the shiver subsided. The light stopped darting. The bed went still except for the heaving of their ragged breath.

It was as if an enormous beast had tried to pick up the house and shake it to death. Failing, it had loosened its jaws and prowled off, still rumbling deep in its throat.

Eli had a superstitious dread the thing would suddenly

turn and come after them again. He didn't move or speak, not wanting to attract its deadly attention again. So he lay, holding Emerson, hoping the worst of the storm was really over.

She didn't speak, either. They stayed silent and clenched together, legs entwined, arms unwilling to let go. He could feel the thud of her heart and of his own.

At last she stirred and sighed. He said, "Are you all right?"

"I think so," she murmured against his chest. "I—I think it's passed."

But still, she didn't move away. He ran his hand over her hair. "That's the wildest time I've ever had in bed. Thank you—I think."

She gave a small, fatigued laugh. "The same to you."

He kept holding her. He nuzzled her ear, and she finally moved away. Reluctantly he let her go. She sat up. "Maybe I can get something on the radio. If we didn't crush it."

He rose on one elbow, watching her. She put one of the earphones to her ear and switched on the tiny radio. It was still clipped to her belt. He probably had a bruise exactly that size and shape on his hipbone.

She fiddled with the dial, then her face became calm, almost entranced. He sat beside her. She offered him the other earphone. He took it and listened.

"The storm has veered from the Keys and gone into the Gulf of Mexico. According to radar, hardest hit was Mimosa Key, fifteen miles north of Key West. There are no official reports from Mimosa, but Mrs. Octavia Luz, of Mimosa Beach, talked to our correspondent by satellite phone…."

The recorded voice of the agitated Mrs. Luz came crackling through the earphone, recounting how the roof was blown off the house next door, but the home had been evacuated, so no one was hurt. Mrs. Luz's husband had his arm cut by flying glass, and Mrs. Luz almost wept when she told how the garage doors had been torn away, and a flying coconut had shattered the back window of the family car.

Eli tried to grin, but it came out lopsided. "She's lucky the coconut didn't kill her husband. Or her."

Emerson put her finger to her lips to quiet him. "Shh. They're talking about Key West."

He listened again. Several docked houseboats had sunk. Trees and power lines were down, roofs and garages and signs had been damaged, but Key West had held its own against the storm. There were injuries, but no fatalities.

Emerson heaved a sigh of relief. "The Captain must be all right. Oh, yes. He's a tough old bird."

He's got a tough granddaughter, too, thought Eli. *Tough and beautiful and classy.* But he didn't say that. Instead he handed her his earphone. "Want to see if we can open the door?"

"In a second," she said. "I want to check those paintings. They got knocked around." She kept one earphone in place and tucked the other into her belt. She got up and knelt beside the fallen paintings. He, too, rose, and stood behind her.

She tsked and clucked her tongue in concern. "I should have braced them in place, protected them better. Oh, well, they can be fixed."

She sounded practical and resigned, but Eli noticed her hands trembled as she checked the canvases. She got to her feet and pushed her hair back from her face. Squaring her shoulders, she said. "Yes. Let's see what's left outside."

She picked up one of the lanterns and unlocked the latch. She swung the door open. And then she gasped and had to turn away from what she saw.

CHAPTER THIRTEEN

EMERSON FELT Eli's hand on her shoulder. His touch had come to feel dependable and good to her. His other hand moved to her chin and raised her face to his.

"You said it yourself, Em. Those are only material things out there. Your sister and grandmother are safe. Your grandfather should be fine. You've come through. That's what counts."

She swallowed and nodded. She had a sudden urge to kiss him in gratitude, but she resisted. Instead she stiffened her spine and turned, again training the beam of her light on the hallway.

The plaster on the walls was pocked as if it had been sprayed by a thousand shotgun pellets. The floor was thick with wet rubbish: tree limbs, leaves and the wreckage of long-familiar objects.

"I have to look at it all," she said, but in her heart, she did not want to.

"Careful." Eli linked his arm through hers. "Watch where you step."

They picked their way down the hall and to the living room. Emerson set her jaw and raised her chin. *Material things,* she kept repeating to herself. *Only material things.*

But although she'd seldom let herself get attached to objects, she found it devastating to see the home she'd known since childhood so despoiled.

The windows were gaping holes. Much of the ceiling

plaster had fallen. The beautiful stained-glass light fixture was gone, probably smashed into a thousand bits.

The piano was still half-buried in the wall, but now two of its legs had snapped off, and the ruined keyboard was like some deathly broken grin. The sofa had been blown against it and lay, wet and upturned and sad as a beached whale.

Only the fireplace seemed unmarred, but its glass doors were smashed and the hearth itself glutted with rubbish. But the stones were in place. *And that's a start,* Emerson thought, raising her chin higher.

The outer walls still soared upward; the wind had not conquered them. Though rubble covered the floor and most of the furnishings were smashed, the house itself stood. It could be a home again—and would.

Yet she felt sick at heart looking at the damage in the other first-floor rooms. Eli still held her arm, and she clamped her hand over his, needing the feel of another human in this desolation.

Together they climbed the stairs to the second floor. Emerson no longer forbade Eli to see this part of the house. She knew she did not want to go up there alone. In the upstairs hallway, more ceiling plaster had fallen, and puddles shimmered in the beams of the lanterns. Windows had blown out, but not all of them. The worst damage to the roof seemed to be over her bedroom. A hole yawned, and tired rain pelted through it.

Holding her breath, she opened the door of the studio. Its usual order was gone, but the built-in counters had stayed sturdily in place. The cabinet doors had blown open, and the floor was littered with painting supplies.

An easel, miraculously unbroken, lay against one wall. Eli lifted it and set it upright. "With luck this place will be good as new in six months."

She nodded, not trusting herself to speak. Next door she found that Nana and the Captain's bedroom was helter-skelter, the bedclothes stripped from the bed and the dresser lying on its side, its mirror cracked.

Claire's room seemed the least touched. Her windows were unbroken, and although fallen plaster dusted everything, her furniture had only danced a bit and not crashed into anything or fallen.

Emerson walked to the dresser and pulled open the top drawer. Carefully she lifted up the top layer of clothes. Beneath them rested Claire's fragile glass animals, undamaged.

For some reason, this inexplicable mercy made a knot in Emerson's throat. Perhaps it was because Claire was such a gentle soul, and these useless little animals meant so much to her.

Emerson pushed the drawer shut again, and said, "I think I've seen enough."

Eli nodded and took her arm again. More than anything Emerson wanted to get to Key West and check on her grandfather, but she knew that it was impossible tonight. She didn't know if her van or Eli's car worked.

The bridge was still out. The highways would be closed. Police would be warning people not to go roaming about. A hurricane left dangers in its wake—gas leaks, downed power lines and washed out roads.

"Let's go downstairs and see if we can get through to Dr. Kim and your sister." Eli's voice was kind.

"Yes."

They made their way back to the first floor. The only habitable part of the house was the hurricane room. After the ruin in the rest of Mandevilla, it seemed a comfortingly safe and solid place.

Emerson sat on the edge of the bed and took Eli's cell phone again. He said, "I'll straighten up some of this stuff."

She dialed as he started putting supplies back on the shelves. On her fourth try, she reached the shelter.

"Monroe County Shelter, Zone One, Gloria Brinkley, Shelter Manager." The woman sounded more drained than before.

"I have a relative there," Emerson said. "My family's gotten separated, and I have to know how he is. I need to talk to Dr. Kim."

"Ma'am," the weary voice said, "we're deluged with calls. I can let you talk to Dr. Kim, but keep the conversation short. And please do not keep calling all night. We're stretched mighty thin here."

"I understand. Just put on Dr. Kim...please."

"One moment," said the woman. An interminable time seemed to pass, but at last she heard Dr. Kim's familiar accent. "Dr. Will Kim here. Yes?"

"Dr. Kim, it's Emerson. How's the Captain? Is the shelter all right? Are *you* all right?"

"My dear," he said, concern in his voice, "we're doing quite well, your grandfather included. But how are you?"

"Fine. Completely okay." That wasn't quite the truth, but it would do.

"And that reporter fellow?"

She stole a furtive glance at Eli, who was watching her so closely that the back of her neck prickled. "The same," she said. "But the Captain?"

"He began to fret about where your grandmother was. He wanted to go home. But then he dozed off. He'll probably sleep through the night. How'd Mandevilla fare?"

"It's standing. But it's badly damaged. He can't come home for a while. A long while." She became even more conscious of Eli's gaze. She said, "We'll have to take him to...you know."

"La Costa Encantada," Dr. Kim said, understanding. "Yes. He's spent happy times there. A good place for you all to recuperate."

"Yes." La Costa Encantada was small, lovely beach community in Puerto Rico. Privacy was guaranteed, and since Puerto Rico was a commonwealth of the United States, there was no need for passports. They could slip in and out incognito.

"Do you want me to help set up the usual travel arrangements?" Dr. Kim asked. "It must be awkward for you there, trapped with the press."

"That would be wonderful." A surge of relief and gratitude filled her. "I'll get to Key West tomorrow. And to the Captain."

"It may be difficult, my dear. You can't drive from Mandevilla with that bridge out."

"I'll get there," she vowed.

He laughed. "If anyone can, it'll be you, Emerson. But take care. I must go now. There's someone injured being brought in. I'm needed."

He was gone before she could say goodbye. She turned off the phone, suddenly feeling small because she kept so much from Eli. But she had no choice.

He said, "Your grandfather's all right?"

She nodded, not meeting his eyes. "He's sleeping. The shelter came through unscathed, thank God. I need to call Claire."

He reached for the phone. "Let me try to get Merriman. He's got a better phone. And he can judge how much Claire and your grandmother should be told about the damage."

She handed him the phone and cradled her forehead in her hand. "Yes. That's better. I'm getting punchy, I'm afraid."

She heard the peeping noises the phone made as he hit the buttons. Like her, he had to try several times before he connected with Merriman.

"Merriman," he began, "It's Eli. I've got good news and bad news...."

MERRIMAN KNOCKED at Claire's door. His shoulders were hunched against the rising wind, which was cold and thick with mist. His heart contracted when the door swung open and he saw her. She gazed at him with a combination of happiness and apprehension.

"Merriman? Is something wrong?"

"I need to talk to you alone," he said quietly. "Is your grandmother asleep? Can I come inside for a minute?"

A worry line appeared between her brows. "She's sleeping very lightly. She napped a lot today. Let me come to your room—"

Merriman's heart rose like a soaring lark.

"Just for a little while," she said. "I wouldn't want her to wake up and not know where I am."

Merriman's brief happiness dived back to earth with a thud.

Claire said, "I'll write her a note, just in case. Then I'll be right over."

"I'll wait out here for you. Better close this door. I'm letting in the cold."

She gave him an anxious little smile that made his marrow melt and his head spin. When she shut the door, it was as if all the lights in the world went out. He stood in the chilling mist, hands thrust in his pockets, dreading what he had to tell her.

A moment later, she eased out the doorway, her raincoat unbuttoned. Merriman slipped his arm around her protectively and hurried her the few steps to his door. He let them inside, then stood staring down at her.

"Do you want to take off your coat?" he said. His own jacket was damp, and his hair hung in his eyes.

She shook her head. "I can't stay that long." She paused, seemed to gather her courage, then said, "You have bad news, don't you?"

He put his hands on her shoulders. "First the good news. Your family's fine, Claire. Your grandfather, Emerson, they're both safe and sound. And the worst of the storm has passed them. You'll be together again soon."

Relief made her posture sag, as if tension alone had held her so erect. But her expression was still wary. "Then what's wrong? Something is. I can tell."

He gripped her shoulders more tightly. "Mimosa Key took the worst punishment. Mandevilla was hit hard. It's still standing, but it's going to need a lot of repairs. Emerson thinks you all should go to— Well, she said you'd know."

"La Costa Encantada," Claire breathed.

"For up to six months," he said.

Claire's hand flew to her mouth in horror. "Six months? That much damage? The things inside—?"

"Mostly destroyed," Merriman said, hating the message he had to deliver. "Except for your room. Emerson wanted you to know your animals are safe. Your glass animals, she said."

Tears welled in her eyes. She fought to blink them back. "It's not fair—"

"What's not fair, honey?"

"That *my* things should survive. My…*trinkets.*" She said the word in self-disgust. "Nana and the Captain had fifty years of memories in that house. Things that can never be replaced—ever."

"But the house is there, sweetheart. And your family's all right—that's what's important."

"Yes. Yes." She blinked back the last trace of tears. "Of course."

She threw her arms around his neck, a gesture that overwhelmed him with tenderness and desire. He embraced her, drawing her close.

"Thank you, Merriman," she said her chin quivering. "You're right. And it's just what Nana will say. But the Captain will be confused. It'll be terrible for him to see so much destroyed. Does he know?"

Merriman swallowed painfully. "No. He has no idea."

She clung to him more tightly. "Emerson and Eli—the hurricane room? Is that what kept them safe?"

"Yes."

"It must have been terrifying." She looked stricken at the thought of what they had endured.

"But it's over. Everything's going to be all right."

A new expression of foreboding crossed her face. "And all this time, Eli's never seen the Captain?"

Merriman tried to reassure her. "No. Not a glimpse."

"Then he hasn't seen…"

Hasn't seen what? wondered Merriman, and the question almost made it to his lips. But he refused to ask it. It seemed somehow wrong to him, dishonorable.

"Then he doesn't know," Claire said, "and he might not guess. And Emerson won't tell. Wild horses couldn't drag it out of her."

Merriman laid his forefinger against her lips. "You don't have to tell me anything. I love you, Claire. No matter what."

"Oh, Merriman," she sighed, rising on her tiptoes.

He kissed her again and again, and they lost themselves in the sweetness of it.

EMERSON HAD WATCHED numbly as Eli talked to Merriman. When Eli passed the phone to her, she summoned all her willpower to focus on what to ask Merriman and what to tell him.

Her calm and concentration were manufactured, but so convincing that she almost fooled herself. She thanked Merriman with a warmth she didn't have to fake, said her goodbye and hung up, exhausted.

Eli was watching with that gaze that missed so little. Merriman might have bought the illusion that she'd worked to create, but Eli wasn't deceived.

"It must be heartening," he said sardonically, "for Merriman to deal with a woman so centered. Nothing shakes the pillar of the family, eh? But you got almost gushy with the gratitude bit. Not like you at all.''

She handed his phone back to him. ''I *wasn't* gushing. I thank God for that man. What would we have done without him?''

''It's good you like him. He's probably going to be your brother-in-law.''

Emerson's spine straightened as if she were snapping to attention. ''I beg your pardon? You don't merely leap to a conclusion. You pole-vault.''

He shook his head. ''No. When he says Claire's name, he sounds like a love-struck kid. I saw it coming. The storm just upped the speed to hurricane force, that's all.''

''Infatuation moves at hurricane force,'' Emerson countered. ''Not love.''

''Ah. But it happened quickly to your grandparents, didn't it?''

''My grandparents are different. They were both—'' She cut herself short, cursing her carelessness.

He'd spotted her near lapse and smiled. ''They were both what?''

''Young. They were both young and had romantic temperaments.''

He said, ''There are stories about how they met and married. There are different versions. Which is true?''

''I don't know what versions you've heard.'' Emerson hedged. She stretched her legs out on the bed and leaned back against the wall. She crossed her arms. ''I'm tired,'' she said. ''I don't want to talk about it.''

''Some say your grandmother was the daughter of a diplomat. Others say her father was a businessman. Still others say he was a professor. The one constant is that she came from a well-to-do family. Her father hired Nathan Roth to teach his children art. He didn't guess he'd run off with his daughter.''

Emerson kept stubbornly silent. She was too fatigued to

risk jousting with him. She didn't want to think about the past. It was the future that nagged her weary imagination.

What if Eli was right? Claire—married? Claire was so shy that she had never even dated. Yet in the back of Emerson's mind, she'd always known it was possible that someone special might come along for Claire. He would be like the prince in a fairy tale, waking Sleeping Beauty.

And, Emerson realized with a pang, Claire would go off with the prince and leave her dreamy, sheltered existence. She would have her own home and—Emerson felt a sharper pang—children.

What's more, this was *right*. Claire was born to love and nurture. She shouldn't stay a spinster, doomed never to be anything more than a dutiful descendent caring for her elders.

Emerson could imagine Claire with babies, a bunch of them. She would be a wonderful mother, a loving wife, a *woman* at last, not someone who has overstayed her time in girlhood and cannot escape.

Eli spoke, interrupting her thoughts. "I'm sorry. That was rotten of me. Pushing for answers at a time like this. You look pensive. My fault?"

Yes, Emerson thought. *No. Yes and no.* "I wasn't thinking about your questions. I was thinking about my sister."

He sat on the camp chair, elbows on his knees and his fingers laced together. "Don't worry. Merriman's a good guy."

"She's good, too. No one's sweeter."

The two of them were silent for a long time. They could hear the steady thrum of the wind, like an anthem to the danger that had passed.

Eli said, "I kind of envy him. Merriman."

Emerson was suddenly afraid to look at him. "I envy her."

"She may go off with him, you know," he said. "His

base is Toronto. It'd be hard for him to work out of the Keys.''

"I expect she will.''

"And then it'll be up to you,'' Eli said. "Watching out for your grandmother and grandfather.''

"And the art,'' she said with conviction. "It's what I was raised to do.''

"That'll be enough for you?'' he asked.

"Yes,'' she answered, but she felt a deep and unexpected sadness.

"You won't look back someday in regret? At the things you didn't do, the paths you didn't take?''

"I don't believe in regret,'' Emerson said. But regret seemed to be what she was feeling.

"Then what do you believe in?'' Eli asked. "Besides your family and art?''

She didn't like the new direction his conversation was taking. His tone had a seductive edge. "I *believe* I need sleep.'' She picked up one of the pillows and tossed it to him. "We can use the bed in shifts. I'll sleep a few hours, then you can have it.''

"You can't sleep on the floor,'' he scoffed.

"At this point, I could sleep on a bed of nails.'' She threw the other pillow at his feet, then the spare blanket that had been folded at the foot of the bed. "Here. You can make yourself a nest or something. Unless you can't sleep on the floor. Then you can have the bed first.''

"I've slept on rocks, I've slept in the jungle and I've slept in a leaky sampan. I could go out in your living room and sleep on the broken glass. This floor? Piece of cake.''

"Enjoy your cake.'' She switched off the lantern on the bedside table. "I'll wake you in a few hours.'' She turned her back to him and lay down.

"Ha,'' he taunted. "You'll sleep like a log.''

HE WAS WRONG. He heard her whimper in her sleep, then cry out. She was moving in the bed, almost thrashing.

Nightmare, he thought. And no wonder, after all she'd been through. A light sleeper himself, he was on his feet in a moment and bending over her. Reaching out, he clutched her shoulder to quiet her. "Emerson— Em. Wake up. You're all right."

The room was nearly dark. He'd set one lantern in the small bathroom, then left the door ajar. He could barely see her shadowy face, the outlines of her body.

She tensed and woke, half rising and grasping his upper arms. Even in the darkness, he could see her panic. "Emerson—"

"Oh!" she gasped, gripping him more tightly.

He shook her gently. "Easy, baby. Bad dreams, that's all."

"Dreams," she repeated, as if she didn't understand.

"Dreams," he assured her.

"It was— You were— We were—" She shook her head to clear it.

"The hurricane?"

"Yes. We were trapped here. A surge came. It poured into the room. From everywhere. I reached for you, but I couldn't find you. The water was almost to the ceiling. I was screaming for you. I thought you'd—you'd—"

"I'm here. I'm fine. We're fine. There was no surge. This room was probably the safest place on the Key."

"W-what time is it?"

He glanced at the glow of his watch dial. "Just after midnight. Go back to sleep."

"No," she said, sitting straight up. She seemed awake but unaware her fingers still dug into his arms. "I don't want to dream again. The floor— I'd rather sleep on the floor. Maybe I won't dream there. You take the bed."

"No. Stay here. You've been battered and bruised and beat up, and you need a decent sleep."

"If I stay here, stay with me," she said, something close to pleading in her voice.

A dart of shock momentarily paralyzed him. Was this, at last, an invitation to make love? Or was she too dazed and upset to know what she'd asked? Did she expect him to lie next to her all night without touching her?

"Are you sure?" His heart beat hard.

"Yes." Her voice was shaky, her breathing uneven.

She lowered herself to the bed again, drawing him with her. He stretched out beside her, hopeful yet unsure. Perhaps she wanted only comfort. He wanted…everything.

Her fingers relaxed and her hands dropped to the blanket. She put her face against his chest. "I'm not used to nightmares."

He let his arm wind around her, demanding nothing, giving only solace—he hoped. Her formidable willpower was weakened, but so was his.

"After bad times, the dreams come." His voice was gruff. "It's a natural thing."

She nestled closer, and he gritted his teeth. He wanted to stroke her bare arm, but he forced his hand to stay immobile. She said, "You mean like posttraumatic stress syndrome?"

"Exactly."

"You've had it?"

He gave a short, bitter laugh. "Oh, yeah. Not real flashbacks. But dreams? Yes."

She was silent a moment. He felt the rise and fall of her rib cage beneath his arm, the feather-softness of her breath against his chest. At last she asked, "What happens in yours? Your nightmares?"

He swallowed, trying to quiet his desire. "Getting beaten senseless in New Delhi. That one comes back a lot. Yucatán. Being ambushed in the jungle. That one, too."

She put her hand lightly on his chest, making his heart

leap and his blood pound. "Mine was so claustrophobic," she whispered. "The room filling up with water."

He resisted the urge to touch her hair, which tickled his cheek. "There was no surge," he whispered back. "It was only a dream."

She paused again, then said, "The worst part was losing you. I lost hold of your hand. It was dark, and there was only the water. The room had become the ocean—so big. It took you, and you were gone. Forever."

"I'm not gone," he said, nuzzling her hair. "I'm here."

"Yes." She settled more closely to him, dizzying his senses, sending fire through his blood. "I'm glad."

He could say nothing. He wondered if she could hear the thundering of his heart.

Her hand moved against his chest, caressing his pectoral muscle, then moving up to his collarbone. She tipped her face so it was next to his throat.

"Before that I was having a good dream." He could feel the nearness of her lips, making his bare flesh tingle. His self-control was going to kill him, he was sure of it.

"I was dreaming of the Captain and Nana. About ten years ago, he got one of his wild urges and took her out in a sea kayak. She hated the idea, but he wanted to, so she went."

Her hand moved up to stroke the hollow of his throat. "Of course, he capsized them," Emerson said, affection in her voice. "Scared her out of her wits. She came stomping back into the house, furious."

I don't want to hear about your grandparents, he thought, his whole body an unbearable ache of desire.

She spoke on softly, her fingers still teasing his hot skin. "She said, 'He could have killed us both, the fool.' She wouldn't speak to him. She stalked upstairs and slammed the bedroom door. He went right after her."

Where's this story going? Eli wondered in despair.

Her fingers tiptoed around his Adam's apple. "They were

up there a long time.'' She almost purred. ''I was in the dining room. It's right under their bedroom. I could hear their bed going whump-whump-whump. Later they came downstairs, hand in hand. And I could tell by their faces they'd been making love.''

She paused, then said, ''Later I teased him. I asked him what went on up there. And he said, in that way of his, 'I had to remind her that life is to be celebrated.' That's what he said in my dream. 'Life is to be celebrated.' It was as if he came to me to tell me that.''

She kissed his neck, and his heart slammed into a wall of pure want. ''Eli,'' she breathed, ''Let's celebrate life. It doesn't have to mean anything more than that. Let's just celebrate that we made it. No strings attached.''

He turned to her with a groan of yearning. ''I thought you'd never ask.''

HIS HANDS FRAMED her face, holding her fast as his mouth took hers in a long and hungry kiss. His arms wrapped her possessively, and she delighted in the feel of his masculine strength.

While she still had the sense to do it, she asked if he had a condom. She panted the question against his lips. ''Of course,'' he panted back. ''I'll get it in a minute.'' They began to give themselves to each other with a triumphant abandon.

As a lover, he was fervent and creative. His lips seemed formed to fit hers exactly, to tease and satisfy, then tease more wickedly and satisfy more wickedly still. He and she explored the secrets and skills of each other's mouths.

Their tongues played, teeth nibbled and nipped. He kissed her eyelids, her jaw, her throat. Lacing his fingers through her hair he lifted it and kissed her behind the ear and beneath the ear, which gave her a tickling ripple all over her body. Then he tantalized by kissing her ear, tracing his tongue in its whorls, breathing warmly against it.

He sat up, pulling his shirt off, then drew her T-shirt upward and freed her from it. Even in the deeply shadowed room, she could see the muscled power of his chest and arms. He undid her bra, then drew her back down to the bed.

She lay on her back while his hands moved over her breasts, cupping and cradling them, gently at first, then with such intensity it transported her. He framed her breasts in his sure hands and began to make love to them with his mouth. His lips and tongue moved from one breast to the other, making her nipples grow taut and even more needful of his touch.

She pushed her fingers into his hair, not wanting him to stop or move from this delicious torture. But then his hand was unbuttoning her jeans and pulling down the zipper. It slipped inside, searching for her most sensitive spots, and when he touched her, she nearly cried out.

He beguiled her, wooed her, made her feel wild and a little mad. When she thought she could stand it no more, he suddenly moved away from her. She felt bereft and reached for him. But he stood beside the bed and, in two swift movements, unfastened his jeans and shed them.

"Now you," he said deep in his throat, "help me." She raised her hips so that he could strip away the confining jeans. He flung them away. Then he bent and rummaged among his own shed clothes. He pulled out his wallet and took out the Mylar packet.

Dropping the wallet, he took her beneath the arms and hoisted her to a sitting position, her legs dangling over the edge of the bed. He'd done it smoothly and without any seeming effort. He pressed the packet into the palm of her hand.

"Will you?" he asked.

"Yes," Emerson said, her breath ragged. "Yes." He looked like a pagan statue there in the near darkness, his body lithe and hard, his erection inviting her.

Her fingers trembled. He sucked in his breath sharply. He braced his hands against her naked shoulders. "Em," he said from between clenched teeth, "hurry. I can't wait much longer."

"I can't, either." But her pounding pulses and tingling body made her fingers clumsy. At last she finished, and he lowered his head and kissed her on the mouth, and they were on the bed again.

He entered her, and a moment later, Emerson closed her eyes and saw the greatest fireworks show in the world. Afterward she snuggled, drowsy and sated, beside him, rubbing her nose against his shoulder, she thought she'd never had a better celebration.

It was so good that they dozed for an hour, woke, fondled, kissed and celebrated again.

CHAPTER FOURTEEN

EMERSON, tingling and content, lay with her cheek pressed against Eli's chest, her hand over the steady beat of his heart. Asleep, he kept one arm draped over her waist.

She liked the warmth of his body next to hers. She liked the tickle of his chest hair against her face, the scent of him, the tang of the sweat from sex.

It was good to be this near a man again. It was particularly good being near *this* man. She stroked his chest, slowly and affectionately. He sighed in his sleep. She smiled to herself, not sorry for what they had done.

Her only regret was ironic. Making love with him had been *too* exciting and satisfying. She would remember it always, and she didn't suppose anyone else would ever make her glow, body and spirit, the way he had.

But she meant what she'd told him. *Let's celebrate life. No strings attached.*

The nightmare about losing Eli had been not merely bad, it had been terrible. She and he had been through too much together not to seal the experience with the ultimate intimacy.

Emerson didn't approve of one-night stands and had never had one. But this was different. They'd outfaced death, so they reveled in life. It was the same sort of impulse that makes survivors of a shipwreck cling together hugging, and impels strangers to kiss when a war ends.

She sighed and kissed his breastbone. In the morning,

this truce would have to be over. But for the time being she settled closer to him and drifted into dreamless sleep, safe in his embrace.

ELI AWOKE with the certainty something was wrong.

With a start, he sat up in bed. He was alone.

He looked about, frowning in disbelief. Where in hell was Emerson? He leaped from bed. The bathroom door was ajar, the lantern's light throwing out a feeble beam. "Emerson?"

No answer. He flung open the door, but she wasn't inside. "Emerson? Em? Where are you?"

He snatched up the lantern and strode to the door to the hall. He wrenched it open and saw the same sad litter of wreckage up and down the passage. But no sign of Emerson.

The only sound was the wind sighing through the house and the occasional bang of a loose board somewhere. "Emerson, where are you?"

No answer came, and he needed none. With a sickening certainty, he knew where she'd gone. Off to Key West to find her grandfather.

He swore, turned back and dressed as fast as he could. When he reached for his cell phone, it was gone. She'd taken it. Of course. It worked better than hers. Hers lay on the nightstand. He grabbed it to punch out his own number, but there was no dial tone. The phone was dead.

He swore again. She had no business being out there alone. How would she even get across that gully, now that the bridge was out? The ditch would still be a torrent of water. Hell, she could drown trying to cross it. He had to go after her.

He strode through the wreckage, wondering how she'd slipped out of the house without waking him. The woman must move as stealthily as a cat. He didn't open the back door because he didn't have to: it was gone.

Through its opening, he saw what was left of his rental car. It was bent like a pretzel around the stump of a snapped-off palm tree. The windshield was shattered, and a small dead shark lay on what was left of the hood.

Eli stepped outside. The morning was still and hot, the sky overcast. He glanced quickly into the garage. The Volkswagen van was still parked there, but part of the banyan tree had smashed its rear and pushed its nose into the concrete wall. Emerson had to be on foot, and that was good; it meant he had the chance to overtake her.

He tried to tune out the destruction around him, but it drove itself into his consciousness. The house looked as if it had been sacked by vandals or hit by a missile.

The yard was a wasteland. Some trees had been torn up by their roots. Others' trunks had snapped. Those still standing were stripped of foliage.

He started down the road as quickly as he could, wondering how the sight of Mandevilla by day had affected Emerson. It had probably wrenched her guts, but that wouldn't stop her, and it wouldn't slow her down.

The road was almost unnegotiable. Every sort of trash cluttered it, from fallen trees to things no longer identifiable. He saw a coral snake slithering along a sodden palm frond.

Eli gritted his teeth and gave the thing a wide berth. He hoped to God Emerson had taken the time to put on boots or hiking shoes. The Keys would be teeming with snakes today, displaced, confused and mean-tempered.

Mentally he went through the ugly litany of dangers a hurricane left in its wake: swarming fire ants and rats, broken glass and twisted metal lurking under the other, seemingly harmless litter. When he caught up with her, he'd give her holy hell.

He knew why she'd stolen out alone. She was going to try to spirit the old man away without Eli ever seeing him. She was no longer the warm and eager woman she'd been last night. She was a rival again, as reckless as she was cagey.

But Eli's feelings were more complicated than rage or resentment. He worried about her. Almost as bad, a sick sense of betrayal rent him. If she meant to take the Captain and slip away, that meant she'd do her best to keep Eli distant from her family, and herself.

If what she'd told him was true, that the Captain had an accident that had somewhat impaired him, why was she still determined to keep Eli away from him? He could think of only one answer. She had lied.

And so what had last night meant? Nothing? A therapeutic roll in the hay? A way to divert him and throw him off balance? Was it *payment?* She had given him sex so she wouldn't owe him anything else?

If he uncovered her family's secret, would she turn around and accuse him of seducing her to get it? She could compromise his reputation, throw his credibility to the dogs. He fought against believing she was that conniving, and yet...

He didn't know. He felt as displaced and full of poison as the homeless copperheads and coral snakes.

He wanted Emerson the way she had been in the darkness last night, eager and loving. But now he wasn't sure if that woman was real or only a character she'd played. No matter which she was, he'd have to choose between her and the story.

And he would not give up the story. He was sure he knew the secret she fought so hard to keep. The Captain hadn't had an accident. He had Alzheimer's or some other form of dementia.

If they'd found him yesterday, she'd have claimed his irrationality was caused by exposure to the storm. She'd say he was an elderly man in shock. But Eli was certain that the family didn't let people see him or talk to him on the phone because it would be instantly clear: his mind was gone.

His painting had changed and deteriorated along with his

brain. Perhaps he went on painting because painting was the thing most deeply imbedded in his being. But how would it affect buyers if they knew that the man himself could no longer judge what he did?

Eli didn't know how guilty Emerson was in this deception, but he was certain there was deception, a great deal of it. Eli's worst suspicion was that the Captain might not be painting at all. If Emerson was knowingly selling forgeries, she could go to prison. And Eli would be responsible.

His stomach pitched in nausea and disgust. His emotions said it would be best for him to walk away from this story. But he would not. Not out of love for her, not out of hate for her, not for any reason.

He took turns jogging and plodding down the road, his mind on fire and his emotions chaotic. A slight wind sighed in the tops of the surviving trees. No birds sang. Ahead he could hear the rush of the water in the ditch, the sound growing more tumultuous as he neared.

He saw most of the grove of tabebuia trees had been broken or uprooted. A tangle of fallen branches lay like a great barren thicket on the other side. Two of the large trunks had fallen across the ditch.

Eli swore. That's how she'd gotten over, using one of the trees for a bridge—if she'd gotten over. Beneath the tree trunks the water ran high and wild. If she'd fallen in, she'd have been swept away by the current.

The sick feeling came back. The water was full of debris, shooting along like missiles. If she'd fallen in…

But then, with a shock, he saw her. She lay on the other side, almost hidden by the thicket of stripped branches. She was motionless. His heart did a sickening flip-flop. She was hurt.

He dropped to his hands and knees and crossed the thickest of the fallen trunks. It was wet and slippery. The bark, splintered, cut into his hands, and the water surged hungrily beneath him. He ignored it, concentrating on Emerson.

She lay in the road, her back to him, one arm thrown out behind her. He sleeve was drenched, her hair wet.

He reached the other bank and made a dash for her, a choking knot in his throat. He crouched beside her, pulling her into his arms, his anger forgotten. He shook her. "Emerson. Em. Talk to me. Please. Wake up. For God's sake—"

She made a face, groaned irritably, and squinted at him. Such relief swept him, he went dizzy with it. "Emerson— what happened? Are you hurt?"

"Leave me alone," she said, struggling weakly to escape his embrace. "I was *resting*."

"Resting?" His voice was incredulous. "You were passed out."

"Was not," she grumbled. "Had to rest, that's all."

"Sure. The best place to catch a few winks. Lying on a pile of trash in the middle of the road."

She pushed her hair out of her eyes, then rubbed her left wrist. "Okay. I kind of fell. But I figured while I was lying down, I'd just catch my breath. I…lost my bike in the water."

His voice rose half an octave. "Your bike? You tried to get a *bike* across that log—that's crazy."

He had a mental image of her struggling to walk a bicycle across the slick uneven trunk. What did she think she was—a circus performer?

"It wasn't crazy. I was going to ride it to Key West."

"Hell, why didn't you just ride it across the log? Standing on your head and juggling oranges?"

"Oh, shut up," she muttered, still rubbing her wrist. "It wasn't like that. It's a folding bike. In an aluminum suitcase. I used to take it back and forth from college."

Her shoulders sagged, and suddenly she looked bereft. "I loved that bike. I'd take it to New York. I bet I rode a thousand miles in Central Park. I even named it. Merlin the Miraculous Folding Bike.''

Eli looked at her in exasperation. He'd seen such contraptions, bikes that folded up as neatly as Swiss Army knives and went into their own lightweight carriers. But even a folding bike was large. To try to carry it over a slippery log was pure folly.

She must have seen the disapproval in his eyes. "I thought I could push it across. Scoot and slide it ahead of me. I couldn't, that's all."

"How'd you plan to get it over the water if those trees hadn't fallen?"

"I don't know. Maybe I would have had to leave it. It was worth a try."

She had a smear of dirt on her cheek, and he couldn't resist wiping it clean. "For that matter, how would *you* have gotten across?"

"I'd have found a way."

"What'd you do to your wrist?" he demanded. She still massaged it.

"Twisted it. Trying to hang on to the bike."

"And that's how you got wet?"

She tossed her damp hair. "Yes."

He gave her an accusing glower. "Nearly went in, didn't you?"

"Yes." Her attitude was defiant. "But I *didn't*. I dangled a little while, that's all. Now let loose of me. I've got to get to Key West."

He held her fast. "You dangled, and it made you so weak-kneed you fell when you tried to stand. You knew you could have killed yourself. I think you passed out. Where's my phone? Lost that, too?"

She wriggled to get free. "I only borrowed it. I was going to send it back. I left you mine."

"Yours doesn't work, and you know it."

"That's why I needed yours," she said with such righteousness he gave a bitter laugh.

"Let me see your wrist."

"It's fine. Go away. You have no right to follow me."

"Maybe I was just following my phone." He seized her wrist and examined it. It was swollen and bruised, but he didn't think anything was broken. He dropped it. "You'll live. To lie another day."

Sparks flickered in her dark eyes. "Whatever *that* means."

He pulled her closer to him. "You've hidden the truth from me all along. It's second nature to you. You sneaked away this morning because you didn't want me to get near your grandfather."

"Wanting privacy isn't lying," she said. She pushed so hard to get away that he let her go. She tried to stand, but her leg gave way, and she started to fall back to the ground. Rising himself, he caught her.

"Banged your knee? Twisted an ankle?" he asked.

"It's only a bruised knee," she muttered. "I'll make it."

"Maybe I'll have to carry you to Key West. Wouldn't that be fun? I could feel so noble, all the way."

"I'll hitch a ride," she said. "There have to be a few cars out there. And you're right about one thing. I don't want you near my grandfather."

"Because of what I'll see? That he isn't the painter he was because he isn't the man he was? That he probably doesn't even know what he's putting on those canvases? That it's habit that drives him, not vision. And he wandered out into that storm because his mind's gone. Very King Lear. Mad and raving."

Her lip curled in contempt. "You know nothing. And you won't. You're like a stalker, you know that?"

"Am I?" He kept his grip on her because he wasn't sure her leg would support her. "Do you always make love with your stalkers? Wrong way to discourage them, babe."

She looked so stricken she surprised him. "I told you. It was a way to—to celebrate that we'd survived. I told you it didn't have to mean anything else."

He bent nearer to her. "That's all it was to you? A kind of mutual congratulations party?"

"That's an ugly way to put it."

"I could put it uglier."

She swallowed, but there was defiance in the set of her jaw. "I'm sure you could. I thought it was something we could share before—"

She shrugged and didn't finish the sentence. He finished it for her. "Before goodbye?"

Her face went unreadable. "You were very good to me yesterday. I...wanted to be close to you. But, yes. We're on different sides. And I won't have you near my family."

"Or you?"

"That would seem to go with the package, wouldn't it?" She said it almost flippantly. "So you can— Just go back to the house. I'll send somebody after you."

He gave another laugh. "I'm not crossing that bloody log again. I'll get you to the highway, help you flag a ride."

"No. I'll go alone."

"It'll take you too long. You can barely stand."

"I'll make it just fine," she countered.

"I'll make you a deal," he said, admiring her at the same time he wanted to shake her. "I'll let you go alone. If you can walk five steps without stumbling, you can go on. I'll stay here and wait for an hour. Give you a head start."

"Fine," she said. He let go, his hands falling to his sides. She took three hobbling steps, limped worse on the fourth, lost her footing on the last. She would have fallen, but he sprinted forward and caught her.

"You flunk." He swept her up into his arms.

"No," she protested. "I don't want you to—"

"Put your arms around my neck," he ordered. "Same deal. I carry you to the highway. We get you a ride. I'll stay behind, give you a head start. But I'll follow you, Em. I will.''

He felt the tension that stiffened her body. In her face, rebellion warred with a strange sadness. But at last she raised her arms and settled them around his neck. He carried her, picking his way through the ruin.

EMERSON HURT all over, but nothing hurt as much as her pride…and her conscience.

She hadn't meant for it to happen this way. With luck, she would have been halfway to Key West before Eli awoke. She had wanted to spirit her grandfather out of the shelter, get him to the marina and hire the first boat that would take them away. She hadn't cared how much it cost.

Then she'd planned to hire a plane to fly them to Fort Myers, where he'd be reunited with Nana and she'd arrange for them all to get to Puerto Rico—including the animals. She'd envisioned herself as Emerson the brisk and dependable, efficient solver of all family problems. Her head would be clear, her purpose steady and her emotions in strict control.

Instead, she had blundered almost fatally. Merlin the Miraculous Folding Bike had seemed like a brilliant idea in the small hours of the morning.

Merlin had been stashed in a storage room off the kitchen and had made it through the storm unscathed. She had taken this for a sign. She'd thought to make it to the highway, unfold Merlin and whiz into Key West, nimbly avoiding obstacles and zipping past any jammed traffic.

She'd refused to worry about getting across the gully until she reached it and saw the situation. At the time, it seemed a simple plan. Balancing Merlin flat in front of her, hanging on to its handle, she would edge across.

She'd thought it foolproof, but it proved only that she was a fool. The case couldn't be pushed smoothly. The tree trunk was too uneven and slippery. The carrying case was not small—the bike's wheels, after all, couldn't fold. Nor was the case light. It weighed almost thirty pounds.

When she'd tried to get it over the stub of a broken branch, it had wobbled, then pitched toward the water. She'd kept her hold on the handle, but the rush of the water hitting the case had nearly yanked her arm out of joint.

She'd lost her balance, but caught at the stump of the branch with her free hand. She'd hung from the tree, half on, half off, before the water's surge ripped the case from her grasp. She'd almost tumbled in after it and had fought desperately to right herself.

She had, but when she'd reached the other side, she'd been overwhelmed by how close she'd come to being swept away. She should have never tried to cross with the bike.

She'd tried to rise, but her body, pushed to the limit, wouldn't allow it. She'd trembled all over, her legs had buckled, and she'd fallen into the dirt and the debris. She'd struck her knee so hard that she'd seen stars, and then for a few moments, only blackness.

The next thing she'd known, Eli had her, and she was crushed by humiliation. She'd never fainted or passed out in her life. He'd found her there, in a swoon like the daintiest Victorian maiden, and it was mortifying.

To her shame, she had to admit she'd done something not merely dangerous, but stupid. And she still couldn't walk straight. Instead of peddling, swift and independent, to Key West, she was being carried to the highway like an ailing baby.

So she clung to Eli's neck, forced to depend on him, even though she didn't know if he would keep his word. Would he truly give her a head start to Key West? If he went honorable and gentlemanly on her at this point, she might never sort out her emotions.

"Do you mean it?" she asked at last. "You'll give me an hour's lead?"

"At least." He didn't look at her. He kept his eyes on

the road, as he negotiated his way through the rubbish and puddles.

If her pride stung, her conscience stung worse. "The way I left this morning," she said, "I thought it was the best way."

"A clean break?" His mouth twisted as he said it.

"Yes. No. Eli, I have to get my grandfather. I *have* to."

He stepped over a tangle of clapboard siding, ripped from someone's house. "What you mean is you have to get to your grandfather before I do. You're don't want me to see him."

She tried to defend herself. "He doesn't want to be seen. It's an issue of rights. Why can't you respect that?"

He stopped, and for a moment, his eyes met hers. "It's an issue of the truth. And you've worked your butt off to hide the truth. It's a very cute butt. I suppose it's a very ugly truth."

"Eli, please—"

But he set out walking again, ignoring her. "We both know what you're up to. So no excuses. And no more lies. As for last night, look at it this way. Some women take money for sex. You'd rather have time. So I'll give you time. One hour. Fair enough?"

She gasped, smarting in resentment. "What a filthy thing to say. Put me down."

"No. It gives me too much satisfaction to have the upper hand. Besides, we've almost to the highway. Listen, you can hear traffic. Not much, but a little."

She went still, listening. She could hear the faint sound of cars or trucks. Soon she'd be able to escape from him. And, she prayed, from her memory of what they'd done together.

He carried her the last five hundred yards. Neither of them spoke. Emerson had tried hard not to let the destruction around her register. But now she saw she would have not recognized this part of the road. The few trees that stood were stripped and barren.

The iron gate to Mandevilla had blown halfway off its hinges. *I'll have to have that fixed,* she thought mechanically. *Or thieves will get in.*

Then she realized how illogical the idea was. There was hardly anything left at Mandevilla to steal. Suddenly she wanted to lay her head against Eli's shoulder and cry for all that was lost.

He maneuvered her body so he could carry her through the gap in the gate. He reached a turn in the road that should be familiar to her, but was turned strange by destruction.

Then she saw it, the highway. A few cars and trucks moved slowly up and down it, carefully avoiding debris. This time her eyes did mist. The highway and the traffic were signs that civilization still endured. The highway led to the Captain. And away from Eli.

He took her to the verge, his face looking as grave as she felt. "Put me down," she said in a choked voice. "I'll try to hitch a ride."

"No. Let me hold you. Somebody's liable to take pity on us sooner. Look desperate and stick out your thumb."

She didn't have to pretend to seem desperate. She stuck out her thumb. So did Eli.

Most of the traffic was going north, out of Key West. But a few vehicles were headed toward it. Emerson was eager for one to stop, yet at the same time, she didn't want it to happen.

Then she saw a yellow tow truck approaching, and as the driver caught sight of them, he slowed. It was going to happen.

The truck pulled over, and the window on the passenger side rolled down automatically. The driver spoke. "You got trouble? Need a lift?"

"The lady does," Eli said. "She's got a relative she's

got to get to. He's at the shelter in Key West. Can you get her there?''

''She hurt?''

Emerson opened her mouth to say not badly, but Eli spoke first. ''She had an accident, bruised her knee. There's a doctor at the shelter. He'll see to her. If you unlock the door, I'll lift her in.''

''Sure thing.'' Emerson heard the automatic locks click.

''What about you, buddy?'' the trucker asked, nodding at Eli.

''I have to stay here awhile,'' he said. He carried her to the door of the truck.

Emerson's arms tightened around Eli's neck. ''Eli,'' she said in a rush. ''Thank you. I wish it hadn't happened like this. Think of yourself in my situation. You'd have done the same—''

He opened the door. ''I know. I probably would. That's what bothers me.''

She couldn't help it. The mist in her eyes turned to tears. ''I hope that in your place, I'd have the courage to do what you did.''

''Don't worry.'' His smile was sad. ''You would have.''

''Goodbye,'' she said, not wanting to let go.

''Give me a kiss,'' he said.

She kissed him and held him tight.

''Ahem,'' the truck driver said at last. ''Excuse me, but I got a Cadillac to tow in Key West.''

Eli broke the kiss. ''Right.'' He swung Emerson up into the passenger seat. To the driver, he said, ''Take care of her, okay?''

''Sure thing.'' The trucker nodded.

To Emerson, Eli said, ''Keep the phone. You can get it back to me later, one way or another.''

''What about you?'' she managed to say.

He held up her phone. ''I've got yours. I'll get it charged up again. Goodbye, Em. *Vaya con dios.*''

He shut the door and stepped backward.

The driver said, "Buckle up, lady." He put the truck into gear. Emerson obeyed without thought. She couldn't tear her gaze from Eli's. She saw a muscle twitch in his cheek.

Then the truck was in motion. She turned so she wouldn't have to see him any longer; it hurt too much. But she could not keep from watching his image in the sideview mirror. A tall, dark man standing by the side of the highway, his reflection growing smaller and smaller until she could see him no more.

CHAPTER FIFTEEN

EMERSON FOUGHT BACK her tears because reason told her that she would be fortunate if she never again saw Eli. As it was, he would be trailing her in an hour.

The trucker, a burly man with a kind air, asked, "You all right?"

She nodded. "I fell and banged my knee, that's all. I got wet and dirty. I look worse than I feel."

The Captain and I will need fresh clothes and all sorts of other things. When will I get them? How?

"My name's Barney Marshall from Big Pine Key." He offered his hand.

She shook it as firmly as she could. "Emerson Roth." She was glad that the Roth name woke no flicker of familiarity in his gaze.

"Your boyfriend back there," the trucker said. "There's plenty of room. He could've come. Seemed hard for the two of you to split up."

"He has other things to tend to," she said vaguely. "I need to get to my grandfather. There's so much to do. Do you mind if I make some calls?"

"Not at all," he said, giving her a discreet sidelong look. "Feel free."

She drew Eli's phone from its holster on her belt. She supposed taking it really had been unforgivable.

She dialed the number of the shelter, which she knew by heart. She was lucky to reach it and to be connected with Kim quickly. "Emerson, my dear? How are you?"

She dodged the question. "A trucker is giving me a lift to the shelter. I had some trouble making it to the road. I could use some clean clothes. The Captain could use a change, too, for traveling. How is he? I need to leave as soon as possible."

"The Captain's fine, but restless. He'll be glad to see you. I take it you can't say much."

"That's right. You said that you could make some arrangements."

"I have. I called the marina. Our old friend Harry Shader's fleet came through in good shape. A call from me, and he'll be waiting at Key West Bight for you. He'll take you to Marathon. At Marathon, Pablo Cordova'll fly you to Fort Myers. And from Fort Myers, he can take you all to Encantada."

Emerson sagged against the seat in relief. "You're a magician."

"As for privacy, they'll ask no questions."

"I know." Shader and Cordova were both trusted men, old friends loyal to the Captain. "How's the sea?"

"Choppy. But Shader'll take his most solid boat, the *Beatrice B.* She's a forty-two-foot trawler with two motors and a cabin. You've sailed her before."

"She's a good one." Emerson said it with a lump of gratitude in her throat.

"As for clothes and such, I'll scrounge what I can. You can use my car to get the Captain to the *Beatrice.* Lock the keys in the trunk. I've got an extra set. I'll take a cab when I have time to pick it up. What about the reporter?"

"Right behind us," she said, stealing a worried look at the trucker.

"Well, nobody should know that Nathan Roth was ever here," Dr. Kim said. "I stashed him in a teacher's office and set up a cot. Told people who asked his name was Cecil Jones and his people were newcomers on Cudjo Key."

"Perfect," said Emerson. If all went well, she and the

Captain would be setting out to sea by the time Eli was crossing the bridge into Key West.

She thanked Dr. Kim, but not as enthusiastically as she would in person. The man was a guardian angel. She hung up and dialed Lori Dorsett, the family lawyer.

Lori lived two islands up from Mimosa Key, and Emerson prayed she hadn't evacuated. She dialed her home number first. Miraculously, Lori answered on the third ring.

"Lori, this is Emerson Roth. Did you make it through the storm all right?"

"Emerson—my God!" Lori sounded both amazed and delighted. "You're all right? Where are you? Did you evacuate?"

"No, but I should've," Emerson said ruefully. "Our place was hit badly. The others left." This was a small lie, but Emerson had hardened herself to telling small lies.

Lori had been in the Keys only a few years. She did not know everything about the Roths, and although Emerson trusted her with much, she hadn't trusted her with the facts about the Captain.

Lori said, "The others went, but you stayed?"

"Yes. I'm going to join them. My grandparents need me. But our place is a mess. I need to delegate you to do a few things for me immediately. If you're not scrambling yourself."

"We came through fine," Lori assured her. "Lost a few shingles, a couple of branches. We were lucky. But, oh, Emerson, what do you need done at Mandevilla? How bad is it?"

"Bad," Emerson said. "The gate's down. I need it repaired immediately. I want a security company to put a guard on the property, full-time. There's a small room off the downstairs hall. There are a few...works...in there. You understand?"

"Paintings? Your family took most of the others?"

"Yes. I need you to get these and put them in safekeeping. It won't be easy. That little bridge got taken out. I need it replaced with something much stronger."

"I'll do my best," Lori promised. "My neighbor's in the sheriff's reserve. Maybe he can help me get to Mandevilla. As for construction—everybody's going to be booked fast."

"I know. And there's insurance. I'll come back here as soon as I can. I'll be in touch every day. You're sure everything's all right there?"

"I meant it. We were lucky. Our office lost some shingles, too, but mostly we got off easy."

"I'm glad. And thanks for being there."

"It's my job, Emerson. Have a safe trip. I'll try to start the ball rolling here."

Emerson hung up, warm with gratitude for people like Lori Dorsett, but suddenly feeling shamed of her lies. They were not large lies, but they mounted and mounted. No wonder Eli suspected the worst.

Emerson turned to the driver. He was trying to look as if he hadn't listened, but she knew he'd heard.

"Mr. Marshall, do you have a telephone book I could borrow?"

"Sure, and call me Barney." He reached under his seat and drew out a tattered Monroe County phone book.

"Thanks, Barney." She took it, looked up the insurance company's number and phoned. She knew Frenchy and LouAnn had evacuated, but she hoped their phone was working and their answering machine was on. Both were functioning, and she left word for Frenchy that she'd need him to help organize a cleanup crew as soon as possible.

By the time she finished the message, Barney was pulling up in front of the shelter, an elementary school on White Street.

"Barney, a million thanks." She fished in her fanny pack and drew out a fifty-dollar bill. "That's for your trouble and your kindness."

"Ma'am, you don't have to do that. Time's like this, folks need to help each other."

"Take it, please. Buy something nice for yourself or your family."

He looked tempted. "Got a little girl with a birthday comin' up."

"Then get her a present with this." Emerson made him take the money.

"You need help getting to the door, ma'am? Your knee—"

"I'll make it," she assured him. Her knee still hurt, but she wanted to see the Captain so much, she could work through almost any pain.

She opened the door and stepped out gingerly. "Ma'am?" he said before she closed the door.

"Yes?" She gazed at him expectantly.

"I hope it isn't out of place for me to say this," he murmured. "When I picked you up, I thought 'look at that poor, bedraggled thing.' Well, you might look a bit scraggly, but after hearing you work that phone, I got to say you're the most organized woman I ever saw."

She gave him a crooked grin, closed the door and hobbled to the front door of the shelter. Dr. Kim was waiting for her and quickly drew her inside, submitting to her hugs and thanks. "Come, come," he said, leading her to a quiet hallway. "Time for that later. This reporter. He's really on your tail, excuse the expression?"

"I'm afraid so."

"Then we have to hurry. The Captain's ready. I packed a pillowcase of things for you. I asked for donations. There's a little of everything. It'll see you through, I hope."

He swung open a door.

Emerson's heart soared when she saw the Captain sitting in a wooden chair by an empty desk. His face brightened when he saw her. He stood, propping himself by leaning against the desk. He held out his arm, inviting her to come to him.

Then Emerson was embracing him. He drew back, looking down at her fondly and beaming with pleasure and pride. "Granddaughter," he said in his slurred way. "Guess what? I've had an *adventure*."

Only the Captain would look at it that way. Emerson hugged him again. "Indeed, you have," she said, holding him close. "And, oh, Captain, so have I."

CLAIRE BLESSED Merriman in her heart when he surprised her and Nana with breakfast. He'd appeared at their door with hot coffee and fresh-baked muffins and scones.

Nana insisted he eat with them. He smiled shyly, his brow wrinkling, and sat on the bed beside Claire. The coffee tasted like ambrosia, and the muffins were still warm. But nicest of all, Claire thought, was Merriman's presence. She'd slept little last night.

She was worried about Emerson and the Captain and sick with the knowledge that soon she would have to tell Nana about the damage at Mandevilla. In addition, there had been no word from Paris about Nana's mother. Never had Claire's family seemed so vulnerable to her.

She was so startled when her cell phone rang that she nearly spilled her coffee. Anxiety stabbed through her. Was it news? If it was news, was it good? Or bad? Fingers fumbling, Claire answered.

"Claire, it's Emerson," said her sister's voice. "The Captain's with me. We're headed toward Marathon with Harry Shader aboard the *Beatrice B.* If all goes well, we'll fly out of Marathon at two this afternoon with Pablo Cordova. We should be in Fort Myers by three-thirty."

Claire couldn't help it. She burst into tears of relief and happiness. "Emerson's coming with the Captain," she said to Nana. "They'll be here at three-thirty."

"Thanks be," Nana said, her hand flying to her heart. "Are they all right?"

Merriman put his arm around Claire, pulling her close. Hand shaking harder, Claire could barely speak. "How are you, Em? How's the Captain?"

"We're fine," Emerson answered. "You're crying. Don't. I'm depending on you. You haven't told Nana about Mandevilla?"

"N-no."

"Then we'll tell her together. But you've got to prepare her."

"I understand. I will," Claire promised. Emerson was right. She struggled to pull her feelings under control. She put her free hand over Merriman's, grateful for his nearness.

"Listen carefully," Emerson said. "We're going to need clothes, both the Captain and me. And he'll need to rest before we fly to Puerto Rico. This is all confusing to him."

"But he's all right?"

"Yes. He's hanging over the rail, looking for dolphins. He's having great fun. So much that it's wearing him out. I'd like to fly out of Fort Myers by three o'clock tomorrow. See if you can get another room at the motel. I'll double up with you, and we'll put Nana and the Captain together. They can have a second honeymoon. Can you meet our plane?"

Claire looked at Merriman, knowing he would take her to the airport. He smiled encouragement. "Of course," she said.

"Good girl. I've got to go now. Before the Captain throws himself overboard to glory in the power of the sea or something."

Claire smiled in spite of herself. The phone went dead. She moved closer to Merriman and met her grandmother's wary eyes. "They're both fine," she told Nana. "They're on a boat, and Emerson said the Captain's having the time of his life."

Nana's hands quivered. "My Nathan. Only my Nathan."

"But Nana," Claire said carefully, "Emerson said the news isn't so good about Mandevilla. It was hit hard. There's a lot of damage. She thinks we should go to Costa Encantada."

"Mandevilla is only a house," Nana said. "I don't care where we go, as long as the Captain is with me, and both you and Emerson are safe."

Claire squeezed Merriman's hand more tightly. "Nana, it's easy now to say that Mandevilla doesn't matter, but later you may feel different—"

"I will *not* feel different then," Nana said proudly. "But I feel different now. I would like to be alone for a time with my thoughts. There's much to think of. Why don't you two take these dogs for a walk or something?"

Her chin trembled, and she looked near tears. But Nana hated anyone seeing her cry. And Claire knew her grandmother had much to sort out. Her love, the Captain, was coming to her. Emerson, too, would join them.

But even as they approached, Nana's mother was probably slipping away forever. That reunion would never occur.

ELI KEPT HIS WORD. He walked to the nearest filling station, which was deserted. There he sat on a concrete bench under a palm tree with tattered fronds. The station's windows were boarded up with plywood. Across the board someone had written, "Can't Reason with Hurricane Season."

That was God's truth. He sat, letting the moments tick away until an hour would be up. He'd let her go. He'd given her time to get ahead of him. Why? He didn't want to think about why.

When the hour was up, he thumbed a ride with a firefighter returning to Key West from Big Pine, as far as he'd been willing to evacuate from home. The firefighter, a chatty sort, told him Big Pine had escaped serious damage and that Eli had been unlucky to be on Mimosa Key.

Tell me about it, thought Eli, but he didn't dwell on the terror. He remembered too keenly what it was like to hold Emerson in his arms, to make love to her.

Coming into Key West, Eli saw the downed limbs, the stripped trees, the uprooted bushes. Streetlights had been blown away, hotel and restaurant signs beaten and broken. Compared to its usual crowds and holiday air, the city looked almost deserted. But the damage didn't approach that at Mandevilla.

The car turned down White Street. Some householders were taking down hurricane shutters or raking the refuse from their yards. A utilities crew was repairing an electrical line.

"Yeah," said the firefighter, "I coulda stayed here. This isn't too bad at all. Hell, down here, we call it 'getting a shower and shave.' Some water comes down, some trees get trimmed, then it's back to normal. Ah, here you are."

Eli tried to pay him. "Naw," said the man, "pass it on. Do somebody else a favor. Good luck, buddy." He saluted Eli, then drove off, leaving him on the sidewalk, staring at the shelter.

He hoped Emerson would come walking out, helping the feeble, feckless old wreck that her grandfather had become. Then it would be over. He'd confront her face-to-face, and she could no longer hide the truth.

But the only person who appeared was a young pregnant woman, leading a small child by the hand. She and the child both had backpacks, and she came down the sidewalk as if she knew exactly where she was going and was glad to be on her way.

He stopped her. "Excuse me. I'm looking for someone. An older man. Tall. He came in with Dr. Kim."

"Dr. Kim?" she said, her face brightening. "Him I

know. An older man? There were several. I didn't notice any in particular.''

"A young woman may have just come for him. A very beautiful dark-haired woman. Her clothes were muddy, but she's striking. She could be in there now—''

"Sorry," said the woman, adjusting the strap on her backpack. "I haven't seen anybody like that. And I want to get home. My husband was stuck in Key Largo. I want to be back when he gets there.''

Eli thanked her. She nodded briskly and marched on. Inside there was the bustle of people, many getting ready to leave. He asked for Dr. Kim. Dr. Kim came to him, looking worn and sleepless, but his eyes full of intelligence.

"Nathan Roth?" he said innocently. "He's a patient of mine, you know. I swear an oath to protect the privacy of my patients. I'd rather say nothing of the man. Nothing.''

"Look," Eli said, "I know he was here. Emerson herself told me. She was coming here for him. Has she showed up?''

Dr. Kim yawned, politely covering his mouth. "You must excuse me. Lack of sleep clouds my mind. Your questions hardly register. It's been a tense time here. Please pardon an aging man for being too weary to answer. I was on my way to lie down. Another time, another day, perhaps when my memory's clearer. Good day, young fellow. Shall I show you to the door?''

Eli knew he'd get nothing from the man. "I'll find my way out," he said gruffly. "Thanks for your time.''

Kim shook his hand, an almost delicate gesture, then turned and left. But Eli did not leave. He made his way from person to person, asking questions, offering money for answers.

At last a grizzled man who looked homeless stared at him cannily, taking his measure. "I was here the whole time," he said. "I saw Kim when he came in. He did bring a man with him. What's it worth to you to hear more?''

Eli offered him a twenty, then a fifty. The man held out for a hundred.

"Something was fishy," the man said, his seamed face twisting into a smile of conspiracy. "Kim put this old guy away from the others. It was like he had secrets about him. Well, the Keys are full of secrets."

"What was this old guy like?" Eli asked. "What kind of shape was he in? Did he seem to have his wits about him?"

"He was cold and wet," the man said, squinting and nodding. "And he seemed confused. But he didn't seem loony if that's whatcha mean. I heard him say, 'My God, Kim, I haven't been this cold since Maine.'"

A small thrill rippled through Eli. *That's Roth. He grew up in Maine.* But he was also puzzled. If Nathan Roth was still rational, why did Emerson want to keep him hidden?

Eli pressed on. "His voice, when he spoke. How did he sound?"

The older man shrugged a skinny shoulder. "Okay. A little slurred. Like maybe he'd had one beer too many."

"Could he walk?"

"He leaned on Kim. Somebody gave him an old cane. He could go fast, considering, with that cane. Must have been a strong guy once."

"Notice anything else about him? Anything special?"

The man smiled, showing stained teeth. "Another twenty tells you."

Eli said nothing. He didn't want to dicker. He laid another bill on the dirty palm. "Details?"

"Gimpy. Favors his right leg. Right arm's limp, withered."

Eli's interest quickened, and he slitted his eyes at the man. "You're sure?"

"Yeah. Fingers curled up like a claw. I notice things."

A stroke, Eli thought. Nathan Roth had suffered a stroke

that had partially paralyzed him. He was right-handed, but his right hand was now useless.

Had he managed to keep painting with his left hand? Or was somebody else forging the paintings? The answer would tell him if Emerson was telling little white fibs or if she was a liar, a cheat and a swindler.

"Did you notice that he left today? With a woman?"

"A woman came a while ago. A looker." He gave Eli a conspiratorial leer. "Oh, yeah. She went off with Kim as soon as she got here. Her and him seemed thick as thieves. Later saw her helping the old guy down the rear hall, toward the back entrance. She had on different clothes. Sweats. She limped bad when she came in, but not so much when they went out."

Kim must have done something for her injured knee, Eli thought. "What else?"

"She had keys in one hand. Like car keys."

Eli felt things dropping into place. "Kim's?"

"I looked out the back window when her and the old guy left. Want to know what I saw?" The grimy hand opened again, beckoning.

Eli wanted the information, and he wanted it fast. He held up a fifty. "Tell me everything you know. Now. Don't play it out."

The man leaned closer, as if about to impart a great secret. "She had two pillowcases full of stuff. I don't know what. She and the old guy got in Kim's car. A silver Honda. Got one of them Key West stickers on the back bumper. One taillight out. Hurricane damage, I reckon. She pulled out fast. Don't know which way she headed."

Eli could guess. Either the airport or the marina. He dropped the bill into the man's hand. He figured him for a street person who'd sold plenty of information in his time.

"Thanks." The man gave his decayed smile. "Appreciate your kindness. I'm a veteran, you know."

Eli doubted it, but gave him a terse nod of acknowl-

edgment. He turned on his heel and left the shelter. He tried
to think as Emerson would. The first thing she'd want
would be to reunite her family.

She'd head for Fort Myers.

But how? The highway to the mainland was mostly
closed; the chatty fireman had told him that. The road had
to be cleared and secured. No, driving was out.

But Emerson was resourceful. He figured she'd charter a
boat or plane. He'd wager more boats were available than
planes. He caught a ride with a fishing guide going to check
on his craft.

When they pulled up at Key West Bight, where most
local boats were moored, Eli saw what he'd expected: a
parked silver Honda. It had a broken rear taillight, the caduceus on the back window and the Key West bumper
sticker that said, "We Are All One Human Family."

The car was empty. There was no sign of Emerson.

A BLOCK FROM the motel in Fort Myers was a small park
and playground. It was an ordinary place, marred by rem-
nants of the storm, puddles and the litter of torn leaves and
downed branches.

But to Claire, this humble park was beautiful as a field
in heaven. The sun shone, the sky was a sea of blue in
which fat white clouds leisurely sailed. The lawn, still
damp, sparkled emerald green, and the world was good.
Emerson and the Captain were on their way. And she was
with Merriman.

The air was sultry, but Claire and Merriman paid it no
mind. Other people strolled the park, and they would look
at the couple and smile because they were so clearly in love.
Claire and Merriman hardly noticed. They were in their
own private paradise.

They held hands, and each had one of the dogs on a
leash. Merriman held in Bruiser, who was high-stepping

and ready to romp, and Claire coaxed along the lagging
Fang, who hated getting his feet wet.

But happy as Claire was to be alone with Merriman, her
thoughts were never far from Nana. ''I know she's pulled
two ways,'' she told Merriman. ''Nothing means more to
her than the Captain. She'll be strong about Mandevilla, but
deep inside, she'll be sad for it.''

''So will you,'' he said.

''But she has more to bear than I do. Her mother's dying,
and she regrets what happened between them. That they're
estranged.''

''Because your grandmother married the Captain? I know
that's the rumor.''

Merriman wasn't being nosy, only solicitous, Claire
could tell. ''Yes. They ran off together. They'd known each
other only a week. It was a scandal her mother could never
forgive. Nana was the only daughter, and her mother said
she'd brought dishonor on the family.''

''But the rest of the family forgave her?''

''Eventually. She never saw her father again, but they
wrote and talked by phone. She's stayed in touch with her
brothers. One lives in Paris and one in Algiers. But none
has ever come to America. No, Nana chose the Captain,
and she wouldn't change that. She only wishes the estrange-
ment hadn't happened.''

Merriman squeezed her hand. ''You said you'd come
with me to Toronto.''

She smiled. ''Yes.''

''It's a long way from the Keys. From your family.''

She took a deep breath. ''I know.''

''I'll be gone on assignment sometimes. You'll be a
stranger in a strange land.''

''I know that, too.''

He stopped walking, and so did she. ''You still want to
get married as soon as possible?''

She swallowed. ''I want to spend a few weeks with Nana

and the Captain. Things are so changed for them. But Emerson will be there for them.''

He let go of her hand, put his arm around her. ''So how soon can we do it?''

She thought. ''A month? Six weeks?''

He drew her closer. ''We can get married at Costa Encantada?''

She nodded and put her hand on his chest, just under his collar. ''Yes. It's a beautiful place. We can be married on the beach.'' She got a bit misty. ''The Captain can give me away.''

Merriman's face went somber. ''You know that means you'll never really live at Mandevilla again?''

''Yes. Oh, I don't want to be apart from you for six weeks. Not even a month.''

''I could come with you. For a while, at least. I'd like that. Just to help you and your family settle in.''

''I'd *love* it.''

She raised her face and he kissed her while the dogs tried to pull them in opposite direction. They ignored the dogs and kept on kissing.

At last she forced herself to pull away, her heart fluttering like a trapped bird. ''Oh, Merriman,'' she said. ''Here we are, necking in broad daylight, and we're going to get married, and I don't even know your whole name. Will you tell me?''

His face went blank. ''Not until we get married. And it's too late for you to back out.''

She laughed at his wariness. ''It's really that bad?''

''Yes. Trust me,'' he said. And as if to prove it, he kissed her again.

CHAPTER SIXTEEN

THE MARINA OFFICE was closed. So was the bar next door, but a pair of sweating men were unboarding its windows and doors. Eli asked if they'd seen an elderly man with a dark-haired woman.

Both looked sly when he mentioned the woman, and the fat one wiggled his eyebrows lasciviously. "I saw *her,* all right. Somebody with her? I dunno. All I saw was *her.* Wouldn't kick *her* outta bed for eatin' crackers."

Eli had a slight but undeniable urge to punch his jowly face. "What about you?" he asked the thinner man.

"They were here about twenty-five minutes ago. She had an old guy with her. Had a cane and a bad arm. He was tryin' to tell her something. But he had trouble gettin' his words out."

Bingo, thought Eli. He thanked the men and made his way around the building.

On the dock, he found people checking their boats for damage or working to repair them. A depressed-looking teenage boy was bailing out a small console boat that had come close to swamping. Eli asked him if he'd seen the beautiful woman and the old man.

The kid squinted up at him and nodded. He pointed farther down the dock. "Yeah. They put out with Harry Shader on the *Beatrice B.* She docks down next to that new Crusader, the *Betty Allsup.* That's the *Betty*'s owner, Walt Queenan, standing there in the red cap."

Eli thanked him and made his way to Queenan, who was

talking irritably into a cell phone. Queenan snapped, "I mean now," and flipped off the phone and shoved it back onto his belt. He looked at Eli in disgust.

"Some bozo had a statue of a freakin' pelican in his yard. It blew through the window of my cabin and smashed my control panel. A damn concrete *pelican*. I'd like to find the fool who owns it and shove it up—"

"Did you see a brunette and an elderly man take off from here with Harry Shader? Not long ago?"

Queenan's face went from angry to suspicious. "What's it to you?"

"I got her cell phone." Eli held it out. It was lipstick red, clearly a woman's phone.

"I heard 'em say Marathon," Queenan muttered. "I heard 'em say something about a plane. Gonna fly out of Marathon."

"Can you describe the man?"

"Talked funny. Moved like he'd had a stroke or something. What kind of cheese-brained dork would buy a concrete pelican? It's wearing a bow tie and a derby. Sheesh. Freakin' moron."

"You know where I could find a pilot to fly me out of here?" Eli asked.

Queenan gave him a bitter look. "If I do, will you have him drop a bomb on the jerk that bought this—*pelican?*"

AT THE FORT MYERS airport, Emerson, so cool to outsiders, found herself in a hug orgy with her family. Even Merriman stepped forward to embrace her. She kissed his cheek. "Thank you," she kept telling him. "Thank you so much."

Claire hugged the Captain so hard that he coughed and pretended that she'd broken his ribs. Then she hugged Emerson even harder. "You did it! But why are you limping? Why are you dressed like that? With the bridge down, how did you get out of Mandevilla? Oh, Em, you *did* it."

"It was a snap." Emerson was flippant to cover her emo-

tions. It was heaven to hold her sister again. She didn't want
to let go.

"Let's get you both to Nana," Claire said. "She wanted
to come, but she's still worn-out from yesterday." She put
one arm around Emerson and one around their grandfather.

Merriman moved to support the Captain on the other
side. The old man threw his chin up and looked at him with
sudden distrust. His brows beetled fiercely. "Who are
you?"

"Merriman, sir. I'm a photographer. I drove your wife
and Claire to Fort Myers. I've been trying to watch out for
them."

"Oh," said the Captain, and immediately lost interest.
"I want my beautiful wife. And then I want my nap."

"You'll have both," Claire promised. "Oh, God, it's
good to see you."

"I've had an adventure," the Captain told Claire with
obvious pride. "In fact, I've had several."

But his speech was slurring badly, a sure sign of fatigue.
He fell asleep almost as soon as he was in the back seat of
the truck. Emerson held his good hand.

Claire, looking in the rearview mirror, caught her eye.
"Em, what happened to the reporter?"

Emerson tensed. "I left him behind. He'll be trying to
follow."

Merriman tossed her a worried glance over his shoulder.
"He's okay?"

"He's okay." She said it tonelessly.

Merriman turned his attention back to the road. "You
could have been stuck with somebody a lot worse. He's
good in an emergency."

"He was fine," she said in the same flat voice. She tried
not to think of Eli beside her throughout the storm, always
coolheaded and dependable. She tried not to think of making love with him. In its way, the experience had shaken
her more than the hurricane.

She gazed down at his phone clamped to the belt she'd put around her oversize sweatshirt. "I have his phone. When this is over, will you give it to him, Merriman?"

Merriman kept staring straight ahead. "I may not see him again. I'm canceling this assignment. I've got a conflict of interests."

He and Claire exchanged such private, knowing smiles that Emerson knew Eli was right. Merriman and Claire were in love, and it would end with him taking her away.

Shyly Claire said, "Merriman's coming to Costa Encantada with us. He'll help us with the animals and to settle in."

"Only if that's all right with you," he said.

"It's fine." She watched them share another smile.

Merriman cleared his throat. "I'll stay three or four days. Then I'll be back when—uh. I, uh, well, we should talk about that later, I guess. We're nearly to the motel."

"Certainly," Emerson said as cheerfully as she could. She knew what they would tell her was coming: a wedding.

"You got an extra room?"

"Yes," Claire said, "the man with the pot-bellied pig and the ferret left."

Normally Emerson would have hooted at such a statement and demanded an explanation. But life had been so topsy-turvy, a pot-bellied pig and ferret next door sounded normal, even prosaic. She should have laughed. But all she felt was a sadness foreign to her nature, and it was sinking deeper and deeper into her being.

THEY ARRIVED at the motel and woke the Captain, who was muzzy and disoriented until the unit door swung open and he saw Nana sitting in her armchair.

His face shone, and he said, "There she is, my love and my dove, my dark-eyed darling."

Nana hurried to him, embracing him and kissing him

long and hard. She drew back long enough to look at him with tears of happiness. "My Nathan. *Plus doux que le miel à moi.* Sweeter than honey." She stroked his cheek.

Emerson, starting to yield to her own exhaustion, felt a lump in her throat. Merriman looked at the couple with an expression of puzzled admiration, and Claire slipped her hand into his. She gave Merriman a look that said *They've always been this way about each other.*

He gave her one that said *We'll be like that, too, when we're old.*

Emerson didn't know how she could read these glances, but she could. She tried to busy herself by kneeling to pet the animals. Bruiser licked her wildly in welcome. Bunbury purred and rubbed against her ankles. Fang got up from his throw rug and nosed at her sweatshirt, snorting a doggy greeting.

The Captain drew back from Nana. "By sea and air I have come to you, my love. I have had a great *adventure.* A number of them, in fact."

Nana took his face between her hands. "Yes, and you are tired, *mon coeur.* Come lie down. I will sit beside you while you tell me."

She led him to the bed and when he stretched out, she untied his shoes and put them on the floor. Then she sat beside him and took his hand. "Rest a moment," she whispered. "Then we'll talk."

But the Captain's eyes were already fluttering shut. Exhausted, relieved to be with his wife again, he was drifting into the healing world of sleep.

Emerson and Claire exchanged guilty glances. Emerson extricated herself from the pets and stood. "Nana," she said, "I have a confession. Please don't be upset, because in the end everything turned out for the best. The Captain wasn't with me. He was at the Key West shelter with Dr. Kim. He was much safer there...."

NANA WAS SHOCKED. She was horrified. She shed tears at the thought of the Captain wandering alone and helpless in the storm. She declared herself angry with him for being so willful and foolish and with Emerson for deceiving her.

This anger lasted all of ten minutes. Nana couldn't scold the Captain. He was asleep. She could scold Emerson only in a whisper, so as not to wake him.

And, being Nana, her anger was quickly changed to concern for the danger Emerson herself had faced. "Oh, my child," she said, her face pained. "You went through hell, but you've survived and brought him back to me. Come here."

Emerson moved to the bedside. Nana took her hand and kissed it. She examined it, the scrapes, the bruises, the bandage on the wrist. "Poor little hand." She touched the wrapping. "And what's this?"

"I twisted my wrist. Dr. Kim bandaged it."

"And you limp. Why?"

"I banged my knee. Dr. Kim bandaged that, too."

Emerson did not mention that she'd tried to get the bicycle across the rushing water. Nana didn't need to know all the gory details.

"Dr. Kim will have a painting, one of the old ones, the *real* ones. And you, my dear, let me kiss your face."

Emerson bent and Nana kissed her on both cheeks, the forehead and mouth. Nana smoothed her hair. "You look tired. You have dirt on your chin and your neck. Go to your room and get some rest. I'll lie here beside the Captain and rest, too. And when we wake, we'll pretend this was all only a nightmare. And we'll move on from it."

Emerson straightened, taking her grandmother's gnarled hand. "Nana, there's also bad news about Mandevilla. Damage. A great deal."

Nana squeezed her hand. "What I love most is in this room right now. It's not at Mandevilla." She smiled at Emerson and Claire, then gazed down at the sleeping Captain. He'd begun to snore.

Claire moved to Emerson's side, taking her by the arm. "Come on, Em. I'll take you to our room. You can clean up and lie down."

Emerson released Nana's hand. "I'll need my designer luggage," she said wryly. She picked up her pillowcase as Claire snapped on Fang's leash. Merriman put the leash on Bruiser and helped Claire stuff a resisting Bunbury into his carrying case.

"No need for you to share the Captain with this menagerie," Claire told Nana. But Nana hardly noticed. She was lost in studying the Captain's peaceful face.

"You and I are bunking together," Claire said to Emerson. "The room's not too awful. It doesn't smell like pig—much."

THE ROOM DID NOT smell like pig—much. There was a hint of the ferret's musky aroma, but mostly the scent of age and neglect.

Emerson thought it wouldn't matter, that soon the little space would be filled with the odors of dogs and cat. Merriman had walked them to their room, leading Bruiser and carrying Bunbury, who mewed piteously until he was again freed.

Merriman kissed Claire goodbye and left. "Where's he going?" Emerson asked.

"Back to his room. And the parrot. But then we're going shopping to pick up a few things for the Captain. I'll make a list. We can get things for you, too. Or you can come with us if you want."

"I'm too tired to shop." Emerson glanced around the room. There were twin beds with mismatched spreads, a single window with broken blinds, and a dented metal bureau. "I made reservations for us at this dump? Next time, tell me to double-check."

"It was the only one that would take so many animals on such short notice," Claire said. "And let's hope there's no 'next time.'"

Emerson nodded. She remembered now. It seemed she had made the reservation in another lifetime. She no longer felt like the same person.

She emptied her pillowcase onto one of the beds and sorted through the things Dr. Kim had scavenged for her. She wrinkled her nose in distaste.

"I'll need a toothbrush," she said. "This one looks used. And a real hairbrush." She picked up a small one that seemed made for a child.

"He could only get me one pair of underpants, and I'm wearing them. And this is his sweat suit I've got on. You could get me another. In turquoise if they've got it. There's a pair of shorts, but they're huge."

She picked up an oversize T-shirt of faded red emblazoned with a picture of a basketball and the words Arkansas 1994 NCAA Champs.

"This is definitely not the fashion statement I want to make," she said, dropping it on the bed. "But I can use it for a nightshirt. Can you buy me enough clothes to hold me until I can go shopping at Costa Encantada? And get me some really good bubble bath? I want to spend the whole night in a bubble bath."

Claire made a rueful face. "There's no bathtub, Em. Just an awful shower. Sorry."

Emerson sighed. "Then the shower it is."

Claire sat down on the other bed and began writing her list. Emerson went into the dingy little bathroom and stripped down. She would have to avoid getting her bandages wet, but this proved easy; since the shower head produced only a tepid trickle.

Claire had already moved her own things into the room, and her scented soap rested on the metal holder in the shower. Emerson took it, rubbed up some suds and began to scrub her aching body.

She remembered showering last night in Mandevilla, thinking of Eli doing the same downstairs. She'd thought then that the two of them had been through hell together. She hadn't known then that they'd barely touched its edge.

Dully, she remembered Mandevilla crashing apart around them. She supposed the sensations of that destruction would haunt her for the rest of her life, stealing back to ambush her in nightmares.

Nightmares. She'd awakened screaming, and Eli was there. Eli, it seemed by then, had always been there. And she'd wanted to be as close to him as she could.

She was washing away his touch in this wretched shower. He had kissed and caressed her everywhere, and she had done the same to him, loving it.

Loving. Love. Don't think those words.

Those words applied to other people, like Nana and the Captain, Claire and Merriman. They did not apply to her.

EMERSON SLEPT for four straight hours. Claire awoke her, shaking her shoulder. "Em? I'm sorry to wake you, but something's happened."

Emerson was alert instantly, like a soldier who'd grown used to alarms. "What is it?" She sat up, remembering in a rush where she was and why.

Claire sat on the bed's edge and took her hand. "The Captain wants to go back to Mandevilla. He says he won't go to Costa Encantada. None of us can get through to him. And Nana's had a call from one of her brothers. They don't expect their mother to last out the week."

Emerson groaned. She didn't need another crisis. She certainly didn't need two. She heaved herself up from the bed. Bunbury, who had been snuggled against her, chirped in protest.

"I brought you a toothbrush and everything. I set it out

in the bathroom and I hung some new clothes in the closet.''

Emerson hobbled to the bathroom, freshened up and put on the lipstick Claire had bought her. It was her favorite color. God bless Claire.

When she came out, Claire shook her head. ''The Captain was doing well. He had a nap. He and Nana even took a little walk around the units. That's when it began to sink in for him, how seedy this place is. He doesn't like it, and he wants to go back to Mandevilla.''

''How's Nana holding up?''

''Better than you'd expect. But I think she's being stoic for the Captain's sake. She's unsettled, though. You can tell.''

Together they went next door. The Captain sat on the edge of the bed, his attitude sullen. Nana sat next to him, her face pale, her hand on his thigh. Merriman, in the chair, leaned earnestly toward the Captain. ''Sir, the road's not open. There's no way to get back to the Keys.''

''Young man, I didn't ask you. We got out of the Keys, we can get back in. Emerson can arrange it. Where's Emerson?''

''I'm here. Merriman's right, Captain. The highway's closed. And we can't go back to Mandevilla.''

With his left hand, the Captain made a gesture of disgust and dismissal. ''That's what everybody keeps saying. Well, none of them have seen it, have they? It was fine when I left. You came from there. Tell them we can go home.''

Emerson came and knelt before him. She put her hand on his thigh, next to Nana's. ''We can't. Mandevilla's damaged. No one can live there until it's fixed. So we need to go to Costa Encantada.''

He fixed her with an angry stare. ''You told me Mandevilla's still standing. I built her to stand, by God. And she does. You said so.''

''Mandevilla stands,'' Emerson said, calling on all her

patience, all her firmness. "You built it well. But the shutters were old. They didn't hold. Half the windows are gone. The roof leaked."

"Piffle," he said, in a huff. "A little broken glass, a little water. We can take that in stride. Where's your gumption?"

Emerson set her jaw. It took all her powers of argument, but at least she convinced him that it would take months to put Mandevilla right. He looked stricken.

"You've always liked Costa Encantada," she pointed out. "And our privacy's secure there."

"Our damn privacy," he said with distaste. "I'm sick of it." Now it was Nana who looked overwhelmed.

"There's a reporter on our trail," Emerson said.

"Damn the reporter, too," fumed the Captain.

Emerson pulled out her heavy artillery. She was the only one in the family who dared butt heads with the Captain when he was in one of his moods. "You're being selfish," she accused. "Think of Nana. She's been so worried about you, and about her mother. Now, instead of being happy to be with her, instead of comforting her, you're adding to her problems."

"Emerson," Nana cautioned.

The Captain looked affronted, but something in his mind seemed to click into place. He gazed at Nana with regret in his eyes.

No one said anything for a long time. Emerson could feel the tension simmering in the room.

At last the Captain turned to her again. "All right, all right. But change your clothes. I won't go anywhere with you, looking like that. You've always been a woman of style. Put yourself right. Then we'll talk."

Emerson went back to her room and changed her gray sweats for the turquoise blue set Claire had brought. She brushed her hair again, pinched her pale cheeks to color them and applied a touch of mascara. "War paint," she muttered to herself and went back next door.

Soon the Captain was almost his usual self, but she could see that he was still troubled. His concern now seemed more for Nana than himself. Emerson at last convinced him that he and Nana would be happiest at Costa Encantada, and they would be back at Mandevilla by Easter.

Claire put her hand on Emerson's shoulder. "Em, you're running on empty. Go back and get a good night's sleep. We'll stay here for a while."

Emerson was too fatigued to argue. "Yes. But promise you'll wake me if there's any news from Algiers."

"I will," Claire promised.

Emerson went back to her room, praying that Nana's mother would hang on to life until poor Nana was at Encantada and more settled.

She went to her room and sat on the bed for a few minutes petting fat, silly, lovable old Bunbury. "You," she told him. "Be glad you're a cat. And get used to traveling. You'll be moving to Canada. Think of it, chubbo. Canadian bacon and doughnuts, eh?"

Bunbury chirped and purred, and Emerson realized she would miss him. Bruiser, jealous for attention, laid his chin on her knee and whined. She scratched his ear. "But you'll go back to Mandevilla. You're a guard dog, aren't you, big boy? And when we're back, we'll run on the beach again and—"

The ring of a phone jolted her. It took a moment for her to realize it was Eli's phone, which she'd put on the dresser. *Oh, please,* she thought. *Don't let it be Claire telling me Nana's mother's died.*

She answered it with foreboding. "Hello?"

"Hello, beautiful." The voice was Eli's, and it made her pulses trip and her stomach flutter. "So how does your family like Fort Myers? The motel's a far cry from Mandevilla, hmm? A real dive."

"What is this? Why are you calling me?"

"Why do you think? I thought maybe you'd want to tell

me the truth—finally. I've seen him, you know. Your grandfather. You might as well come clean, Em.''

Anger surged through her, and fear, a confused host of other emotions jumbled up with them. ''Where *are* you?''

''Right outside. Not thirty yards from you. The jig's up, Emerson.''

HE HEARD HER angry gasp. He said, ''You're alone over there. May I come in? Give me a statement, then take me to talk to your grandfather. We can clear this up.''

''No. You *can't* come in. You can't talk to my grandfather. If you don't let us alone, I'll call your editor and complain.''

Eli sat in his rented car, watching her window, imagining the flash of anger in her eyes, the color rising in her cheeks. ''If you're going to call him, do it on your own phone, all right? I've recharged it. And I want mine back.''

''I'll give you your bloody phone,'' she snapped. ''But you're not coming in. Where are you?''

''Parked across the court. By the coffee shop. A gray Ford. You look good in that turquoise outfit, by the way. It's your color.''

The phone went dead. He watched her door. He knew in which units the family and Merriman were. He'd bribed the sullen girl at the desk, given her twenty dollars. And he'd watched.

Emerson's door flew open and she came striding across the parking lot. She still limped, but it barely slowed her. She came straight for him, purpose in every line of her body.

My God, he thought, *she's a magnificent creature.* There were lights by each unit, and he could see her clearly. A faint drizzle had begun, but she ignored it.

A complex mix of emotions warred in his chest. He got out of the car. More than anything, he wanted to put his arms around her, draw her close. He wanted to bury his face in that silky raven hair, then kiss her mouth, her eyes, her throat, her everything.

She stopped and held out her hand. "My phone?"

He laid it on her palm. "*My* phone?"

She slapped it into his hand.

"You're not even going to thank me?" he asked.

"Thank you." She jerked up her chin sarcastically. He saw that in spite of the resentment that animated her, she was tired. Not only tired, but frightened, and perhaps as bewildered as he was.

"Emerson," he began, wanting to tell her he was sorry to do this, that he wished it was all different. "Listen to me, please—"

But she shook her head and held up her hand, a signal for him to stop.

"No. Thank you for everything. But I won't listen to you, and I won't talk to you."

She looked as if she might weep out of weariness and frustration.

"I know the facts. He's had a stroke. I talked to people in Key West who'd seen him. At the shelter. At the marina."

She clenched her teeth. "You're really a relentless son of a bitch, aren't you?"

He had a hollow feeling where his heart should be. "Yes. I am."

"This is cruel. Couldn't you at least give us a day or two to recover?"

"You'll be gone in a day or two," he said.

"My grandparents have been through hell. They've just been reunited. Don't come barging in to ruin it."

"Where are you taking them? My guess is Puerto Rico. You've gone there before by charter flight. Costa Encantada, right?"

Her mouth twisted in disgust. "Your detectives dug that

up, too? Well, you can't get into Costa Encantada. It's a gated community. High security."

"I won't have to, if you level with me."

Tell me the truth, Em. If he's still painting, even left-handed, you've done nothing wrong, not seriously wrong. You're in the clear. Clear yourself. Please, Em.

"Go away." Her voice was full of bitterness. "Leave us in peace."

"You knew I'd follow."

"I'd hoped you'd have the decency not to. Leave." She turned to go.

He played one of his trump cards. "I saw them walking earlier, your grandparents. He uses a cane. Favors his right leg. His right arm's limp. The hand's withered. He can't paint with that hand, can he?"

She swung around to face him. "Dozens of artists have overcome physical setbacks and kept working. If you don't know that, you're in the wrong business."

"And some couldn't keep working," he said with cynicism. Toulouse-Lautrec. A stroke stopped *him.*"

"Renoir," she returned. "His arthritis was so bad, he had to have the brush strapped to his hand. Matisse—when he couldn't use a brush, he used scissors and made collages. Monet kept painting even with cataracts. When Degas went blind, he used touch and changed from painting to sculpture."

"I'm not interested in them. I'm interested in your grandfather. Did he teach himself to paint with his left hand? Use his mouth to hold the brush? Or is somebody else painting those canvases for him? Because they've changed, Em. You can't deny it."

"The others changed, too," she retorted. "Renoir, Matisse, Degas—"

"If I saw him paint, your case would be proved. But you won't even let me see *him.*"

"I told you, he doesn't like people seeing him this way."

"You said it was because he's deaf. He and your grandmother were deep in conversation. He can talk. He can hear. Did the stroke impair his mind? Are you afraid he'll blurt out something I shouldn't hear?"

Emerson stepped closer, her eyes sparking dangerously. "He's old. He gets confused. He gets upset. I'm not going to let you give him the third degree. My God, after what he's been through these last few days?"

"Your grandmother promised to talk to me. She hasn't. Will she honor her word?"

Emerson pushed against his chest, hard. "She *couldn't* talk to you. There was a *hurricane,* you dolt."

His nerves, too, were worn thin. He didn't like being pushed, he didn't like her constant evasion, and he took a step toward her. "Will she honor her word? If not today, tomorrow?"

She pushed him again, harder. "No! We're displaced. Our house is in shambles. Our possessions are gone. My grandmother's still shaken, and her mother's dying. Dying! What are you? A vulture? A hyena? *Leave us be!*"

Her taut self-control snapped. She began to beat on his chest and shoulders. "Leave us be, leave us be, leave us be," she ordered in a frenzy.

He seized her wrists, and when he saw her wince, he cringed. He'd forgotten she'd hurt her wrist. He gentled his grip, but he hung on.

"Let go!"

Her cheeks were wet, and he couldn't tell if it was from tears or the rain. Suddenly he was sick of himself, of his constant hounding of her. She'd never give in. Never. "Oh, Emerson," he said, sad to his marrow. "Why did it have to come to this?"

Her jaw tightened. "Because of you. You made it happen."

He stared down at her, riven by conflict. "I'll go away. On one condition. Let me kiss you one last time."

She glared at him in disbelief, trembling with anger. "You'll really go away?"

"Yes."

"And not come back?"

"Not unless you ask me to."

"That will never happen."

He moved closer, breathing hard. "I know it won't."

"And your precious story?"

"I'll write what I know."

"You don't know anything."

"Then I'll write what I suspect. I've put the answer together. Not all of it, but most. After that, it's up to the authorities to investigate."

"If you make false allegations against us, I'll sue you. I'll do my best to ruin you."

"I know that, too," he said. She meant it. And he understood why. She was a tigress when it came to those she loved. Beautiful, fierce and except for her family, solitary. Almost as solitary as he was.

He bent his face to hers. He kissed her. Not passionately or possessively, though he wanted to. It was a long kiss, full of tenderness and regret.

She suffered it. She didn't respond at all. And when he drew away, he spoke, his lips still close to hers. "Goodbye, Em."

For a moment, he thought he saw sadness in her eyes. But she looked away. "Goodbye," she murmured. She moved to free herself from his touch. He let her go.

She turned and moved as quickly as she could back to her room.

He stood for a long moment, staring after her. The drizzle had turned to rain and was coming down harder now.

He got back into his car and drove off, not caring much where he went.

CHAPTER SEVENTEEN

EMERSON WAS PUTTING on her baggy nightshirt when Claire came in. Bunbury went to rub against her, and Bruiser danced around her in joy.

Claire said, "The Captain and Nana are wearing down. It's been a long day. And no word about Nana's mother. I brought the phone with me. If word comes, I'd rather we got it first."

"Good thinking," Emerson said. "Maybe...somehow... we can make it less hard on her."

Concern showed in Claire's eyes. "Em? Is something wrong? You look like you just lost your best friend."

Emerson almost flinched. "Nothing's wrong. I'm tired, that's all. I'm going back to bed."

"Are you sure? Because—"

"I'm sure," Emerson said sharply, pulling back the faded bedspread. "What time is it?"

"Ten o'clock. I'm not tired. I'm kind of restless. I'll read awhile."

Emerson climbed into the bed. The sheets were limp and smelled musty. She watched as Claire crouched, affectionately petting Bruiser. "Where's Merriman?"

"In his room," Claire said, turning her attentions to Bunbury. "He's got a book, too. We each bought one when we were out today."

Emerson couldn't plump up her flat pillow, so she punched it. "You're really going to marry him?"

Claire gave her a wide-eyed look. "I know it's sudden. Don't you approve?"

"Sudden, schmudden," Emerson said with irritation. "It's just you haven't had much privacy, have you?"

Claire looked wistful. "I didn't want to leave Nana alone for long."

"Even when she was asleep?"

"Especially when she was asleep. She could have woken up disoriented and been upset."

Emerson punched her pillow again. "You're too good to be true. You always have been. So have you spent any time at all alone with the man? I mean any *real* time?"

"Well, we took the dogs on a long walk to the park. Almost forty minutes. And we did all that shopping. That took almost three hours."

Emerson gave her an exasperated look. "And you probably spent it all shopping."

"We had a lot of things to get. Oh, all right. We parked by a lake a few minutes and kissed."

"It's shocked I am," Emerson said, clutching her heart. "Snogging in a public place. There goes the family honor." She fell over backward on the hard mattress.

Claire frowned. "Are you making fun of me?"

"Yes."

"Why?" Claire sounded wounded.

"You love him? He loves you?"

"Yes and yes."

"But you're here with *me?* You're going to read a *book? He's* going to read a book? Why aren't you in his room? You could find out if he's blond all over. He could find out about that funny little mole on your—"

"Emerson!"

Emerson pulled the sheets up to her chin. "Okay. Be a prude."

"I'm not a prude. I've had some very…amorous urges lately. So, frankly, has he. I can tell."

"Really?" Emerson was dying to know the details, but knew Claire would never tell. "So why aren't you in his room?"

"He didn't ask me. He's too much of a gentleman."

"He didn't ask because he thinks you're too much of a lady. He's afraid he'd offend you. Why don't you go to him?"

"Em, I couldn't do a such a thing. I couldn't."

Emerson sat up straight. "Listen, little sister. Life is short. I became very aware of that last night. If you love him, go to him. He probably wants you so much it makes him crazy."

"But what would I say?"

"Tell him I kicked you out. Your reading light kept me awake. Ask if the two of you can read together. The rest'll take care of itself. Trust me."

Claire rose, a thoughtful expression on her face. "You won't tell anyone?"

Emerson rolled her eyes. "Just go, will you?"

Claire smiled. She picked up her book and opened the door. She said, "I'll be back by morning."

"Fine."

And then she was gone. Emerson blinked fast and felt a knot in her throat. It was the right thing to send Claire to Merriman, she was sure. But she felt empty and apart, a solitary person in a world made for pairs. She switched off the light and turned on her stomach, burying her head beneath the pillow.

"I don't mind being alone," she whispered to herself. "I don't. I don't."

She thought of last night, of making love with Eli. That's what it was, she finally admitted. They hadn't *had sex.* They had made love, and she had felt love.

WHEN MERRIMAN opened the door and saw Claire, his heart somersaulted in his chest. He felt a dopey smile curve his mouth. His throat had gone tight, but he managed to say, "Everything all right?"

She looked up, blushing and clutching her paperback to her chest. "Emerson said I should come here if I wanted to read. She said the light kept her awake. Is it all right if I come in?"

"Of course," he said, hardly believing this miracle. He held the door open for her. She slipped inside, then turned away from him, as if too bashful to face him.

She gazed at the parrot's cage, covered on the dresser. Merriman heard the bird muttering sleepily and hoped it would shut up and drift off to dreamland. "Pretty?" mumbled the parrot. "Pretty?"

Very pretty, Merriman thought. *Heart-stoppingly pretty.*

He bustled to straighten the bedspread. He'd been lying on it, fidgety and unsatisfied. "You can sit here," he said, his throat still clamped by nerves. "I—I'll sit on the other bed."

She did. He did. An awkward silence enveloped them. She placed her closed book in her lap. He picked his novel off the night table. "Have you started yours?" she asked in a small voice.

He cleared his throat. "Um. Not really. Having trouble getting into it. Did you have time to start yours?"

"Actually, no. Emerson was in an odd mood. I think she wanted to be alone."

"Oh."

She opened her book, and he opened his. They each stared at the first page of a chapter. Merriman could not comprehend a single sentence. The words danced idiotic and meaningless before his eyes.

The minutes stretched out, excruciating. Suddenly Claire spoke. She kept her eyes on the page, and her words came out in a breathless rush. "Merriman, I can't stand it. I've never liked lying, and you're the last person in the world I want to lie to."

He blinked in surprise, and his heart turned another somersault, one crazed with impossible hope.

She seemed in an agony of self-consciousness. "I didn't come here to read. I came to…be with you."

"Oh, thank God," Merriman said, flinging the book aside. It hit the parrot cage, woke him from his drowse and made him swear and flutter.

Neither Merriman nor Claire paid attention. He was at her side on the bed in one swift movement. His arms went around her, pulling her close, and hers circled his neck. His mouth pressed down eagerly on hers, and he lowered her to lie next to him on the bed.

He drew back to look into her eyes. "Claire, do you want to make love?"

She nodded, her face so sweet and shy, he ached for her. She whispered, "I don't know how. Will you show me?"

"Yes," he said hoarsely. "Oh, yes."

THE NEXT MORNING Emerson watched Claire put the leashes on Fang and Bruiser. Claire said little, but her cheeks were pink as roses. She wore a mysterious smile, as if she'd discovered a secret, and it was wonderful.

Well, they did it, Emerson thought. *And obviously it went well.*

A moment later, Merriman knocked and came in. He greeted Emerson and spoke with her, but Emerson knew she was merely a phantom to him. The only real thing to him was Claire.

They left to walk the dogs. Emerson brushed her hair and went next door to see her grandparents. She was grateful no call had come about Nana's mother.

She kissed both Nana and the Captain good morning. "Tell me what you want for breakfast. I'll go out and get it. Then we need to pack. The sooner the better."

"Is something wrong?" Nana asked, worry in her eyes. Emerson phrased her answer carefully. "That reporter got in touch last night. He says he'll leave us alone, but I can't be sure. We'll be safer from him at Costa Encantada.''

"I'm tired of hiding things," the Captain grumbled. "There's nothing to be ashamed of. Some day the truth should come out."

"No, no." Nana laid her crooked fingers on his shoulder to soothe him. "We've talked of that."

It was early in the day, he had slept well, and his mind was clear. He patted her hand. "Sorry, my dove. It was thoughtless of me."

He bent and kissed her forehead. Nana smiled, but then her smile faded. "The reporter was here? He followed us? You saw him?"

"I talked to him." Emerson tapped her phone. It was a misleading statement, but a true one. "Now tell me what you want for breakfast. Then we'll leave for Encantada as soon as possible."

THE COTTAGE AT Encantada was small, but lovely. Years ago, when the Captain's reputation was at its height, he'd bought the place for a song.

A part-time caretaker kept it in shape, and several times a year, Emerson rented it to carefully screened applicants. The rent paid its basic upkeep and taxes. But lately, since the family had less money, she'd often thought of selling it. She knew the Captain would protest, for he would see its loss as an emblem of failure.

For now Emerson was deeply grateful the place was still theirs. The cottage was set on a small hill overlooking the beach and the Caribbean. The hurricane had not touched this side of the island, and the storm was but a memory here. The sea was a vista of tropical blues and greens, and the sky was flawless and unclouded.

The cottage was flamingo pink, with white trim, and it had a porch that ran the length of the house, facing the beach. It was a sturdy little dwelling in a beautiful and private setting. To both east and west, the nearest neighbors were half a mile away.

But Emerson had to admit that the cottage had fallen into neglect. This neglect was not terrible, but it was more visible each year. The heat and the sea took their toll. Since the paintings no longer sold as briskly as they once did, she'd tried not to run up new bills.

But even though the house needed a coat of fresh paint, inside and out, and even though the appliances were old, and there were ceiling fans instead of an air conditioner, the cottage had the feeling of a haven. Emerson saw both the Captain and Nana visibly relax once they were unpacked.

Merriman stayed three days. Then Emerson drove him and Claire to the San Juan airport. When they said goodbye, she strolled away so she wouldn't have to witness all the tears and kissing.

The next day, she, too, departed, leaving Claire in charge. There was much for Emerson to do, most of it painful.

She caught a bumpy puddle jumper flight to Key West. She had reserved an SUV, a motel room at the edge of the city and two storage units in Sugarloaf Key.

Then she set off for Mandevilla to see what could be salvaged. All along the highway, she saw signs of the hurricane's destruction: missing windows, tattered roofs, ruined trees.

She stopped at Lori Dorsett's law office. True to her word, Lori had seen that the gate was repaired and that a security man was on the site at all times. She hadn't been able to get a new bridge put up, but there was a jerry-built walkway. She'd rescued the paintings, which were stored in her spare bedroom. Emerson thanked her profusely, then set off, sad and apprehensive, for Mandevilla.

When she made the turn off the highway, she remembered how Eli had carried her there. She remembered his kissing her and his strange gallantry in giving her a head start. Now, gallant no longer, he was probably in New York, pounding out his wretched story about her family. What did he know for sure? What would he dare to hint?

But there was too much else to worry about. She was sure that there was enough trouble and loss waiting for her at Mandevilla not to waste time obsessing about Eli.

She came to the gate and let herself in with the key that Lori had given her. When she reached the spot where the bridge had been, she parked the SUV next to the security car and crossed the makeshift walkway. The water in the gully was only a dirty trickle among the rubble now.

The road was still littered with debris. Her heart began to beat painfully hard, until she could feel the pounding even in her throat, a choking sensation.

Then she saw Mandevilla, not quite a ruin, but ruinous enough to bring tears to her eyes. A man in a security officer's uniform sat in a lawn chair he must have brought himself; she'd never seen it before. Beside him were a thermos and a stack of magazines. He was a burly man with a close-cropped head and sunglasses. He heaved himself up from the chair when he saw her. His plastic name tag said D. D. Krepspa. He wore a gun on his hip.

His voice was abrupt. "Ma'am, this area is protected by the Lower Keys Security Company and is off-limits to the public."

Emerson looked him up and down as she took off her backpack. "I'm not the public. I'm Emerson Roth. My grandparents own this place." She reached into her backpack, pulled out her wallet and flashed her driver's license as professionally as a detective might flash his badge.

"Oh," he said, shifting his belt under his bulging stomach. "They said you'd be along."

"They were right." Her tone was brusque. She didn't like this man, although she knew he had to be here. She saw that the magazines he'd been reading were comic books about superheroes. She wanted to be alone with her shock and grief. She didn't want to share the moment with this overweight stranger.

He was chewing gum, and he cracked it. "Got hit pretty hard, eh?"

That was such an understatement, she didn't bother to reply. She merely shrugged. She decided it was a good thing, after all, that Krepspa was here. She no longer had the urge to cry. Not with him watching.

She put her wallet back in her purse and pulled out a set of work gloves. She'd come from Encantada dressed for work. She wore jeans, a long-sleeved work shirt and an Aussie hat.

He looked at her with amusement. "What you think you're gonna do? All by yourself?"

She looked at him squarely. "I came to start cleaning up this mess."

He glanced at the ravished house. "It's too big a job for one woman."

She pulled on her gloves and yanked down her hat brim in determination. "Mr. Krepspa, you'd be surprised at what one woman can do."

ALL DAY Emerson worked to salvage the salvageable. She felt as if she were part archeologist, part rescue worker, part bag lady.

She quickly learned that some tasks were done better with the brain and feelings switched off. *Nana's oriental tapestry is ruined. She'll be sad, but pretend not to be. That's too bad. Go on. Keep working.*

My wardrobe's a mildew farm. My shoes are warped and moldy. My lingerie has jungle rot. My bed has become a breeding ground for fungi. Too bad. Go on. Keep working.

Most of the good china's smashed. Most of the everyday china's smashed. The kitchen table and chairs are kindling. The piano can never be fixed. The antique curio cabinet is

ruined. The Captain's rocking chair can never be repaired.
Too bad. Go on. Keep working.

She gathered the small treasures that had been spared;
there were a surprising number of them. Those that had
been broken, she bagged as garbage.

Although her clothes were ruined, most of Claire's were
spared. Some of Nana's and the Captain's would still be
good. Emerson was efficient, and she kept track of what
was gone and what remained. She took pictures with a dis-
posable camera for the insurance company. She made lists.

She catalogued what she needed to bring the next day:
more garbage bags, a shovel, a janitor's broom, packing
boxes, plastic sheeting. Throughout the day she took breaks
to make calls to the insurance agent, to construction com-
panies and to the New York gallery. She did not waste a
moment.

Toward sunset, the shifts changed and a second man
came, bearing his own lawn chair, thermos and a box of
doughnuts. Emerson was exhausted. She'd made innumer-
able trips to the SUV, driven a load of recovered keepsakes
to the storage shed and taken a separate load of clothing to
the cleaners.

She picked up a teakettle and an armload of linens for
her last trek of the day to the SUV. She would go back to
the motel, spend an hour soaking in the bathtub then start
filling out insurance forms.

The linens from the linen drawer were damp and mil-
dewing, but the cloth was strong enough that Emerson
thought the cleaners could save them. When she added nap-
kins to the stack of tablecloths, a memory came surging
back.

There was one room she hadn't searched. It was as if she
had purposely forgotten its existence: the hurricane room.
Some part of her bent on survival had suppressed all
thought of it.

Now she walked down the hall almost mechanically and

opened the door. There, in the fading light, was the bed on which she and Eli had made love. The covers were still rumpled. Over the table next to the bed was the little wall safe. With unsteady fingers, she dialed the combination and swung open the door. There, as if nothing at all had happened, stood the figurine of the dancing Ganesh.

All the emotions Emerson had held back swept through her in an overwhelming tide. She picked up Ganesh and held him against her chest, bowing her head over him.

She pressed her cheek against the cool china and envisioned the Ganesh dancing on Eli's forearm. She saw its ears wiggle. She gave a kind of helpless hiccough that was close to a sob. She looked at the Ganesh and thought *I should smash you because you make me think of him.*

But the dancing figure looked incongruously merry with its plump human body and elephant's head. It also looked wise, as if it knew something she did not.

She could not hurt him. She left the kettle in the hurricane room and carried Ganesh away from Mandevilla.

EMERSON WORKED a second full day at Mandevilla while D. D. Krepspa sat in the shade reading his comic books. This day he brought a portable CD player and filled the air with disco music.

He told Emerson, rather grandly, that he'd help her but he was forbidden to leave his post. She took a break at noon, but was not hungry. She walked to the blue hole. The devastation of the trees along the way saddened her, but when she reached the water, in its middle, she saw two brownish green lumps, one with a gleaming yellow center.

It was Gollum, the alligator. Somehow the old devil had survived the storm. She smiled, glad for a familiar face, even if it was his.

On the third day, Frenchy and his wife LouAnn came to help her. She felt that at last the cleanup seemed to be truly progressing. Frenchy had arranged for three men to arrive, too, strong and honest workers who would help clear the worst of the heavy wreckage out of the house.

Emerson planned to work another two days, then fly back to Costa Encantada to make sure Nana and the Captain were adjusting to the changes. But the next morning, Claire called.

Claire's voice was shaky. "Em? Do you think you could come home right away? It's happened. Nana's mother passed away. Her brother called early this morning."

Emerson was still in her motel room. She'd been bent over, lacing up her work boots when the phone had rung. Now she sat up ramrod straight. "How's Nana taking it?"

"Harder than I thought. She's locked herself in their room. She doesn't even want to talk to the Captain. Em, I really think it'd be good if you—"

"I'll be there as soon as I can," Emerson promised. She hung up, phoned Frenchy and asked him to oversee the cleanup at Mandevilla for a few days. Then she called to book a ticket for San Juan.

As she held the phone, waiting for the ticket agent to check his computer, she covered her eyes with her hand and thought, *Does trouble never end?* Then she raised her face, and her eyes rested on Ganesh, eternally dancing in spite of everything.

THE DRIVE to the airport was a blur, so was the flight to San Juan. She took a bus to the largest village near Costa Encantada. Claire was there, waiting for her in the rented Jeep.

The sisters embraced, and Emerson volunteered to drive. Claire was shaky with emotion. On the way to the pink house, she told how Nana had paled when she'd heard the news. She hadn't broken down and wept or made any sort of scene.

She'd simply said, "It is over. I must be alone now."

Claire had heard a muffled sound coming from behind the closed door.

"I think she was wailing," Claire said, her chin quivering, "but that she blocked her mouth with a scarf or something. That she didn't want us to hear."

Emerson shook her head. Nana had seldom talked about her mother, but both Emerson and Claire knew she'd never stopped loving her. Nana had wished the older woman would forgive her, but her wish had gone ungranted.

Emerson took a deep breath and tried to say the sensible thing. "Nana chose what she chose. She could have been a good girl and stayed home and obeyed. Or she could have the Captain."

Claire nodded. "She'd do the same thing again."

"She gave up everything she knew for love. And it's a good thing she did, or we wouldn't be here."

Claire smiled. "I'm glad I don't have to choose with Merriman."

Emerson slid a sideways glance at her sister. "But you're leaving everything *you* know. You'll be in a different country."

"It's not the same. We'll all still communicate. And visit."

"You're not afraid to go that far away?"

Claire, the shy, the stay-at-home, raised her chin with confidence. "I'd go to the ends of the earth to be with him."

Ah, Emerson thought, *there's more of Nana in you than I ever suspected.* She gripped the wheel more firmly. "And when's the wedding?"

Claire looked happy and dreamy. "In five weeks. It'll be very small. Just the family. Then we'll go to the Bahamas for a honeymoon. We'll be back for Bunbury and the parrot. Then on to Toronto."

But Claire's smile faded as they neared the pink house. She and Emerson were both thinking of Nana.

THE CAPTAIN SAT in the living room in a wicker rocker, a solitary figure. He greeted Emerson with a hug and a kiss. "It's good of you to come. It'll help her to know you're here."

"She's still by herself?" Emerson asked, straightening his crooked collar.

He gave a curt nod. "It's how she coped with her father's death. You're too young to remember. She knows the funeral will be today. She'll mourn privately. Then, tomorrow, she'll come out. She won't want to say much about it. It's her way."

He knew Nana through and through, and he was right. The next morning, she emerged from the bedroom. She embraced Emerson and accepted her sympathy graciously, but quickly changed the subject.

"How kind of you to drop everything and come. How is Mandevilla? How is our Key? The Kims, how are they? And their house, how did it fare?"

While Emerson answered, Nana set about brewing a pot of the strong Turkish coffee she loved. The Captain sat in a kitchen chair, watching her with admiration in his eyes. Claire bustled about, taking apple tarts from the oven.

The kitchen filled with delicious scents, the familiar aromas of home. Nana poured the coffee into demitasses. "Sit, sit," she said. "Let's have breakfast with our Emerson. This family has much to talk about. There is a wedding to plan."

CLAIRE'S WEDDING was simple and beautiful. Nana had made her dress, which was long and of white silk. The gown was simple, and Claire's veil was held in place with a crown of wildflowers.

Merriman in gray slacks and a blue blazer looked at her as if entranced, trying not to smile too broadly, his brow furrowed. Raphael Mendoza, a preacher from the village, performed the ceremony, which Claire and Merriman had written together.

The weather was so perfect it seemed it had made itself blissfully radiant for the occasion. The sky shone, a cloudless, tender blue. The sand of the beach dazzled with its whiteness, and the sea was calm and colorful as a jewel. The barest of breezes blew, ruffling Claire's veil and Merriman's fair hair.

When Pastor Mendoza pronounced them man and wife, the Captain cried with emotion. Nana's eyes grew bright with tears, but she stood straight and did not shed them. Emerson, although her heart rose, hurting, in her throat, did the same as Nana.

There were embraces and kisses and laughter and good wishes, and then goodbyes. Merriman took Claire away, dressed in a traveling suit of white linen. The pastor took his leave.

It was over. Emerson was bursting with happiness for her sister, but she missed her already. And something else haunted her, a sense of incompleteness to which she did not dare give a name. She disguised this feeling, or thought she did.

For two days, she stayed with Nana and the Captain. Then she went back to the rigors of her routine. Mandevilla was almost cleaned up. She'd lined up a contractor to begin to restore the house. She fought her way through tangles of red tape about insurance.

She worried about money. She made several trips to New York. That the Captain and Nana had been displaced by the hurricane was in the news, but not a major story. The fact earned only a paragraph in the arts section of a handful of newspapers and magazines.

But the news made no difference in sales. Collectors no longer fought to outbid each other for the paintings. The gallery manager told Emerson frankly that there were rumors about the worth of the Captain's later work; people whispered that he could no longer paint.

Emerson knew these rumors were what had brought Eli and Merriman to Mandevilla. She had wanted to lay the gossip to rest, but she had failed. Even now Eli must be writing the story that the paintings were tainted by the rumor of fraud. The Captain's faded fame might be replaced by a swell of infamy.

But for now, a few of the smaller paintings still interested potential buyers. Soon Emerson would have to tell the agent to cut the prices on the larger ones. Insurance would never cover all the expenses of the hurricane, and she was worried about Nana and the Captain's financial security. Well, Costa Encantada could be sold. If worse came to worst, Mandevilla itself could be sacrificed.

Disheartened, Emerson returned to Key West. Tomorrow a crew would start building a newer, stronger bridge. She had a small mountain of messages waiting for her at her motel. Wearily she took them to her room and started to sort them. She didn't even want to look at the e-mails that would be lurking in wait on her computer.

As she scrutinized a landscaper's bid to replace trees, her phone rang. Absently, she picked it up. "Hello. Emerson Roth speaking."

"Emerson, the Captain and I want you to come to Encantada as soon as possible." Nana's voice was taut with tension.

Emerson's pulses jumped. "Is something wrong?"

Nana said, "We have heard from your Mr. Garner. He is coming to see us tomorrow. About his story. My love, we need you to be here."

Eli. Nana's words were like a knife through the heart. Emerson should have known he would break his promise to stay away. He was coming with accusations, trying to force the truth from them—she knew it. Well, she'd fight him to the end.

"Emerson?" Nana said.

Emerson set her jaw. "I'll be there."

CHAPTER EIGHTEEN

EMERSON PULLED UP to the house in her rented Land Rover. Another strange vehicle was there, a black Jeep. Eli's. She knew it with eerie, stomach-shaking certainty.

She got out of the Land Rover and mounted the pink steps. The sea wind blew her hair. She had worn a simply cut dress in bright turquoise. Once he'd said it was her color. Had she worn it out of vanity? Or belligerence? She didn't know.

She knocked at the door, and Nana answered, her face strained with anxiety. Eli had put that look on her face, and Emerson felt a powerful wave of resentment toward him.

Emerson hugged and kissed her, then drew back. "Nana?"

Nana nodded, seeming to read her thoughts. "Yes, he is here. He's been here almost an hour. He would like a word with you alone. He wants to know if you will walk on the beach with him. Or would you rather be inside?"

"The beach," Emerson said numbly. "Where's the Captain? Has Eli— Has the Garner man upset him?"

"The Captain is fine. He's in the studio. He'll meet with Mr. Garner when you get back. He wants you to be there."

Emerson pressed her lips together and nodded. Nana turned back and walked into the house. She carried herself with such stoic resignation that Emerson's indignation at Eli shot up another notch.

Too restless to stand and wait for him, she descended the stairs and stood with her back to the porch, staring out at the azure-and-emerald sea. She took a deep breath. It was a gentle day, much like Claire's wedding day.

She heard a door open and shut behind her, and her body stiffened. She gritted her teeth and waited, nerves humming. She heard his footsteps on the steps.

Then he was beside her. "Emerson," he said in a low voice.

She faced him, steeling herself. "What are you doing in my grandparents' house? Are you going to hound them to their very graves?"

"No." His dark eyes looked her up and down. She'd tried to forget how handsome he was. The lean face with the strong cheekbones and sharp jawline shook her heart. The wind tossed his hair.

He wore tan jeans and an open-necked shirt of pale yellow, the sleeves rolled up to his forearms. He didn't try to touch her. His hands were jammed into his front pockets.

She had to look away, so stared out at the water again.

He said, "Will you walk with me? There's something I want to tell you."

She carried a purse and a straw sun hat. She moved to the Land Rover, opened the door and threw them onto the front seat, an almost contemptuous gesture. Still she didn't look at him.

"All right. We'll walk. What do you want to say? Why are you here?"

She set off toward the shore, and he stayed beside her, matching his pace to hers. "I called your grandparents yesterday. I said I wanted to talk to them. And to you."

She shot him a glance that was half angry, half fearful. "Is it about your damn article? I just got back from New York. The rumors about the Captain are growing. That's your doing, I'm sure."

"It's not my doing," he retorted. "I haven't said a word about him or Mandevilla."

"Then why are people talking?"

He gave a shrug that was eloquent with frustration. "A few people are talking. People who know art. His name made the news because of the hurricane. A few journalists tried to reach him. He was, of course, unreachable."

"How did you get to him?" she demanded. "I gave this number to nobody."

"I called Dr. Kim and explained the situation. He told me."

The statement threw her off balance. "Why would *he* help you?"

"Because I told him I wanted to apologize for putting pressure on your family. There were things I wanted to say in person."

She'd reached the water's edge. She kicked off her sandals and took them in hand, trying to act nonchalant. She walked at the surf's edge.

"If you're going to apologize about your story, don't be a hypocrite. It won't—"

"There isn't going to be any story." His voice was so sharp, so pained, that she stopped walking. She stared at him in disbelief. He stopped, and his gaze held hers.

She found it hard to breathe. "You were afraid of a lawsuit. Well, that shows some sense."

His mouth twisted. "I'm not afraid of your threats. I've been threatened before. There's no story because there's no proof."

Her eyes widened. "You said you saw…"

He shrugged again and shook his head. "I saw an elderly man with a withered hand. I had some people tell me he looked as if he'd had a stroke. What did they know? One source was some gin-soaked panhandler. Another was a guy mad as hell about a cement pelican—"

Emerson blinked. "Cement pelican?"

"It doesn't matter. None of these people was a doctor. None of them knew if he could still paint or not. At the end, all I had was what I started with, gossip and scuttlebutt. Guesses and speculation.''

He was clearly disgusted with himself for his failure, but she was limp with relief. ''You didn't write it?''

He shot her a glance that simmered with emotion. ''Oh, I wrote it, all right. Or tried to. It was lousy. It stank. It made me sick. Tabloid trash. I never showed it to my editor. It was so bad, I got drunk three nights running. I finally burned it. You win, Emerson. Does that make you happy?''

It clearly hurt him to make his confession. But she made her voice cool. ''Yes. It does.''

''Then some good came from it. And I'm sorry for— what was your word?—*hounding* you. And your family. When I met you, I wanted to stand high in your regard. Instead, I dropped low. And for that, I couldn't be more sorry.''

Bewildered, she threw out her hands. ''But why? Why did you want my regard?''

''Because you're you,'' he said.

She could think of no reply. She stood mute, and the cold surf swirled around her bare feet. A chill rippled through her.

He spoke through clenched teeth. ''I told your grandparents that I cared for you. That I love you. I tell you that because you deserve to know that you've humbled me. Completely.''

She shivered and moved away from the reach of the foaming water. ''We're still on different sides,'' she said. ''There can't be anything between us. No good can come of it.''

He smiled cynically. ''I know. It's impossible. You have to protect them—'' he nodded toward the house ''—from the likes of me.''

She bit the inside of her lip. What he said was true. She had to protect them. It was what she did. If Eli didn't unearth their secrets, one of his kind would. He might foreswear the hunt, but he was still one of the pack.

"There's nothing more to say, then, is there?" she asked, trying to keep her voice steady.

His face became set, expressionless. He glanced up at the sky. "Maybe. A little. Your grandfather wants to speak to me. And you. Shall we go back to the house?"

She ducked her head. "Yes."

They walked in silence for a moment. Then he said, "I heard about your sister and Merriman. Congratulations."

"Thank you."

"He's a good man."

"Yes." *You brought him into our lives,* she thought. *You brought him to Claire.* But she didn't trust herself to say that.

He said, "And you're healed from your injuries? Your knee? Your wrist? All the scratches and bruises?"

"All healed." *On the outside.*

"Good." They mounted the stairs. When they reached the porch, he paused and said, "After I talk with your grandfather, I'll be leaving. I have an evening flight back to the States."

"Oh." She had to act as if it were of no consequence to her. She couldn't say *Please don't go back to that life.* Or— *Take me with you.* Neither was possible.

She opened the door, and he followed her inside. Nana sat in the wicker rocker, her hands folded in her lap. She looked at Emerson and Eli with something like trepidation. "Ah. You're back."

She lifted herself out of the chair, reluctance in the motion. "The Captain will see you. Come, I'll take you to him."

She led Emerson and Eli down the hall to the little bedroom that served as the studio. The Captain stood by the window, leaning on a cane. He hadn't had a haircut since coming to Encantada, and he looked like an aging lion with a silver mane. His seamed face was serious, but he smiled when he saw Emerson.

He held out his good arm, and she went to him and kissed him on each cheek. He kissed her back. Then he held his left hand out to Eli. "I'm Nathan Roth. Your prey."

A muscle jerked in Eli's cheek, but he clasped the other man's hand firmly. "I'm Eli Garner. I was the predator, yes. I'll apologize again, if need be."

The Captain gave a grunt of disapproval. "No. Sit down." He lowered himself to a flowered couch and sat at one end. "Come sit beside me," he told Emerson, patting the cushion.

She did, glad for his closeness, but uneasy, too. She prayed he would say nothing that would set Eli back upon his track.

"And you sit there," the Captain said, gesturing at the far end of the couch.

Eli obeyed. Emerson pressed closer to her grandfather.

She looked around the familiar room and knew Eli could not stop himself from looking, too. He would take in every detail. That there was one window that overlooked the beach, and that the easel was set near. On the easel was a painting, half-finished.

Before the easel sat a padded chair, empty, and next to it, a small work table, with a pallet, brushes and paints. An easy chair, in the same floral pattern as the couch, graced the opposite wall. Bookcases and cabinets took up the rest of the space.

"Nana, sit," Emerson entreated.

"I would rather stand," Nana said, her mouth a controlled line. Her back erect, her hands clasped, she stood by the door.

The Captain leaned around Emerson to speak to Eli. "Did you tell this girl what you told us? That you care for her?"

Emerson, startled, gave her grandfather a reproving look.

"Yes, sir." Eli's tone was fatalistic.

"Did it do you any good?"

"Captain!" Emerson protested.

"No, sir," said Eli. "I didn't expect it would."

"Hmph. Nor did we. Though she wants you, I warrant. We knew she'd been pining for something since you left. We assumed it was you."

"Captain! I never said any such thing."

Nana gave her a stony look. "Sometimes you don't have to say."

The Captain went on. His voice was strong today and hardly slurred. "Mr. Garner, our Em is not a free woman. She's bound by ties of duty to us. So my wife—my beloved wife—and I have decided to release her. Sir, we will tell you the truth about the paintings."

Emerson, appalled, clutched his thigh. "Captain—no." Her head and heart both reeled. Had Eli somehow *planned* this? Had cunning been behind his every word to her and to her grandparents?

She pleaded with him. "Don't. He's tricking you. Captain—"

Nana interrupted her. "Emerson, it is our decision. We've spoken of it often these last weeks. The time for hiding the truth is over. Your grandfather wishes it. And so…so do…I."

The Captain put his hand over Emerson's. To Eli, he said, "We've read your work. It's good work."

"Fine work," murmured Nana.

The Captain said, "Emerson told Claire some of the things you did when the two of you were trapped at Mandevilla. Claire told us. You risked your life for me. And for Emerson."

Nana shot the Captain a resentful look. "You were so awful to run off into the storm. *Mon dieu.* If I had known, I would have died."

"Well, yes, that." The Captain looked embarrassed,

something that seldom occurred. "Nevertheless, Mr. Garner, of late we've decided it's time to tell the facts. They must be told to a responsible journalist. And after your phone call yesterday, we agreed it would be fitting to tell them to you."

Emerson leaned toward Nana, imploring her, "After all these years—"

"It is time," Nana said.

Eli looked almost as dismayed as Emerson felt. "I didn't come here for that."

"No," Nana said. "You came here for her. And she will not feel free to be with you until the story is told." She gripped her hands more tightly together. "Six years ago, Mr. Garner, my husband had an auto accident. When we were on holiday. He was badly hurt, as you can see. His hand—he would never use it again."

The Captain frowned. "Skull fracture. I had mood swings. Still do. Spells. So, I just hid away. When I was lucid, I knew it was necessary. Anyone could see that this hand could never paint anything."

He plucked at his own sleeve to emphasize how useless his arm and hand were.

"But the paintings kept coming," Eli frowned.

"Of course, they did," said the Captain. "But I didn't paint them."

"Then they're forgeries," Eli returned, looking sickened. He stared at Emerson as if saying *Tell me it's not true. You didn't do this.*

The Captain said, "They aren't forgeries. They are all genuine Roths. From the first to the last."

A dubious realization lit Eli's face. The Captain nodded. "One of the Roths was a good painter. That was me. But one is a great painter. That is my wife. My love and my dove? Show him."

Emerson, her heart thudding, watched as Nana moved to the easel. She sat down before it and took up a brush. She squeezed a dab of acrylic onto the pallet. She began to paint.

"I'll be damned," breathed Eli.

"We thought it a fine joke at first," the Captain said. "My paintings weren't selling. I knew hers were better. But she was too modest. And there was her family. She'd scandalized them by marrying me. She wouldn't scandalize them twice."

Eli turned to Emerson. "Is this true?"

She fought back tears. "Yes. Yes. All the paintings are hers."

"But they changed," Eli persisted. "Why?"

Nana, with fierce dignity, met his eyes. "Because I changed, with my husband hurt so badly. And age changed me. My energy is not what it was. Illness changed me. My hands are crippled. They do not do my bidding as they once did. What had begun with lightness of heart had turned into a great burden. But everyone thought he was the painter, and how else were we to make our living?"

Eli shook his head. "You pulled this off for *years*. My God. What kept you going?"

The Captain reached for his cane and rapped its tip on the floor, a sharp crack. "Why, the art, boy. The art. She's a great artist. But she didn't want the world to know."

"My mother was very strict to her faith," Nana said, sadness in her eyes. "She thought the making of images sinful. And for a woman to do it, more sinful still."

"But, Nana," Emerson said, "why are you telling now? You swore you would never tell. Because your mother would never forgive you."

Nana stared at her for a long moment. Her chin trembled. "She did forgive me, love. At the last. The very last before she died. My brother told me. She said she loved me and forgave me everything. She departed this world with no resentment in her heart."

"You didn't tell me?" Emerson was both shocked and hurt.

"It took time to sort out my feelings," said Nana. "The Captain has grown tired of the deception. So have I, oh, so long ago. But Claire was to be married. We didn't wish to draw attention to ourselves until that was done, and they had time to settle."

The Captain shook his head and looked at Eli. "I was hired to teach Lela's brothers in Paris. Not her. Her mother would have none of that. But Lela came to me, saying she wanted to paint. Her mother believed it a terrible thing for a woman to do. But to waste that genius? Criminal. At first I didn't mind the charade. There was no malice in it. Only her modesty."

Nana turned her face away. "I don't want to talk anymore. My feelings are too strong. I wish to be in private."

The Captain struggled to his feet. "And I'm tired. This has taken a good deal out of me."

He turned to Emerson and Eli. "Deal with it," he said.

He and Nana leaned on each other and moved to the door. She paused and raised her face to him, her eyes shining. "You were wonderful, my dear. A marvel."

"Yes," the Captain said, "I was rather good, wasn't I? Taxing, though. Taxing."

They stepped into the hall, and the door shut behind them. Emerson and Eli sat at opposite ends of the couch. She looked at him warily, filled with uncertainty. "Well," she said coldly. "You finally got your story, didn't you?"

"That's not what's most important to me right now," he said, his face as tense as hers. "The question is, do I get the girl?"

Emerson couldn't answer. She stared at the unfinished painting, her eyes brimming dangerously. Like Nana, she had the desire to flee, not to let this emotion be seen.

But with a swift movement Eli was next to her, one arm around her shoulders. "Because I want the girl, Em. I want her more than I want the story. I want you more than anything. I love you.''

And then he was kissing her, and she was kissing him back, and she was laughing and crying at the same time because it was true: she was free, now, free to love him.

ELI CANCELED his flight back to the States. He could not part with Emerson, not so soon. Late that afternoon they were going to walk on the beach and watch the sun set.

But just before they were to leave, Nana drew Emerson aside. ''A moment alone with you, please?''

Eli nodded his understanding. ''I'll wait outside.''

Nana waited until he was gone. ''He is a good man, Emerson. I saw it from the first. You will marry him, will you not?''

Emerson smiled. ''Yes, Nana.''

Nana hugged her. ''Ah, I knew it! Your babies, what beautiful hair they will have. All dark and wavy. I can't wait to see.''

Emerson laughed. ''Babies? We haven't even been engaged a day.'' Then she grew more serious. ''But *how* did you know I loved him? Did it really show?''

Nana gave a little huff. ''I knew the moment I saw you in Fort Myers that something had happened. As if you could hide it from me, of all people. Emerson, I have *loved*. I know love when I see it.''

She embraced Emerson again. ''The Captain is greatly relieved to be shut of this secret. Know that is true. And I am relieved that you are shut of it, too. Now go to your young man. He awaits you.''

She kissed Emerson's cheek. ''I must go boil an egg for the Captain. He is tired and wants soothing food. Go, my love.''

Emerson left and ran lightly down the porch stairs. Eli caught her in his arms and whirled her around until she was dizzy.

"Em. My Em. I like the sound of it," he said, breathless when they stopped.

"So do I." She tightened her arms around her neck. "Oh, Eli, it's a long story you'll have to write. You'll have to be here lots. Again and again."

He kissed her, a long, intriguing kiss that addled her with wanting more. Then he smiled down at her and said, "I don't think it's a long story."

Her mouth fell open in disappointment. "You don't?"

"It covers half a century. It's a long *book*. There'll be a resurgence of interest in the paintings—a big one. I'll need lots of interviews and background. And on-site research. Maybe I'll have to move to Key West for a while."

"Oh, yes," she said, "a long while. Really long."

"A lifetime," he said. "Em, I want us to be like your grandparents. I want to have and to hold you and cherish you, from this day forth, as long as I live."

"I want it, too. To love you all my life."

He kissed her again. His hands moved up and down her body. Beyond, the sea's murmur grew more urgent. The tide was rising to the pull of the unseen moon, and it would not be denied.

THE CAPTAIN PEERED out the studio window at the pair. "Look at them," he said to Nana. "Kissing like all get-out. Why, I swear, they're almost the way we used to be."

"Almost." Nana's tone was full of nostalgia.

"Gad," said the Captain. "Gad." Then he turned and frowned slightly. "Is my egg ready?"

"Yes, love. It is."

"Good." He turned back to the window again. He smiled and shook his head. "Ahh. Seeing them, it's good. It makes me remember. It's almost like being young again ourselves."

"Yes, my sweet dear," she said, taking his hand and

drawing him toward the kitchen. "And that is as it's meant
to be. For we are young again in them, are we not?"

"Indeed, my love and my dove. I feel that we are. Yes.
That's one of the great things about love." He kissed her.
"It goes on and on."

Hand and hand they walked down the hall.

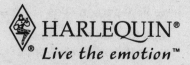

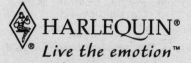

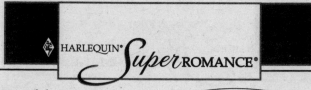

HARLEQUIN *Super*ROMANCE®

Men of the True North—
Wilde and Free

The Wilde Men

Homecoming Wife
(Superromance #1212)
On-sale July 2004

Ten years ago Nate Wilde's wife, Angela, left and never came back.
Nate is now quite happy to spend his days on the rugged trails of
Whistler, British Columbia. When Angela returns to the resort
town, the same old attraction flares to life between them. Will
Nate be able to convince his wife to stay for good this time?

Family Matters
(Superromance #1224)
On-sale September 2004

Marc was the most reckless Wilde of the bunch. But when an
accident forces him to reevaluate his life, he has trouble accepting
his fate and even more trouble accepting help from Fiona Gordon.
Marc is accustomed to knowing what he wants and going after it.
But getting Fiona may be his most difficult challenge yet.

A Mom for Christmas
(Superromance #1236)
On-sale November 2004

Aidan Wilde is a member of the Whistler Mountain ski patrol, but
he has never forgiven himself for being unable to save his wife's
life. Six years after her death, Aidan and his young daughter still
live under the shadow of suspicion. Travel photographer Nicola
Bond comes to Whistler on an assignment and falls for Aidan. But
she can never live up to his wife's memory…

Available wherever Harlequin books are sold.

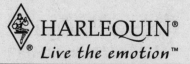

HARLEQUIN®
Live the emotion™

www.eHarlequin.com

HSRWM

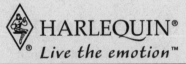